DELICIOUS HUNGER

TRANSLATED BY

DELICIOUS HUNGER

HAI FAN

JEREMY TIANG

TILTED AXIS PRESS

TRANSLATOR'S NOTE

One of the events at the 2023 Singapore Writers Festival, 'Wonders of the Rainforest', was described in the program as an author-led walking tour that would 'immerse in the greens that run through Singapore and Malaysia'. This would have been unremarkable if the author in question had not been Hai Fan, who spent thirteen years in the rainforests of Malaysia and southern Thailand as a member of the Malayan Communist Party (MCP, or Magong—a contraction of **Ma**laiya **Gong**chandang, the Chinese name of the party).

It's one of my great regrets that I was not in Singapore for this event—not just for the spectacle of the authorities blithely sending a group of civilians into the rainforest in the company of a former Communist guerrilla but also because I would have loved to have spent time with Hai Fan in the natural world. Palpable in every one of the stories in this collection is the deep connection that the Magong had with the rainforest around them, which Hai Fan maintains to this day; the last time we met, he presented me with a hardened bit of meranti resin, to make sure I knew what it looked like as I translated.

The book's affinity with nature raised an interesting challenge: rendering the names of plants. I set out to identify every plant mentioned, a daunting task as vocabulary specific to

Singapore and Malaysia mostly does not make it into Chinese dictionaries, and plants in the region are known by a variety of names in different languages. Even when I'd managed to track down a plant, I still had to decide which version of its name to use—the common English name (but when so described, this often only means 'common' in the west), the Malay name by which it would have been more widely known in Malaysia, or something else. With the 独角莲, for instance, the English name 'voodoo lily' was somewhat problematic, so I translated the Chinese literally—'one-horn lily', which happens to be an evocative description of the plant's appearance, with the trade-off that using a non-standard name makes it impossible to google.

I generally try to sort these issues out on my own. Partly because it's fun (possibly related: I enjoy crossword puzzles more than is seemly); partly out of a vague belief that the average reader of a book does not get to question the author, and so wanting to rely as much as possible on the text itself before invoking the phone-a-friend lifeline; and partly because I didn't want to bother Hai Fan, whom I knew was hard at work on a new novel.

There was one plant that I couldn't track down, though. I only even knew that it was a plant because of a reference to its branches; it's mentioned once in the book: 黄郎仔, which means something like 'yellow chap'. Finally, I caved and asked Hai Fan, who laughed. 'I don't know what those are called either,' he told me. 'They were everywhere, bushes with yellow leaves. None of us knew their proper name, so we just called them 黄郎仔.'

I toyed with the idea of showing him a selection of yellow-leaved tropical plants to see if he could ID one of them, but appealing as the idea of a botanical perp line-up was, I decided that if the comrades hadn't known the actual name of the plant, then neither would I. If it had shown up more often in the book, I might have gone with something along the lines of 'little yellow guy'—but with only a single mention and no further context, that would have been distracting. It's now in the book as 'yellow bush', and that will have to do.

I had initially translated 民运 as 'People's Movement'—a literal rendition of these characters, which I thought gave a reasonable sense of what this branch of the organisation was. As we went through the manuscript, Hai Fan asked me to transliterate this instead as 'Minyun' (sometimes romanised as 'Min Yuen'), and to add an explanatory note here giving a fuller sense of their role. The Minyun was essentially the civilian branch of the MCP, whose job was to mobilise nearby villagers in support of the MCP guerrillas, including through the purchase and transportation of supplies, as well as to help run these villages, providing them with education, security and conflict-resolution.

Names are unstable, arbitrary things. As noted in the book, the comrades all took on new names upon entering the rainforest, partly to symbolise a new beginning, partly to shield their previous identities so no one could implicate anyone else. These names often had a significance of their own, with comrades who joined up at the same time adopting names with one character in common. While there was little consistency in the romanisation of names at the time—黄 could be rendered as Wong, Ng, Ooi, Wee or Huang—I have opted for pinyin for the comrades' chosen names to reflect that Mandarin was the language most commonly spoken in the rainforest (with the exception of Lim Kuan, a Teochew speaker).

As it happens, my own name has also changed, albeit for less interesting reasons. Back when I was an actor, there was already someone in Spotlight working under my government name, so I began using my mother's surname instead. 'Tiang' is an arbitrary spelling, probably based on what a colonial officer thought he heard while recording an ancestor's name. The Chinese character, 程 ('Cheng' in Mandarin), means 'journey'. In any event, neither 'Hai Fan' nor 'Jeremy Tiang' actually exist, legally speaking.

My approach to translating the other proper nouns in this book has been somewhat impressionistic—I am, in general, a proponent of vibes-based translation. For instance, is 霹雳河 the Perak River or Sungai Perak? I remember calling it 'Sungai Perak' growing up, so I've gone with that. Will readers not from the region deduce that 'Sungai' is the Malay word for 'river'? Not necessarily, but there's enough context for it to be clear that 'Sungai Perak' is the name of a river, and that 'Perak' is the name of a state. Elsewhere I have translated literally— why lose the immediate mental image conjured up by 'Three Forks River'?

Purists might take issue with this piecemeal approach, but I've always thought that linguistic consistency is a virtue more prized by people from monolingual societies, which I very much am not. Life in Singapore and Malaysia takes place in a patchwork of many languages and cultures, a multitude reflected in Hai Fan's writing—with its fragments of many Chineses, transliterated Malay, English, and Thai words—and also in this translation.

—Jeremy Tiang

EDITOR'S NOTE

A RAINFOREST OF INVISIBLE SILENCE

Nature and timing, the real living of the ground. Planting crops like cassava. Blast fishing. Self-sufficiency in the rainforest. This ebb from the outside world of KFC, 'snack vendors in small-town alleyways, of the city's hawker centres' and ticking watches, to the mist fall of the rainforest. This is the world of *Delicious Hunger.*

The synergy between Hai Fan and translator Jeremy Tiang is palpable when you read the text. The experiments that the translation into English presented was in stretching the form of the work into zig zags and poetic enjambment to feel at one with the rainforest, while retaining Hai Fan's deliberateness with his matter-of-fact tone and emphasis on the ridge of a combat knife or the headiness of someone's sweat in close quarters.

Something that has been on my mind while working on this text has been the thought of coping networks during condensed periods of violence and grief. In 'Mysterious Night' Ah Wei longs to dry Jingfang's laundry and fill her bottle, in his grief realising all the times he'd taken for granted the one who was closest to him. Without a coping network, without his home in the rainforest, Jingfang, Ah Wei becomes a 'stray cat'. We are invited into a collection where coping continually changes shape.

Fog arrives as a 'rising tide' in the rainforest, often covering the entire camp. It falls upon its visitors like silence. Ah Wei goes silent from the pain he experiences. In 'Hillside Rain' Donghua grieves in silence and in 'Magic Ears', even the talkative Lu defends himself in his heart against jabs instead of falling out with his comrades. Yejin silences his feelings in 'Wild Mangoes', with the numbing words of 'feelings are just feelings, though'.

These are the silences that are not perceived so easily. They are the missing words and gaps of visibility in a climate that could easily absorb the lives we come to know. In 'Delicious Hunger', an invisible rainforest comes to fruit before us. Non-kinetic actions of military life and nation building fall to the wayside.

Speaking with Jeremy, I would often ask, 'How can we increase the intimacy here?' and use rhythm to show the pace of this life, the misting energy in the air. One of my favourite sections to work on was in 'Magic Ears' as the unit is pulled into a tight spot, 'torn uniforms' and thorns 'tearing tearing tearing' bump words into a poem of chaos, the skin of uniform and nature intertwining. The poetry was always there. That freneticism of silence and choice. As Jeremy said to me, 'Hai Fan has so much sincerity in his writing'—a sincerity that is magnified by a rejection of writing that is solely meant to educate, and instead showcases an experience through the vehicle of the surreal literary—suggestive, ever-present, a natural world of its own.

—Tice Cin

MYSTERIOUS NIGHT

1.

Hoo... hoo... hoo...

A distant animal cry.

Barely audible, even carried by the gusting hill winds, but the comrades in the camp heard it right away. They stopped whatever they were doing and pricked up their ears.

Old Jiang had been writing, but now his pen was still. He looked up, thoughts still etched on his face, a glimmer of hope in his eyes. He stared in the direction of the sentry post. Could Ah Wei and the others be back from their recce?

Hoo... hoo... hoo... Yes, that was the signal. Someone asking to be let in.

The sentry responded with an identical cry. An urgent shout from the mound: 'They're here! They're here!' Guanghua, voice raised in excitement.

'Who? Who's here?' asked the sentry, joy and surprise mingled in her voice.

'The work team! They're here!'

Ah, the work team! Could it really be them?

The assault force unit had been camped here more than a month. The order came down from above: they were to meet another work team to receive important documents, materials, and personnel, then liaise with a trekking unit heading south from the Thai-Malaysian border for a handover. Ordinarily, waiting in the belly of the lush green rainforest, they'd have been fine—a dozen people could easily live off the land. But the Orang Asli croplands got swept up in the battle, and everything changed. Now they had to be deep undercover to keep the Enemy from sniffing them out. Anything noisy— hunting, blast fishing—was forbidden. Under Enemy fire, they'd managed to grab a couple of sacks of dried cassava, which they were rationing out a little at a time. A month ago, the quartermaster Uncle Tian led a detachment to dig up buried rations, only to find a black bear had got there first, leaving nothing to be salvaged. It was not yet the season for hill fruits such as mongon or bora, so all they had to fill their bellies were foraged vegetables: mountain taro, pak choi, sand ginger. Hunger gnawed at them, ground them down, weakened them. When the male comrades went shirtless into the gully to fetch water, Old Jiang's heart tightened painfully to see their shoulder blades and ribs growing more prominent by the day, like river rocks in a drought. Guanghua came back from patrol the other day and reported finding a patch of stone pig intestines—a sort of edible plant—that would feed them for seven or eight days. How much would that help, though, without rice or meat? Old Jiang was well aware that danger lay all around them. Even without the threat of the Enemy, the comrades had been hungry for a while now, deprived of vital nutrients. There were limits to what their bodies could withstand. There'd already been malnourishment in the unit. Several of the men started bleeding for no reason, the women's periods were much heavier than usual, and one comrade was even martyred as a result. Although he tried not to show it, these gathering dark clouds made him anxious. He'd started weighing how much longer they would be able to stay here. Yet rescheduling the drop-off would be a major disruption to other assault force squads, as well as the larger deployment strategy. Besides, for all he knew, the long-awaited work team might show up the next day. That was how the comrades felt every minute of every day—a mix of hopeful urgency and readiness for yet more disappointment—as they waited, and waited… Could it be that the team had actually arrived?

The words made Old Jiang's face heat up, and warmth spread through his body.

'They're here, they're here! At last!' he exclaimed, grabbing his notebook, ready to dash out.

'Old Jiang!' Ah Wei, a comrade in his late thirties, whooshed over like a gust of wind. A wound had recently been paining him greatly, sinking his normally bright disposition in gloom and silence. He'd gone entire days without speaking. But now, his pallid face was flushed with excitement, and his eyes gleamed beneath his thick brows. 'Old Jiang, it looks like the work team.'

'Sit, take your time and tell me.' Old Jiang put a hand on Ah Wei's sweaty shoulder and pressed him down onto a wooden block, then took a seat himself. He breathed deeply, trying to calm his churning emotions. 'What happened? You found new tracks?'

'Yes, by the big river. Footprints—people running. Yesterday, by the look of them.'

'Oh!' Without them noticing, Old Jiang's tent, made of two sheets of plastic, had filled with people. At Ah Wei's words, their tense faces drew closer.

'How many?' asked Old Jiang.

'We followed the tracks a little way. It looks like twenty or fewer of them. Then they crossed.'

'Crossed the river?'

'Yes. They swept their tracks clean on either side. Guanghua found the stick.'

'This one!' called Guanghua, brandishing the narrow wooden pole split at one end.

He was right—this was the sort of implement rear-guard comrades used to cover our tracks. Everyone's faces slackened, and some lips even stretched into smiles. They started to guess who the sweeper might be.

Old Jiang held the sweeping stick, frowning. Why had they crossed over? The maildrop and meeting point were both on this side of the river. This was odd. 'What else did you find?'

'A pile of shit!' Guanghua blurted out. Everyone looked at him strangely, but he didn't care. 'Buried in the sand near the river, the way our comrades do it. When I dug it up to see, it had a whiff of fried bee hoon.'

'How can you tell apart different types of shit?'

'That's easy!' He spread his hands smugly. 'You shit whatever you've been eating. Fried bee hoon has a charred smell, so of course your shit smells of it too.'

Everyone burst out laughing, carefree now the waiting was almost over.

'Sounds like those tracks belong to our work team.' Uncle Tian straightened his cap, still dubious.

'But,' said Old Jiang cautiously, 'if this is the work team, why cross the river instead of coming to meet us?'

This key question had everyone stumped. The commotion suddenly quieted.

'Did you follow the tracks across the river?' Old Jiang asked.

'Yes. We didn't stop till we found where they'd spent the night.'

'You found their camp!'

These places were inevitably covered in tracks, so it should have been easy to tell if they'd been made by our comrades. Ah Wei's words livened the group up again.

'Did you see hammocks?' asked a comrade urgently.

'No!'

'A fire pit?'

'Also no!'

'Just tell us!' Even elderly Uncle Tian, normally so calm, was agitated. 'What did you find?'

'A level patch where they must have slept. The leaves had been flattened. No fire pit—they probably didn't cook. You know when we're in a hurry and don't want to leave a trail, we eat fried bee hoon from our rations rather than light a fire, and sleep on the ground rather than set up hammocks. Just get through the night and move on. Oh, there were traces of blood on the kapok puffs…'

'A casualty?' Guanghua interrupted.

'That's what I was thinking,' said Ah Wei. 'Maybe they got too close to the Enemy, and there was a skirmish? A casualty would have slowed them down, so they missed the handover. Their first priority would be getting the injured person back to base, rather than searching for the message drop.'

He looked at Old Jiang, seeking his opinion.

It's true, this was worth looking into. They'd been waiting for the work unit, and here at least was some sign of them. This hypothesis was reassuring—they could imagine the detachment, having crossed the river, frantically seeking their comrades.

Old Jiang sat in silence, hands intertwined. His thoughts shifted with the comrades' conjectures and responses. He understood how they felt—wouldn't you be overjoyed if something long-awaited suddenly showed up one morning? If only he could be like them, experiencing nothing but joy at the prospect of an imminent handover.

Ah Wei watched Old Jiang, silent and apparently deep in thought. He suddenly remembered the item in his pocket, and gingerly fished it out. 'Here you go—a footprint. We found this on the road.'

'A footprint?' Old Jiang took the object, no larger than a mango, but exerting a magnetic pull on the dozen or so pairs of eyes fixed on it. Old Jiang placed it on the bamboo table, and carefully pulled away the wild yam leaf it was wrapped in.

A squishy chunk of yellow clay, about half the size of his palm. On it was, unmistakably, the markings of a shoe. Someone called out, 'It's one of ours!'

'That's definitely a comrade's!'

Uncle Tian put on his glasses and studied the clod carefully. After quite a while, he looked up and said with certainty, 'This is a comrade's shoe.'

The comrades nodded eagerly. As their quartermaster, Uncle Tian handled all their gear. No one knew their equipment better than he did.

'That means the work team's here!' he concluded, shoving back his cap in a habitual gesture that revealed his deeply lined forehead. He removed his glasses and grinned, exposing a broken front tooth. Everyone felt much less anxious now. Seeing the footprint was like glimpsing the work team itself, rushing day and night to reach them.

'But comrades, look closely. Something's not right.' Old Jiang suddenly stood and pointed.

'What's wrong?' Guanghua had only just sat down on a bamboo stool, but bounced to his feet again. He bent forward to stare at the piece of earth.

Uncle Tian put his glasses back on.

'Look, the pattern's perfectly clear, like you'd expect from a new shoe.' Old Jiang's eyes narrowed. 'Our work team's been on the road a long time now, marching day and night. Wouldn't their shoes be more worn down?'

Everyone thought they'd found the answer, but grew uncertain again now that Old Jiang had put a big question mark over it. 'The situation Ah Wei described earlier didn't seem right either, did it?' He paused, looking around at his comrades. Everyone was staring back in confusion, so still they might have been carved from wood or moulded from clay.

'For example, why did the work team cross the river? Even if there'd been an injury, they only had to say the location of the message drop and there were plenty of other comrades who could have gone looking for it. It's the scouts, not the HQ, who decide on the route. Then look where they spent the night. That's not the way we camp, but we ignored that because everyone wanted it to be true. Doesn't it actually sound much more like an Enemy camp? Look at the sweeping stick.' He lifted the pole from the table and brandished it. 'Our comrades guard these like their rifles. Who would ever throw one away, unless it was broken? And to toss it by the side of the river where anyone could see it? Comrades, we ought to have spotted these discrepancies. We wanted it to be them so badly, because we've been waiting so long, and didn't consider other possibilities. Of course, it could still be true. If only it is! But if not, if this is the Enemy, then we're in danger.'

Having blurted out what was on his mind, Old Jiang looked around for his comrades' reactions. No one stirred, as if they'd been crushed by disappointment.

From several hilltops away, a lonesome wild pheasant cried out desolately *oh hee, oh hee.*

'B—but… th—that's…' In his agitation, Guanghua started to stammer. 'If we c—can't tell if it's the Enemy or our comrades, wh—what should we do?'

What should we do? Old Jiang had an answer in mind, but wanted the comrades to come up with a solution themselves. He sat in silence, looking expectantly at them.

As everyone eagerly debated the question, Old Jiang realised something and turned to glance at Ah Wei, who was slumped to one side. His brother-in-arms, whom he'd brought south from the border zone, wasn't saying a word. Head down, he looked dazed, his flush of excitement replaced by a greenish hue. The light in his eyes had gone out, and sweat poured freely from his forehead.

2.

After leaving Old Jiang's tent, Ah Wei retreated to his sleeping space. He'd spent the night apart from the others ever since Jingfang was martyred. Guanghua had invited him to bring his hammock closer several times, but he always declined. 'It's easier to find a space to set up on my own.' Then he'd settle by a tree near the sentry post.

Sitting on the gnarled, protruding roots that writhed like pythons, he felt despair for the false happiness he'd willingly embraced just now—in fact, for most of today. Now regret coiled around him, a gnawing venomous snake. He curled up, head buried in his large hands, skinny fingers digging into his tangled nest of hair, eyes shut tight as he resisted the buried memories trying to resurface.

Yet there it was, right in his ear: the clear *png* of a bullet hitting a roasting cassava, sending up a plume of sparks. He flung himself to the ground and rolled behind a tree, shielding himself from the thick cloud of bullets and returning fire. And then? He remembered lying there and watching Jingfang, a few paces away, fall heavily to the ground…

He hadn't seen this coming. They'd needed to stockpile rations while waiting for the work team, so Old Jiang sent him, Jingfang, and two other comrades to the Orang Asli cropland to buy cassava, which they would roast and store. The job had gone smoothly, and they met a middle-aged Orang Asli named Dalay, who called them 'Langway' (meaning 'good people', the Orang Asli nickname for the comrades) and said his father had been close to the Langway in the old days. He even had a five-pointed red star insignia, given by the Langway to his father as a memento. He'd kept hold of it, because seeing the red star was like seeing the Langway themselves. His words moved and encouraged them.

And so, Ah Wei decided to stay near the cassava planting grounds for a couple more days, taking the opportunity to dry some more for their stores.

Jingfang was against this plan. She reminded him of Old Jiang's orders to carry the vegetables deep into the rainforest before roasting them, but he ignored her. They had to 'Trust and rely on the revolutionary masses,' he said. 'What a girlie,' he muttered to himself. 'Afraid of everything, seeing wolves and tigers at every turn.'

Then those gunshots at dawn. Jingfang on the ground, dragging herself towards him, leaving a bright red trail behind her. He returned fire from his refuge among the trees, then dashed out to pick her up and carry her to the shelter of a mound of earth. A stabbing pain in his right calf. Splotches of blood soaking through his grass-green puttees, dyeing them almost black. During a break in the firing, he scooped up Jingfang and both their rifles, and hurtled towards the nearby hill.

They stumbled through the gully. Volleys of mortar explosions echoed through the hill range all around him, whizzing through the air, *shrr shrr*, scattering flurries of leaves.

On his back, Jingfang moaned, 'Water… water…' He was unbearably thirsty too. Finally, he set her down gently. As soon as she touched the ground, she passed out. The front of her shirt was soaked with warm blood.

She never regained consciousness.

The night before Old Jiang's commando unit headed south, they all vowed to 'Spill the last drop of our blood in the rainforests of the fatherland.' During the counterrevolutionary purge a few years ago, he and Jingfang had been tortured: tied up, isolated, interrogated, forced to confess. How many times had they proclaimed, *Let the struggle test our loyalty to the revolution!* When Old Jiang announced he was leading a unit south, how ardently they fought to join him, as much for Old Jiang's sake as for their own need to wash off the shameful stains and restore their revolutionary glory! Seen in that light, Jingfang's death was merely a fulfilment of her promise. A justified death with no regrets.

Only… why did she have to die because of his carelessness? Why hadn't he listened to her warning? He was the one who ought to have died! Yes, him, not Jingfang! When he was accused in a struggle session of not respecting female comrades, he couldn't defend himself, nor did he try, but he also didn't pay much attention to the critique. He'd still called them 'girlies', and thought they were only good for trifling work, lacking vision and ambition. When Jingfang was alive, she was the one who'd dealt with daily chores for both of them: hanging their clothes out to dry, filling their water bottles, packing their equipment, cleaning out their hut. He'd been perfectly capable of doing these things, but believed he ought to save his energy for more important tasks. And now, every one of these jobs that used to be Jingfang's pained him. How he longed to dry her laundry and fill her water bottle. Why hadn't he when he'd had the chance? When rations were distributed, Jingfang would always give him half the contents of her mess tin. The comrades poked fun, but Jingfang would retort, 'He needs the food, he works harder.' When they'd been forced to stop hunting, on the few occasions a little fish swam into their trap, Jingfang would still give him her share. Everyone knew, and miaowed mockingly, 'Hey, kitty, your owner's looking for you.' Ha ha. And now he had no owner. A stray cat. If anyone but Jingfang had suggested roasting the cassava deeper in the rainforest, would things have turned out differently? Why do human beings always take for granted those closest to them? He felt he'd never wash away the puddle of blood Jingfang had left, moist and sticky, on his back.

Still it seemed he'd failed to learn the lesson of the blood. It had barely been three months, and already he was blundering again into blind optimism. As Old Jiang said, 'If this is the Enemy, then we're in danger.'

Ah Wei rubbed his temples. When had they become so clammy with sweat?

Someone tapped him lightly on the shoulder. He turned to look. Old Jiang.

'Look at you. Your hair's as wild as the undergrowth.'

Once, back at the border zone, Old Jiang had cut his hair. He remembered asking how a commander like him had learnt to cut hair, and Old Jiang smiled: it was a skill he'd picked up back in the day, back when he was a regular soldier.

After coming south, it was Jingfang who cut his hair. Which meant it had been a few months since his last haircut. There were no mirrors here, and he no longer had any idea what he looked like.

'Come on.' Old Jiang prodded his shoulder. 'You'll feel lighter without all that hair. Might lift your spirits. You're not getting enough to eat, no point wasting energy sprouting weeds from your head.'

3.

This wasn't Guanghua's first time as a scout.

He was small and agile and had run the mountain route many times before coming south. The dense rainforest was an old, familiar friend. He liked to say, as the more senior comrades did, 'Thunder god rules the sky, but trekkers own the earth', to describe the carefree lives of the trekking team, free from all restrictions. Of course, after joining the assault force down south, his environment changed, and so did the logistics of facing the Enemy. There'd been a few dustups and skirmishes, and now he was even more vigilant. When he was working undercover, the Party sent him to be a contractor at a construction site, firstly because his earnings came in useful, and secondly so he could temporarily house new recruits before they joined the ranks. In order to blend in, he started smoking. After his return to the field, life was so monotonous that he found it impossible to quit. When tobacco was hard to come by, he would grab aromatic leaves from the rainforest at random. One variety, known as 'wild grape', looked like tobacco when you cut and dried it, and made the same puffing noise when smoked. He'd also enjoyed chatting with a cigarette in his hand, expounding about everything under the sun. It was only what happened later that made him give it up. Old Jiang told him to take out a new recruit to gather some rattan. All around their campsite were the iron sentries (that is, landmines) he'd been responsible for placing, and so he led the way. He'd thought they were a good ten metres from a mine when, just as he passed a meranti tree, there was an enormous bang behind him. The new comrade, five or six metres away, was sitting in a puddle of blood, having stepped on the landmine Guanghua had set with his own hands. How had he made this mistake? How? He'd rather have stepped on the mine himself! But there was no way to change what had happened. When he self-criticised, he could only blame his own 'liberalism' and 'carelessness'. He hadn't paid enough attention to his work! That's when he finally gave up smoking for good.

After Jingfang was martyred and he saw Ah Wei moping around all day, he started going over for a quick chat with him every so often. He also privately asked Old Jiang to send them out together. *More than anyone, I know how he feels.*

Hearing Old Jiang's analysis of the situation yesterday made his scalp tingle, and sent flames shooting up his neck and temples. *The commanders really do see things differently from us!* he thought, annoyed at how easily he'd succumbed to mindless hope, gaining a deeper appreciation of the hidden dangers lurking within the unknowable rainforest. He held his loaded

M16 at his waist, barrel pointed straight ahead, thumb on the safety. His wide-open eyes were on full alert, scanning the path ahead. Several times, a swaying branch or nearby rustling caused him to spring behind a tree like a leopard, cautiously looking out for any movement. This was the same path he'd taken on patrol yesterday, but his emotional state was completely different. One day ago, he'd been excited, impulsively sprinting alongside the footprints, his comrades' familiar faces flashing in his mind one by one. Old Jiang's hypothesis poured cold water on his overheated brain, and now he was quietly ashamed of his rash conclusions and inability to see past the surface of things. When they called for a further recce, he volunteered right away.

Ah Wei followed Guanghua, keeping an appropriate distance between them at all times. His sharp eyes scanned their surroundings nonstop. If a footprint looked odd or a tree had been climbed, he stopped for a closer look. From time to time, he also glanced back at Junqiang and Ah Hai.

Late last night, he'd sat on his hammock, unable to sleep. The words Old Jiang said to him during the haircut kept swirling through his brain: 'The Enemy can only defeat you if you've already defeated yourself. There'll be many battles, but we have to stand strong and stay upright!' Yes, he'd suffered through the counterrevolutionary purges, the myriad troubles of the assault force, the pain of losing Jingfang. Old Jiang also said, 'Is growth ever easy? Even a snake has to shed its skin several times!' He had to take a step forward, to burst from his guilt and sorrow like an insect from its cocoon!

All of a sudden, Guanghua stopped and darted behind a tree, then slowly studied the path ahead. After a long while, he tiptoed a few steps forward and looked around again, before finally waving to Ah Wei, who had ducked behind a mound. The group nimbly stepped forward.

In this pheasant plain (that is, a rainforest clearing created by pheasants dancing and thrashing about in the throes of their mating ritual), the leaves on the ground had clearly been stepped on. Guanghua squatted and carefully started lifting them, looking for anything suspicious.

'Well? Did they spend the night here?' Ah Wei walked over to Guanghua, still studying their surroundings.

'Yes! Look.' Guanghua stood, thrusting a handful of ashes at Ah Wei.

'Hey, come see, there are hammock marks,' called Junqiang, waving at them from where he was standing by a little tree about as thick as his thigh.

Sure enough, there was a mark all around the trunk where a hammock had been strung up. In front of it was a hill palm grove that had been recently trodden on.

'This is definitely where our comrades spent the night! Look at these ashes. They can't be more than a day or two old.' Guanghua bit his lower lip, looking at Ah Wei doubtfully.

'Search the area!'

They split up and scrutinised every inch of ground. When they regrouped, Guanghua was holding three sticks that had been sharpened at one end, and said with certainty, 'It must be our comrades! That's a cooking tripod, and there's leftover firewood next to it.'

'But I found this.' Junqiang opened his palm to reveal the gold foil of a cigarette packet and the packaging of some medicinal powder. These were items usually found in huge quantities at Enemy campsites, not anything our comrades would have.

'That's strange.' Guanghua turned the packet over in his hand, scratching his head.

'I've counted the hammock marks—about ten people slept here. But looking at the ground, at least twenty or thirty passed through.' Ah Wei held the tripod in one hand and the medicine packet in the other, glancing at them in turn. He mumbled, half to himself, 'Could they both have been here?'

'You mean both the work team and the Enemy passed by this spot?'

'Yes. If the Enemy found traces of the work team and were hot on their heels, they'd have been here one after the other, and left two sets of markings.'

Guanghua and Junqiang exchanged glances, each sunk deep in thought.

'That means—' Guanghua pointed at the path ahead of them, winding its way through the rainforest. 'The Enemy might be there, and so might our comrades.'

'Yes. We'll need to be very careful. Remember what Old Jiang said. We have to think of this as a hostile situation. That's the only way we can keep hold of the initiative and get a jump on them.'

With that, Ah Wei waved them on. Their footsteps were lighter now, and their eyes sharper. They kept moving, passing tree after tree.

Guanghua stopped again and bent to pick something up. He beckoned to Ah Wei, who ran over. Guanghua handed him the object and whispered, 'A grain of rice! It's fresh!'

'Then the work team is right ahead.'

In front of them was a little hillock. Halfway up the slope, another road slithered between the lush trees. They couldn't see the peak.

'It's almost noon. Could they be at the top of that hill eating lunch?' The thought flashed through Ah Wei's mind. 'But if that's the Enemy, that could be bad—it's not good to move when your Enemy's still.' He pulled them all behind a tree for a whispered discussion.

'I don't think we should follow the trail. If it's the Enemy up there, we're bound to lose.'

'We could hack our way through the brush to the side, get above them, and see.' Everyone nodded at Guanghua's suggestion.

'Remember, if it's the Enemy, we'll go back to camp at once, assuming we aren't discovered. If they engage, we'll fight viciously, and regroup at the maildrop afterwards. Don't forget these may be our comrades, so don't shoot without making sure. Don't hit the wrong target!' After these final instructions from Ah Wei, the group slipped silently into the hillside.

The sun was dazzling through the treetops, and mountain breezes whistled past them. The mist had cleared, and the rainforest looked bright and new. The tangle of doubt inside them would soon be resolved. Were they facing a battle, a joyful reunion, or...? It was as if they each had a little motor in their chests that could be heard chugging away.

4.

Although Ah Wei's detachment only consisted of four people, they took the hearts of all the comrades with them. When they hadn't returned by nightfall, everyone's anxiety was tinged with fear.

'Why aren't they back yet?' The question hovered over every comrade's mind, and Old Jiang imagined all sorts of possibilities. Of course, the detachment had been prepared to spend the night out, and they wouldn't come back till they'd got to the bottom of the situation. Nothing for it but to wait patiently. Old Jiang spread open the document he'd stopped halfway through the previous night, but before he could start reading, he heard the faint ringing of the alarm bell, followed by a flurry of hurried footsteps disappearing into the distance. He sensed the Enemy right away, and his head snapped alertly in that direction. The comrades had put down what they were doing, and were taking their positions behind trees, rifles at the ready. He grabbed his own rifle, slung the ammo pouch over his head, and hurried out of the tent. A comrade came over and, gesturing at Sentry Post Three, murmured, 'The alarm went off. Uncle Tian led the combat team to the defence line.'

'Did you see what it was?'

'Too dark. All we saw were moving figures by the gully.'

As they spoke, the two men walked swiftly to Sentry Post Three.

There, Uncle Tian had already deployed the rifle defences. Old Jiang sat hunched at the foot of a jackfruit tree, one of the map points identified by Uncle Tian.

'What's up?' he asked quietly.

'We can't see anyone, but it doesn't seem like there's a lot of them,' Uncle Tian replied, also squatting. He patted Old Jiang on the shoulder. 'Go on back, we can deal with the situation.'

'I'm not scared. It's just as safe here.'

'Look! Someone's moving,' the sentry cried out.

Old Jiang and Uncle Tian rose slowly to their feet, hugging the tree trunk, and stuck their heads out on either side. Sure enough, a few dozen metres away by the gully, a tree was swaying gently. Their rifles immediately swung towards it.

'Hold fire, we don't know if that's the Enemy,' Old Jiang ordered. They'd left a message telling the work team to meet here, so this might be their comrades.

Then, all of a sudden—

Thwapp! From the gully came the sound of a wooden mallet hitting a tree, followed closely by several more thuds.

'The signal!' said the sentry in a hushed voice.

Old Jiang and Uncle Tian glanced at each other, then gestured for the sentry not to respond. Several pairs of sharp eyes stared in the direction of the noise.

Thwapp! Thwapp! The same number of thumps, clearer this time: the agreed-upon code.

'Signal back!' called out Uncle Tian jubilantly, forgetting to keep his voice low.

This exchange instantly dispelled fears of the Enemy, but everyone's nerves were taut as a bowstring. When something so longed for finally appears, the resultant joy will be mixed with tension. Besides, the suspicions raised by the tracks yesterday still lingered. The eyes of the group moved instinctively to Old Jiang. How much doubt and happiness were mingled in that brief look?

Old Jiang's own gaze was fixed tightly on the source of the noise, though his grip on his rifle had slackened.

A few figures slipped out from behind the tree, each holding a rifle. They moved towards the sentry post.

Through the undergrowth, pushing aside vines, they came closer and closer. Now there was nothing blocking their view, the comrades immediately noticed the red star gleaming in the last of the sun's rays, pinned to a cap—and beneath it, wasn't that the familiar face of a brother-in-arms? One we'd thought of frequently despite an absence of more than a year.

'Comrade Xiangxin!' Old Jiang stepped into the open, waving at the skinny, middle-aged man.

'Ah... Old Jiang!' At almost the same instant, the new arrivals caught sight of him and cried out joyfully, sprinting like wild deer towards the sentry post.

Old Jiang shot forward like an arrow and gripped the warrior's hand, swaying slightly. 'It's been hard on you.'

There were tears in the fighter's eyes as he looked at his commander. 'No, you've had to wait so long, it's been harder for you.'

The sentries, so anxious and battle-ready just a few minutes ago, were overcome by happiness. There were eight other comrades besides Xiangxin. Now they all cheered and called out greetings, their laughter rippling nonstop like the wind through the treetops.

Old Jiang shook hands with every comrade, but kept looking around as if waiting for something. Behind him, Uncle Tian asked, 'Hey, why isn't Old Cheng here?'

'That's right, how come there are so few of you?' These questions quietened the hubbub, and dozens of blazing eyes fixed on the newcomers.

'Oh, we were... separated from Old Cheng and the others,' said Xiangxin quietly, his voice scorched by guilt and unease.

'What!' Someone couldn't help exclaiming.

'It was like this.' Xiangxin turned to face Old Jiang. 'Twenty of us set out together. Ten days ago, we were supposed to ford the big river, but the water was flowing too quickly at the crossing point. We found some rocks that rose above the surface, and fixed bamboo poles to them as handrails. Maybe we made too much noise—an Enemy patrol heard us and set an ambush in a ditch near the river. Luckily, our scouts spotted their tracks on the hillside. Right away, Old Cheng gave the order to scatter. No sooner were the words out of his mouth when the gunshots started. The nine of us were sitting ducks, so we hit the ground and returned fire. About twenty minutes later, we were able to retreat, covering each other. The Enemy was strafing us from above, blocking the way ahead, so we had to breach the dragon's mouth and escape upstream into the gully.'

'What happened to Old Cheng and the others?'

'They were on the other side of the ridge, safe from the Enemy. They must have gone back the way we came. While we were returning fire, some of us heard a whistle in the distance, but weren't sure where it came from. Afterwards, we waited by the message drop, but—'

'No news?'

'Right. And that's how we got split up.'

Old Jiang had been listening in silence, wheels turning in his head. He'd imagined various possibilities, but now that the actual situation had been revealed, he fell back into thought. The key question was where Old Cheng and the other comrades ended up.

'So this means Old Cheng and the rest are on the other side of the big river?'

'Very likely. We'd spent all day walking upstream, but didn't find anywhere to cross.'

'In that case—' Out of habit, Uncle Tian adjusted his ratty old hat. 'Those tracks Ah Wei found across the river might belong to Old Cheng's group?'

'Tracks?' A few of the comrades exclaimed at virtually the same moment.

'Yes, and there was a crossing point—but also some warning signs,' Old Jiang answered. His eyes drifted towards the burgeoning density of the rainforest. At this moment, the sun slipped behind the hills, and the darkness around them began to thicken.

A lone bird returning to its nest, startled by something, let out a long cry as it swiftly passed over the roof of their hut.

'But look at us, chattering away. You haven't even bathed yet.' Uncle Tian smacked his forehead, suddenly realising he hadn't prepared the guest quarters. He waved the newcomers into the camp. 'Come on, let's get you settled, we can talk more later.'

5.

The night slowly crept over them. A rising tide of thick fog rolled in, spreading amid trees that rustled like crashing waves, covering the entire camp. Just a few paces away, trees and bushes loomed darkly, outlines indistinct. Through the dense layers of foliage, a few stars were dimly visible, holes pierced through the black dome of the heavens, luring you to investigate the mysteries beyond. Nameless insects chirped discordantly in the hilltop breeze, the rainforest talking in its sleep.

Old Jiang paced around the campground with his hands behind his back, deep in thought. The events of the last few days turned over and over in his head. Even after a conversation with the recently arrived comrades, he couldn't get to the bottom of this. This unsettling situation was like the mysterious night before him, shrouded in mist, the truth obscured so no one could see or feel what was there. His mind focussed on a single task: gathering everything that had been seen and heard these last few days, in order to deduce who was wandering the rainforest, friend or foe.

In his thirty-odd years, this wasn't his first time lost in a fog, and he hoped it wouldn't be his last. Many things remained confusing, even after years had passed. Before coming south, when he got caught up in the border zone counterrevolutionary purge, hadn't it been just as hard to tell friend from foe? He couldn't convince himself, and the commanders couldn't convince him, that nine-tenths of his comrades were in fact traitors who'd infiltrated their ranks! Of course, he was well aware that the ranks were susceptible to sabotage from such interlopers—he'd seen it for himself several times during the Japanese resistance. But to say these strapping, honest men and women were Enemy agents—no, he couldn't believe it! He'd recruited many of them in the farming villages when he and the other older comrades went in, guiding them step by step on their journey, educating them till they were ready to enlist. They'd been living with the comrades day and night in these rubber tree hills. How could they possibly have secretly received spy training? Their family backgrounds were laid bare, even back a generation or two. How would they have transformed into Enemy agents overnight? Even his own lover was accused! It was ridiculous, bitter, sad, painful—and he couldn't expel these feelings from his heart. Yesterday, while cutting Ah Wei's hair, he'd said, 'Everyone experiences loss, and sometimes this leads to a lifetime of sorrow.' That was heartfelt. Back then, watching the commanders ordering nooses to be placed around the necks of those comrades he knew so well, he'd been helpless with rage. He'd been in HQ himself, but how could he possibly go against instructions from Central Command? The evidence that seemed so certain, all those mutual accusations, went against common sense. He was plunged into a bewildering fog. Some comrades refused to accept the slightest stain, and defended their revolutionary purity and pride, but couldn't preserve their lives. Others managed to survive, but at the cost of going with the flow, accepting the guilt heaped upon them, and dragging other comrades down. He remembered one time, after they'd moved south, Jingfang came to see them and burst into tears, right there in front of her cousin Jingying, his wife. She confessed she was the one who'd given up Jingying's name, implicating her in a counterrevolutionary plot she'd just made up, and that's why Jingying had been seized, placed in isolation, and interrogated. At the time, Old Jiang hadn't been able to make any sense of it. Relying on his decades in the Party to protect him, he'd untied Jingying—but that was all he could do! Jingfang said, 'I had to go on living. If they'd purged me, I'd never have been able to prove my loyalty and innocence.' Watching Jingfang weep and beg forgiveness, Old Jiang had felt he was the one who should be pleading for mercy. He'd recruited them both, yet was powerless to defend their revolutionary honour or preserve their young lives. He comforted Jingfang, 'No one here doubts your sincerity or virtue.' Jingfang shook her head tearfully. 'That's no use. I made a confession—it's all in my file!' When Ah Wei came back wounded that day with news that Jingfang had been martyred at the Orang Asli croplands, Old Jiang hadn't shed any tears. He couldn't have articulated what he felt, a vague sense this was fate. Right away, he'd made a bold decision: he asked for the exact location of Jingfang's death, then led three comrades there through the night, hacking their way through the rainforest, following a narrow path along a steep hillside, till they reached Jingfang's corpse and brought it back before the Enemy could find it. He hadn't been willing for Jingfang to suffer any more humiliation, not even in death.

To this day, he couldn't understand it. Where had this enormous counterrevolutionary wave come from? How could the commanders, whom he'd esteemed so highly before, see the situation so differently? Whose conscience and reason were to be trusted, his or the commanders? Doubt and bewilderment beset him. He'd had to quietly warn himself not to allow his faith in the leadership to be swayed or questioned.

Then in the early seventies, he'd learnt that he would be leading a newly formed assault force down south. How excited he'd been at the news! For the chance to once again set foot in his fatherland, of course, but at the bottom of his heart was a flicker of joy at escaping the whirlpool of the counterrevolutionary purge.

The assault force had put their lives at risk and suffered the storms of fortune for several years now. They'd wandered lost, gone hungry, fallen ill, been betrayed, faced the Enemy—doing battle with the heavens and fellow human beings. Yet no matter how unfavourable their situation, he'd always remained confident. Just like this chaos and confusion before him now. When the sun rose the next day, dispelling the mist, who knew what daylight would reveal? Still his heart was calm. Comparing this to the fog and fear of the purge, he abruptly remembered a saying the old comrades had: 'The battles you fight with a rifle are easy, it's the ones you face unarmed that are hard.'

The struggle was complicated, so naturally their brains had to be complex too. Old Jiang believed this situation would be a crucible for the comrades, both in thought and deed. Especially Ah Wei. Would he see it that way? When he'd cut Ah Wei's hair yesterday, as he tousled that bird's nest, he'd felt sadness and pity. Ah Wei was a wiry guy from Guangxi, not particularly tall; in fact, before he joined up, his nickname was 'Shrimpy'. Would he be able to withstand these repeated torments?

Ah Wei hadn't been able to see the man behind him, only felt his hair falling to the ground, just like when Jingfang used to do it. He understood perfectly clearly that these hairs could never return to his head. All that sprouted there now were endless doubts.

Next, Old Jiang casually asked after Ah Wei and Jingfang's child, the one being raised by his aunt in the village. Ah Wei had seen him before heading south, at the Party's arrangement.

'That little devil. He must be six or seven now?'

'Yes, he's starting school next year.'

'The hope of humanity lies in our children, after all!' Old Jiang brushed hair clippings off Ah Wei's ear. 'But we have to give the children hope too.'

Ah Wei stood up from the wooden block. 'Old Jiang, let me handle the recce tomorrow. Whatever we do badly, we have to correct ourselves.'

So where was Ah Wei at this moment?

Png! A rifle went off, then a whole string of them, reverberating through the night air. The melee ratcheted up the comrades' nerves, and in a short while, more than twenty of them were clustered around Old Jiang at the campsite, bringing with them conjectures, questions, and unease.

'It's directly southwest,' said Uncle Tian, striding through the crowd with a compass. 'Exactly where Ah Wei and his team were heading.'

'Sounds like both sides are exchanging fire,' said Xiangxin, but this hardly explained the situation. The comrades asked themselves: Who were the two sides? Old Cheng and the

Enemy? Ah Wei and the Enemy? Or could Ah Wei and Old Cheng's detachments be firing on each other?

6.

Gunshots speared the fog of night, piercing the stillness of the rainforest. Ah Wei and the other three crouched behind two meranti trees, both larger than they could put their arms around. They took big, ragged gulps of air, listening closely as the gunfire died away.

'That came at just the right time!' Guanghua spoke first, unable to suppress his glee. They'd all been thinking this anyway, and no one answered. They got out their towels to wipe away their sweat, faint smiles playing across their faces.

All the questions raised by their afternoon discovery were now answered in a single burst of gunfire!

Guanghua, leading the way, had almost reached the hillock when there was a sudden rustling from the shrubs in front of them. He instantly ducked behind a tree, where he found Ah Wei already hiding. Straight ahead, voices were speaking Malay. They could hear every word.

'Babi. We've been running like mad all day, chasing, chasing, and we didn't even smell the Communists' farts.'

'I promise you the Magong didn't get far. The tracks we found this morning were new—they must be right in front of us. And they don't even know they're about to die! Heh, with these disguises, they might even come running to us. You scared they'll get away?'

Then pissing sounds. A couple of Enemy soldiers who'd wandered away to relieve themselves. Desperate for confirmation, Guanghua risked a quick peek. Sure enough, a dozen paces away, two bearded, ferocious-looking Enemy soldiers were peeing side by side. The startling thing was their outfits: not the usual camouflage, but the same grass-green uniforms and red-star caps worn by the comrades, down to their rubber-soled shoes. Guanghua felt a surge of agitation.

'But if you don't manage to catch the chicken, you lose the handful of grain. What if the Magong surround us? We're just one squad...' said one of the soldiers a little anxiously, fastening his trousers.

'Don't be scared. Listen,' said the other, patting his shoulder, 'Central Command's sending a platoon up from downstream as backup. They'll spend the night at our old camp at Three Forks River, and should be with us tomorrow at the latest. They've also sent reinforcements to a few more rainforest bases, all battle-ready. Just one radio message and the Magong will have nowhere to run. This was a secret mission—no airborne troops. They'll never know! Heh, this is our best chance! If we lead the victory charge, we won't be sergeants anymore! Time for promotion!'

Their laughter made Guanghua's trigger finger itch. If only he could pump these men full of bullets right now. He glanced sidelong at Ah Wei, who was flushed, dark eyes blazing, gun hand sweating. Too many thoughts churned through his mind. Here, falling into their laps like a miracle, was the perfect chance to eliminate the Enemy and steal their weapons, an opportunity he hadn't had since coming south. In the heat, sweat trickled down his spine, making his shirt stick to his back, just like the blood Jingfang shed that day. A single shot, and those two gleaming black M16 rifles would be theirs for the taking. Two Enemy soldiers laid out on the ground, an offering for Jingfang's heroism, and perhaps a way out of his personal dark night. But a gunfight would surely lead to pursuit, which would make finding the work team impossible!

Ah Wei's teeth clenched. He reached out a trembling hand to clutch Guanghua's shoulder, tamping down his inner turmoil. His expression said: *Don't move.* Their blazing eyes followed the two retreating backs.

Ah Wei tugged at Guanghua's sleeve, and nodded at the tree Junqiang and Ah Hai were hiding behind. They quickly stepped back and vanished into the shrubs.

'We should have shot them, Ah Wei. Why didn't you?' Guanghua snarled, waving his fist.

'The Enemy is very likely going after the work team, encircling them. If we don't warn our comrades in time, they'll be massacred,' Junqiang said anxiously.

'But how can we alert the work team? The Enemy's ahead of us.' Ah Wei was silent for a moment. 'We have to fire a rifle. That's the only way to tell them the Enemy is coming.'

'Yes! That's it! Bang, and the comrades will be on their guard.'

'No, shooting will reveal our position, then we won't be able to do the handover,' said Junqiang, thinking of Old Jiang's instructions.

'Then what?' asked Guanghua.

Indeed, it looked like meeting the work team would be difficult. What a dilemma. Firing a rifle would throw unforeseeable obstacles in the path of their mission. Not firing would leave their work team comrades in the dark about the evil fate about to befall them. Ah Wei turned over these possibilities, his brows knitting into a single dark line.

'How about this: What if we trick the Enemy into shooting? Like this...' Ah Wei squatted and brushed aside some fallen leaves, then drew his battle plan in the soil. The others gathered round.

'Yes, this should work!' Guanghua stood and dusted off his hands, suddenly in high spirits. 'Come on, let's not let those pigs get away.'

They knew a quicker route, and would be able to get in front of the Enemy. Guanghua and Junqiang led the way, advancing towards Three Forks River. Ah Wei and Ah Hai brought up the rear, deliberately leaving obvious tracks to lure the Enemy into following them.

7.

The sun sank towards the west, its slanting rays penetrating layers of branches to listlessly dapple the forest floor like fallen leaves. The ocean of trees slowly darkened.

From a nearby valley suddenly came the enormous crash of a tree falling over. The trunk landed heavily, while branches broke off and continued skittering downhill. The ground itself trembled. Echoes flew through the air, startling roosting birds into flight. The monkeys were alarmed too. A hundred feet in the air, they leapt around their perches, letting out peculiar cries.

Then the rainforest was still again, and dusk rose thickly from the valley. The rainforest became unknowable, mysterious.

The passage of time didn't affect the group's concentration. Operating between two Enemy forces, they were on high alert, every nerve quivering, hunger and exhaustion forgotten.

Three Forks was up ahead. Guanghua and Junqiang returned jubilantly from their recce to report to Ah Wei. 'Sure enough, the Enemy is bivouacked in the old camp at the chicken heart ridge.' (A raised area where two rivers met). 'Just one platoon. They're in the gully now, bathing in the river.'

'Excellent! The troops who're after us must be less than an hour away. It's getting dark soon. They'll pitch camp at the

Dragon Mouth, and they'll want to get water from the river before settling in for the night.' Ah Wei sounded jubilant, his eyes gleaming with high spirits.

From the treetops, a hornbill let out its distinctive cry of *gwah-ah, gwah-ah, gwah-gah-gah-gah-gah.* Then a burst of flapping, and six or seven of them soared over the forest, ink-black wings spread wide.

Night descended suddenly.

The hills were full of leaves rustling, mingling with the slosh of water hitting river rocks in the valley, as if nature itself were snoring. At the chicken heart ridge, four dark figures took advantage of this cacophony to cover their footsteps, slipping nimbly into position. From their hiding place behind a tree, four pairs of sharp eyes turned at the same moment to the newly erected Enemy camp. All was dark, without so much as a lick of flame. If not for the fireflies zipping casually past, it would have seemed like there was nothing at all in front of them. Thanks to the recce, they were absolutely certain that the entire platoon was there, and could even deduce where the sentries were located.

Png! Like a shooting star, a bullet rose in an arc of light from the bottom of the gully, heading straight for the Enemy's sentry post. The gunshot echoed through the hills, shattering the silence of the night.

Png! Png! Png! The sentry shot back, but not knowing where this bullet actually came from, all he could do was sweep his rifle blindly across the chicken heart ridge.

Png! Pngpngpngpng! The second Enemy encampment, thinking they were suddenly under attack, quickly returned fire. Two dragons on opposite peaks, blazing with silvery light.

'Let's go!' Ah Wei called out quietly. As the gunfire masked their movement, the four figures descended into the gully and headed upstream.

When the incandescent flare rose over the valley, it illuminated the bodies of several dead or dying on both ridges. At the bottom of the gully, there was nothing to be seen.

8.

Long, balmy arms of morning sun roused the slumbering rainforest. A million glittering rays broke through the wasteland of sky, pushing aside the thick foliage. Through the ink-dark crowns of trees came a dazzling spill of light, countless rays as radiant as tiny golden needles, impossible to ignore.

The highland mists were thick in the rainforest. They swirled through the air like gauzy material, a mesh finely sifting the brilliance of this new day. Everywhere—on the vast tree trunks, the parasitic ferns, the twirling creepers, the blooming flowers, the grass, and leaves—were dots and dabs of luminosity, speckled and quivering.

The rainforest pulled itself free of nightmares, and woke up from its lethargy.

Ah Wei and the other three had spent the night dozing against a meranti tree. As soon as the first greyish patches of light appeared on the trunk, they were up and ready to hit the road. Walking along, they startled awake several monkeys who'd been snoring among the branches and now chattered furiously at them. Leaves rustled as they tramped on.

'Goddamn it! Of course we run into a big gang of them, just when we can't shoot,' Guanghua grumbled to himself. His unruly stomach gurgled as he imagined the aroma of roasted monkey meat. They hadn't eaten a bite since the previous afternoon. Hunger, thirst, and exhaustion were making their footsteps sluggish, but excitement kept them going.

Abruptly, Guanghua stopped in his tracks to grab a twisting, woody vine about the thickness of his wrist, looking it up and down as the others drew closer. Ah Wei nodded approvingly, and Guanghua got out his knife. He slashed the vine twice, hacking off a five- or six-foot section, which he handed to Ah Wei. Repeating this manoeuvre, he produced three more. The four men held their segments of vine overhead, cut ends to their mouths. Moisture trickled out as if from a tap, sweet and clear.

'Delicious! Better than Coca-Cola.' Guanghua was in paroxysms, licking his lips.

Ah Wei handed the spent vines to Junqiang, who flung them behind a tree. 'Get some rest,' said Ah Wei. 'The road out of Big Dragon is up ahead. Don't step forward till you hear movement.'

Before they could even mop the sweat off their brows: *shrrr-shrrr*, a pause, *shrrr-shrrr*. The sound of comrades clearing a path. They exchanged glances, and Ah Wei's eyes told Guanghua to start moving towards the junction.

On the great dragon path was a hunched-over soldier clearing dried leaves off the road with a sweeping stick, step after step. A few feet behind him was a strapping youth with a rifle by his side, eyes blazing as he kept a look-out. Still leaning against the tree, Guanghua rubbed his eyes and had a closer look. Wasn't that Zhijian from the work team? A dozen yards on was a row of figures. He could just make out Old Cheng and Binghua, and Little Fen the medic.

Unable to hold back any longer, he called out, 'Zhijian!'

The hunched-over man immediately jerked upright, searching for the voice.

'Ah! Guanghua!'

In these harsh surroundings, after so many reversals, the comrades-in-arms were finally united. Their eyes glittered with tears, and each clasped the other's hands tightly.

'Old Cheng, how did you end up here?' Ah Wei asked solicitously, patting the tall but emaciated man on the shoulder.

'It's hard to explain.' Old Cheng's brow furrowed. He had a question of his own. 'Did you hear the gunshots last night?'

'Yes! That was the Enemy.'

'A good thing that happened. If not, we might have been ambushed. After seeing the message Xiangxin left us at the message drop, we prepared to pull back out, and had to pass by here.'

'The Enemy set a trap for you,' Guanghua interjected.

'What's going on?'

'That's... hard to explain too!' said Ah Wei. He looked at the vastness of the great dragon path. 'Let's keep moving. We went through quite a few twists and turns to meet you. Let's wait till we're with Old Jiang and the rest, then we can talk as much as we want.'

Without them noticing, the sun had emerged over the hills. The towering peaks gleamed.

A faint breeze rose, and every leaf on every tree and shrub went into its dance.

IN THE LINE OF WORK

At nine in the morning, I was busy in the medical centre when someone from down the slope called out, 'Haishan, Haishan!'

Even without looking up, I could tell it was Lim Kuan—I knew his gruff voice well. But why so urgent?

I quickly looked in that direction, and there he was on a ridge of earth, about thirty metres down a steep slope, left hand grasping a slim tree trunk, right hand raised high and waving at me.

I half-leapt half-ran to him. He was breathing hard, his short, plump body trembling, sweat beading on his forehead. He met my gaze, eyes apologetic.

'What's going on? Where's your metal leg?' I asked, glancing down.

'Look.' He pulled up his trousers so I could see his truncated calf, like a withered branch stripped of its bark, dangling in the air, the stump scraped red, raw and bloody.

'Aiyah!' I exclaimed. 'Quick, I'll carry you up and staunch the bleeding.' As I spoke, I knelt in front of him.

He climbed onto my back and wrapped his arms around my chest. 'I was trying to hop up here on my own. It's all swollen —that makes my stomach churn.'

'How did you hurt yourself this badly?'

'I was engraving a steel fankok, but a word wasn't clear in the original, so I went to look it up in the dictionary. Forgot my leg was gone. Just stepped and ended up on the ground.'

'Why such a rush?'

'I keep feeling as if my leg is still there.' I was gently dabbing a clump of cotton wool on his wound. Curiously, he asked, 'Hey, where your finger is right now, I feel as if my toes are still moving. Why is that?'

'Why? Heh heh,' chuckled Huang, a medic who'd overheard our conversation. 'You want to set forth again, you old devil. It's got you so confused, even your stump is trying to sprout a new leg.'

That sent the comrades around us into gales of laughter. 'What's so funny?' said Lim Kuan, all worked up. 'I'm serious.'

'Who says we aren't serious?' retorted Huang, who teased Lim Kuan rather frequently. Still grinning, he added, 'Doesn't everyone know that our Ling Guang is the front scout of our trekking team?' He warbled, '*Warrior hearts must turn south in battle.*'

'That's where I was deployed! Duty called. When they say set out, we set out. When they say stay, we stay. No arguments.' Lim Kuan sounded serious, raising his voice to cut through the laughter, almost bellowing. I was wearing a surgical mask, but a moment ago had been yukking it up with everyone else. Hearing Lim Kuan's words, I hastily sobered up, reminding myself not to join in the joking so easily—what if I accidentally hurt the feelings of a comrade? Particularly Lim Kuan, my childhood friend who'd only just recovered from his injury, only just started making strides in his new position.

★

Lim Kuan and I had been childhood playmates. We were both Teochew, like everyone else in our village. I'd heard a few sections of our unit had a lot of Teochews, so everyone could speak their own language regularly. Where we were, though, us Teochews were a minority. He and I only got to exchange occasional words in our language. Most of the time we spoke Mandarin, but neither of us could quite get rid of our accents. At the welcome gathering on our first evening, Lim Kuan made a speech, but as soon as he opened his mouth, a ripple of laughter went through the crowd. He'd wanted to say, 'Thanks to the Party and our comrades, for this get-together'—but 'Party' came out as 'patty', and 'get-together' more like 'gag-togagger'! They nicknamed him Ling Guang, deliberately mangling his name.

He and I joined the Underground around the same time. We'd just graduated from middle school, and the Organisation put him in comms, which meant he was always running around. As for me, I was stuck at home rearing my family's pigs, so the task they gave me was studying traditional Chinese medicine. We embarked on our new lives, and yes, my life did change, but not all that much. A couple of years went by, and I was still me, the same well-behaved schoolboy.

It wasn't like that with Lim Kuan. Each time he came back from the outside world, he was noticeably different—he dressed more fashionably, wore his hair long, started growing a beard, took up smoking, and even his way of talking got coarser. One time, he came to visit me while I was out. I came home to find a startling figure in my house: yellow-and-red batik shirt, green thirty-inch flared trousers, unruly hair, straggly beard, thick-rimmed glasses, smoke trailing from his cigarette. Taken aback, I blurted out, 'Who are you looking for, sir?'

He turned around, whipped off his glasses, glared at me sternly—and couldn't stop himself bursting into laughter.

We both knew that, given the circumstances, his get-up was in the line of work. How else could he get past all the inquisitive spying eyes on every street corner? If I'd had to transform myself so thoroughly, I'd surely have felt ill at ease, rather than taking to it as easily as he had. Back then, I said to him, 'I take my hat off to you.'

'What for?

'You're a completely different person!'

'You think this doesn't bother me?' He jumped to his feet, gesturing vigorously with his right hand, scattering cigarette ash across the floor. 'You know, my ba has just been glowering at me, not saying a word. Then, just now, he stuffed two dollars into my hand, pointed at my hair, and yelled, "I didn't raise you to be a hooligan. Ten years of school was wasted on you!" Then he screamed at Ma—said all that studying had turned me into a pig.'

I'd never heard him mention any of this. His ba, Uncle Seng, was one of the most steadfast elders in our village. I'd never have expected him to lose his temper like this.

'How could I explain this to him? Who would believe this is in the line of work?' he muttered to himself. Then, with a shake of his head, 'Forget it.' With that, he settled back into his chair, hoisted his thigh, turned to one side, and raised the cigarette butt once more to his mouth, squinting as he drew hard on it. Wisps of white smoke seeped from the corners of his mouth, as if he were expelling all the sorrow buried in his heart.

This problem wasn't solved until the Organisation activated us. This was in 1973, by which time I'd been studying traditional medicine for several years—finally, I would be able to put it to use. Meanwhile, Lim Kuan had been working day and night to bring on a new batch of guerrillas. We both jumped for joy when we got the summons.

The night before we left, he took me to say farewell to Uncle Seng. He was afraid that if he went alone, the old man wouldn't believe him, and would try to stop him, assuming Lim Kuan was up to no good. Unexpectedly, when he'd heard what we had to say, Uncle Seng lowered his head and was silent, leaving us anxious. Finally, he looked up and took hold of his son's arm. 'Zo ni' (Teochew: 'why') 'didn't you say something sooner?' With that, he insisted on dragging us into the village for a meal.

We'd been to the Teochew fried kway teow stall beneath the banyan tree countless times, but never feeling the way we did, our bellies full of words we didn't know how to express. The old man ate a couple of mouthfuls then set down his chopsticks and squinted at us through his glasses, first at me then at Lim Kuan, as if meeting us for the first time.

We were almost done eating when he finally spoke. 'I'd be lying if I said I wouldn't miss you. You raise a child all these years, then he leaves, and you don't see him anymore—' His breathing got heavier, his chest rising and falling. 'You chose your own road. I can't say you're doing the wrong thing, serving the People. Which family hasn't suffered in our New Village? The "state of emergency" and May thirteenth. Our lives are cheap as dogs and pigs. Just one thing: If you're going to do it, then do it properly. No changing your mind, no going back and forth.' His eyes flashed at Lim Kuan, holding both encouragement and a warning. 'If you dare to turn around, just you watch—I'll break your legs in two!'

Once we were inside, the old man sent a letter by messenger, and stuck a hundred ringgit inside. Lim Kuan showed me the letter, just a few lines long. As far as I can remember, it went: 'Your old ba is doing just fine in every way, don't worry about me. When you're out there you have to give it your all, no shortcuts, stay focussed. Make sure you get on well with everyone. When one of you has a problem, the rest will jump in to help.' The old man loved his son so. If he could see Lim Kuan today, one leg sacrificed to the Revolution, how it would break his heart.

*

I saw with my own eyes the moment Lim Kuan lost his leg, and I helped him with my own hands. There were so many long, sleepless nights when I helped him get through his pain.

Right after we joined up, we went through three months of basic training. I was deployed to the medical corps, while Lim Kuan stayed with his old expertise, communications. Of course, this meant something completely different in the rainforest than it had in the outside world. Out there he'd had the two wheels of his bicycle, but in here there were only his two legs; out there he'd dressed casually, in here he was in full battle gear with a rucksack that reached above his head; out there he'd raced down streets and alleys, in here he forged through an ocean of trees. Yet no matter what, for the sake of the Revolution, he would go wherever the Party told him. Like all comrades from the cities and towns, Lim Kuan slowly had to get used to the rainforest environment through rigorous training, until he could finally grasp the ways of the hills and rivers. By the time of his third wilderness expedition, he was being recognised as the best scout, the 'locomotive' of the southern trekkers. The comrades joked that he was living up to his nickname, 'Ling Guang' as in 'brilliant light'. The condor has taken flight, they exclaimed.

I couldn't help feeling far inferior. Never mind rainforest expeditions, I wasn't even chosen to carry out regular tasks like transporting rations. Even when I went out to gather medicinal herbs, I had to be accompanied by a 'hill sprite', for fear I would get lost in the rainforest. Naturally, the constant stream of medical tasks greatly increased my professional knowledge, but still I wasn't satisfied. I wanted to go on a long expedition. Before each trip, there'd be all kinds of preparations: gathering dried rations, sewing water sacks, frying bee hoon, packing medicines, and so on. Seeing the signs, I grabbed this opportunity to persuade everyone, from the branch committee to the Party committee, expressing my determination and laying out my reasons. In a word, I wanted to be included.

I asked Lim Kuan for help too. Each time he came back, he'd always regale me with exciting stories about the expedition: fishing with explosives, hunting, chasing elephants, gathering turtle eggs. Envy took my breath. Would he sing my praises in front of the unit leader to increase my chances? He responded to my request with a howl of laughter, then patted me on the shoulder and said, with both jubilation and empathy, 'Rather you than me. If I'd been stuck working in camp, I'd have died of boredom.'

I'd done it. My name was included in the 1977 expedition as the unit's medic. By coincidence, Lim Kuan would once again be the advance scout.

Everything went swimmingly on the way there. Our burdens were heavy and we moved slowly, but the comrades forged on with a single heart, united in our struggle over hills and across rivers, breaking into territory secured by the Enemy, advancing step by step until we finally reached our destination and linked up with our trekking comrades.

Now that we had accomplished our mission, we were able to set down the burdens on our hearts, and our backpacks were much less weighty, allowing us to lighten our footsteps.

In order to shorten the journey, the troop got ready to ford Sungai Perak upstream, at one of the wider bends. A year ago, a comrade had been swept away by the undercurrent while traversing a river, and leadership had sent a telegram to say: *It is essential that you do a thorough recce, to seek out the safest crossing point for this and future expeditions.*

We reached the southern bank of the great river at noon and paused to rest as a smaller group set out to find a stretch of water with no unexpected currents. Our plan was to wait for nightfall, when we could cross under cover of darkness.

At four in the afternoon, we began cutting down bamboo stems and weaving vines between them, to create shields. Soon the hillside had a hundred-metre-long stretch of bamboo poles standing upright, throwing up clods of earth and startling the macaques, who cried out *hoo-wah* as they leapt from the branches.

We crept down to the river at seven, holding our bamboo shields before us. By then the golden sun had dipped below the green hills, and the river that had been glittering with ten thousand points of light had turned inky black in an instant. Seven or eight hornbills rose in a flock and darted across the river, leaving their *gok gok* cries amid the vegetation. Wisps of fog rose from the water surface and dispersed.

Unit Leader had calculated that as we were in the last third of the lunar month, the waning crescent moon would only be visible in the later part of the night, and we could take advantage of the pitch-black hours after dusk to cross the river.

The river wasn't too wide here, but with the fog blurring the boundaries between rainforest and water, it looked infinitely huge. Life proliferated in the rainforest during the day, thrumming with sound and movement, but now a vast black gauze had descended. Through the gloom drifted pale glimmers: fireflies, tender spots of desolation. The river's rushing filled our ears, and its dimly gleaming surface seemed unfathomably broad.

Lim Kuan and Li Gang, both skilled at watercraft, slid soundlessly into the dark river. Each held a bamboo screen as camouflage, rifles balanced atop. Their task was to reach the other shore and, upon ascertaining there was no Enemy activity, light a fire to signal it was safe. They would then cover the rest of the unit as we crossed.

The two men slowly progressed through the water, until all we could see were two black spots like bobbing coconuts. Watching the borderless dark engulf them, I felt an unexpected wave of terror sweeping over me, leaving me barely able to breathe.

As they reached the midpoint, a blinding flame suddenly appeared among the dingy shadows of the far shore! At virtually the same moment, a few dozen metres of riverbank seemed to catch fire, and a *pngpngpngpngpng* of gunfire rose like a thunderstorm.

Our guards immediately returned fire, covering the duo in the water. But some comrades saw that with the first gunshots, Lim Kuan and Li Gang had disappeared beneath the surface.

Change of plans: we trekked through the night, getting to the pre-arranged maildrop as quickly as possible. No one said anything along the way. My heart might as well have been a chunk of lead. I might not have had any fighting experience, but it was clear how much danger they were in, stranded unarmed in the belly of the river, Enemy fire pouring down on them. Even with night providing cover, it only took one unseeing bullet to hit its target. What would happen to them? I didn't dare imagine.

That night we waited huddled against trees by the maildrop till nearly sunrise. Amid the *chee cha* of the dawn chorus, the pre-arranged signal finally sounded. Our sentries responded, and the other unit slowly appeared from the morning mist, stumbling towards us.

An icy wind blew right through my spine, a premonition. 'They're in trouble,' I muttered to myself, staring so hard my eyes felt on fire.

'Haishan! First aid kit!' yelled our leader, who had sussed what was going on. He shot towards them like an arrow, accompanied by a couple of comrades.

Our leader was a strapping older comrade, with white hair and a broad forehead above two thick salt-and-pepper eyebrows. He'd joined up at the age of thirteen, and several decades of guerrilla life had left him completely unflappable, the quickest to respond in any crisis. Without hesitation, I did as he said. By the time I had the kit laid out, Lim Kuan was in front of me, breathing hard, so drenched he might have been pulled from the water just that moment, face ghastly white, an evaporating haze steaming off his back. Seeing me, he blurted, 'Li Gang's injured!' He raised his left hand and jabbed the middle finger into his shoulder blade. 'A bullet entered there and went right through him. He's lost a lot of blood.'

'And you?'

'Me? I'm fine.' He sat on a protruding root and slumped against the tree trunk. 'Fuck it, how did the Enemy know we were crossing there? Lucky those scaredy-cats fired while we were still so far away, otherwise...'

Now that our brothers-in-arms had returned, everyone felt a little calmer, though our situation remained dire: the skirmish, exposing our movements, meant more Enemy soldiers in the hills to flush us out. Once it got light, their helicopters would hover by the river, dropping bombs indiscriminately. Meanwhile, our trekkers would have to turn back with limited rations, and Li Gang was injured. Our fighting power was nothing like before. The most urgent task was to shake off pursuit. We'd loop round the bend in the river and cross further upstream, but even three days' journey might not be enough to break through the Enemy cordon. And how could we find another crossing point under their tiger-like gaze? No time for delay. But what should our next move be?

Lim Kuan went up to Leader and said, 'I know a way.'

Leader was sitting on the ground, deep in thought. He turned now to look at Lim Kuan and, as if reading his thoughts, said, 'Head upstream to the fork, and cross at Chicken Heart?'

'Yes. The Enemy won't dare to go there, so we can get the jump on them.'

'That's a minefield. We skirmished there with the Enemy year before last, and they blanketed the hillside. The way the Orang Asli tell it, even a deer couldn't get across!'

'We won't take the dragon path, but cut along the half-row.' (That is, halfway up the hillside.) 'Then once we're past the dragon mouth, we'll make a run for it. There's so much open ground there, they can't possibly have put mines at every step?'

'I thought of that too.' The leader was silent for a moment, sucking on the cigarette that drooped from his mouth, its glowing tip almost at his lips. With a grunt he rose to his feet, dropped the cigarette butt, and stamped on it. 'Let's do it!'

This was only my first expedition, and far more twists and turns were coming up than I had expected. Now a minefield? My heart was at sixes and sevens. What would this be like? I wasn't afraid, only anxious. Perhaps Li Gang's injury was casting a shadow over me. I looked ahead at Lim Kuan leading the way, and couldn't shake the feeling of unease.

By contrast, Lim Kuan seemed calm. The next day, we crossed the river fork and went up the dragon ridge, where we found several craters left by exploded mines—some as large as cooking pots, the smaller ones like bowls—snapped wires still protruding from the soil. Lim Kuan pointed them out to Leader and said, 'In a few years, when the batteries and detonators have stopped working, we can come back and collect the explosives.'

It was hard going along the hillside, a steep slope without an inch of level ground. We had to walk with one foot higher than the other, spattered by the loose soil. Branches entwined with vines stuck out across the path, so dense they looked impassable, but we could only grit our teeth and force our way through. A couple of comrades took turns carrying Li Gang piggyback, and I followed behind, holding aside thorny limbs that might otherwise strike the patient. After a good while of this, my palms began to throb with pain, and I could see the other comrades had cuts on their faces, necks, and arms.

Evening took forever to come. Looking at the route, we worked out that by lunchtime the next day, we'd be at the great river. Once we were across, the Enemy would be left safely behind. In the wide-open land, we could spread our wings, and home would be—not far away. At the thought, we let out a collective breath.

Who could have predicted what came next? Soothed by the rush of the river, we were mopping the sweat from our faces when an earth-shaking explosion—*hrrrng lrrrng*—had me instinctively flinging myself to the ground. Leader's voice rumbled, 'Don't move, look out for mines!'

'Leader!' Rongjun the scout cried hoarsely, dashing over sprayed with dirt. 'Lim Kuan stepped on a mine.'

My brain froze. *Hrrrngg.* I stared at the ground. Then I gathered myself, ready to sprint over.

Leader reached out to stop me. 'Step where I step.' He walked ahead of me, taking big strides.

Lim Kuan was slouched in the head scout's arms, left leg held high, foot missing. The bloody shredded flesh of his wound was smeared with dirt. Something like a giant rubber band drooped from the stump, and blood gushed like a spring.

'I sh… shouldn't have stepped on that root,' he said guiltily to Leader. His huge eyes blinked slowly, his face was white as paper, a vein twitched in his forehead. Drops of sweat the size of beans rolled down his cheeks, leaving brown streaks in the grime.

'Don't say anything,' said Leader, reaching out a hand to stop him.

I immediately began applying a tourniquet. This was the biggest injury I'd ever had to tend to on my own. Feeling a jumble of emotions, I cleaned the dirt from the wound and cut off the dangling tendon. Lim Kuan's leg was shaking from tremendous pain. I tried to be as gentle as I could, keeping a close eye on his reflexes. His eyes were wide, he bit down on his lower lip, the muscles in his face convulsing, breath was coming in harsh bursts, his uniform was soaked through with sweat.

When I finished bandaging him, he went limp as cotton stuffing—but there was no way we could stay here. The Enemy had surely heard the blast, and if we didn't move right away, we would probably be attacked or ambushed. Our only option was to get going, carrying our two injured comrades.

'Sl... slow down.' Lim Kuan's head, which had been resting on a comrade's shoulder, jerked up and he spoke with difficulty. 'Sh... shoe. M... my shoe. D... don't let th... them see...'

Leader understood, and gave an order that the pieces of Lim Kuan's shoe, blown apart in the explosion, should be gathered and buried.

We managed to cross the river, but would the Enemy catch up? Which way should we go the next day? Were Li Gang and Lim Kuan in danger from their injuries? Our minds, full of these questions, felt stuffed with straw, and no one could rest easy. More than ever, I felt the burden on my shoulders was heavier than I could have imagined.

I stayed awake all night, watching over Lim Kuan. I'd given him a sedative, and he managed to doze through the first half of the night before being roused by the gunpowder burns, which made him feel like his whole body was on fire. He had a temperature of 104. Delirious from agony, he kept muttering, 'I'm sorry' and 'I shouldn't have stepped on that root.' When the pain was unendurable, all I could do was offer him my arm to hold onto. His fingers dug into me like pincers, leaving my flesh swollen and numb. I would have happily taken on more discomfort, if that would have lessened his burden. At one point, he begged me in a trembling voice, 'Sing for me... sing something.' And so I did: *Hometown river flows through dreams / Warrior hearts surge, homesick / Fatherland mountains urge us on / And warrior hearts must turn south in battle / My childlike heart will not age, it remembers mother warmth...*

Leader didn't sleep well either. Whenever Lim Kuan stirred, he came running over to pace around his hammock. In the small hours of the morning, he gave up and spread a plastic sheet by a tree trunk, so he could doze sitting up. I saw the amber glow of his cigarette flickering in and out of view, all through the night.

And still we had to get moving. With our advance scout out of commission, the only other person who knew the route well was Leader himself. He took me aside before we set out. 'Haishan, I'll leave Lim Kuan and Li Gang in your care. I have to lead the way.'

Leader would be the advance scout? Surely that wouldn't do. Especially after our commanders' repeated instructions. But if not, what were we supposed to do? When Leader walked past us with his rifle in his arms, every one of us wanted to reach out and stop him, but nobody could find the words.

'No way,' said Lim Kuan. As soon as he heard what was going on, he'd asked the comrade piggybacking him to hurry up front, so he could grab Leader by the sleeve. 'You can't be in front!'

Leader smiled evenly as he turned and said quietly, as if coaxing a child, 'I know the way well. We'll cut straight ahead and get back to base a little sooner. We don't have much rice or medicine left.'

'Someone else could lead the way.'

'Who?'

'Me.'

'Definitely not. Whoever heard of a wounded advance scout?'

'I won't be in front. The second in line can carry me piggyback, and I'll call out directions.' He said this very seriously, with great determination. He was in much better spirits this morning. After staunching his wound, I'd given him an anti-inflammatory and a glucose injection, which brought his temperature down a little, though it was still hovering around 102.

'No, I'll go first.' Leader wasn't giving way.

'Just let me do it for a couple of days. How else are we going to get through our own minefield?'

Indeed, straight ahead lay dragon ridges strewn with mines by previous trekkers. Without Lim Kuan to guide us, we'd have to make a detour, and our already diminished store of food and medicine would surely run out.

'Please?' said Lim Kuan, gripping Leader's shoulder in his anxiety. 'It's all in the line of work.'

'I'll do it.' Liyan, a petite comrade, suddenly stepped forward. She was an experienced trekker, and her eyes shone with confidence. 'I helped set those mines, and I remember where they were. I'll be the advance scout.'

'All right, and I'll help guide the way,' Lim Kuan chimed in.

And so Lim Kuan was back in the advance party. Leader told me to stick close to him. Riding tall on a comrade's back, his lips pressed firmly together and his fierce eyes fixed on the path ahead, as he called out directions to the rest of the unit.

Forging a new path through the hillside frequently meant having to bash through undergrowth and shrubs, navigating thorny thickets full of plants we couldn't name, catching and tugging at us. A vine with fish-hook thorns kept catching Lim Kuan's earlobes and temples, until they were streaked with blood. Every now and then, a twig would hit his leg stump, causing such agony he couldn't stop sweating.

I followed behind, staring at his back, full of a rushing agitation I couldn't have described. Was it something like compassion? Pity? Admiration? Respect? I couldn't tell. As I ruminated, my eyes prickled. I'd known Lim Kuan more than twenty years, but only now was I seeing how strong his life force was, what magnificent sparks it could produce. Where did this strength come from? I felt as if I'd only just gotten to know him, and spent a long time thinking about this.

★

Most of a year went past in a flash. Lim Kuan received excellent treatment in the unit, and his injuries recovered day by day. His left foot had been sacrificed to the war, and his calf shrivelled like a tree trunk stripped of its bark, clumping into scar tissue that would never heal.

The workshop made a prosthetic which I brought to him one morning. He turned it this way and that, examining it closely, then lowered himself onto the bed, stump drooping, and asked me to help him put it on.

'Fits perfectly,' he said in Teochew, smiling. Joyful as a small child, he wanted to get to his feet right away.

'Not yet!' I hastily grabbed him by the shoulders. 'We haven't put in the sponge padding, and the skin on your stump hasn't toughened yet. You'll bleed.'

'So when can I walk?'

'When your skin is up to it.'

'I'll go out with this leg one day. Do you think I'll still be able to trek?'

'How do you mean?' I gave him a startled look.

'The Party put so much effort into training me, and I know this route better than anyone else. Tell me, how could I not continue?'

I stared at him blankly, uncertain what to say.

'Don't believe me?' He looked displeased. 'Don't you remember? All the way back, even with my leg bleeding, I still remembered the way. So why couldn't I do it now, with my metal leg?' Looking me in the eye, he added with emphasis, 'It's all in the line of work.'

'No, no, I believe you,' I hastily replied. It was true—how could I not? When he once again invoked the line of work to express his determination, the words were a red thread linking together my memories, drawing them out: walking out of the school gates and joining up together; him working as a messenger, us both in fatigues; setting out together, him being carried on a comrade's back and still guiding us... What abrupt changes we'd lived through! The only unchanging thing was the work, a rock-like article of faith, the forge he lived in every minute of the day, making him ever stronger.

I gently stroked his iron leg, imagining the hardship he would now have as a guerrilla, and felt a burst of sorrow. My eyes dampened, and I couldn't bear to look up at him.

★

Not long after this, the print room got someone to bring Lim Kuan a steel board and metal pen, asking him to practise carving waxed paper.

He took the items and froze, staring at them in confusion. 'Can I...?'

The man who'd once spent all his time roaming, now had to sit down quietly; a hunter who habitually had his rifle in his hands as he wandered the hills looking for prey, now had to grasp a slender writing implement. He had to set down all that was familiar to him, and begin this unfamiliar work. Another fork in the road of Lim Kuan's life.

He didn't hesitate too long. One sunny morning, he cleared a space on the bamboo table by the door of our unit, set down the steel board and stylus, sat upright before them, lowered his head, and began taking his first steps towards this new position. I kept an eye on him, solemnity welling up in my heart. When I went over for a closer look, the pale blue waxed paper already had a few neat rows of writing carved into it, beneath the title, 'In Memory of Norman Bethune'.

★

'Hey, Ling Guang, what's the big rush? You came out without stopping to put on your metal leg?' Seeing that Lim Kuan seemed serious, Huang quickly changed his tone. He'd asked exactly the same question I had, shaking me from my recollections.

'Heh, I don't know how it happened. All I could think of was I needed to look something up in the dictionary, and next thing I knew, I was on the ground.' He glanced around at everyone, shaking his head. 'Besides, I need to be in a rush! Things keep going wrong. "The People's rights" appears several times in the document, and I spelled it as "writes" all the way through—dozens of times!' He held out his palm and demonstrated the wrong character. 'You can't imagine how long it took to carve away all those mistakes—a whole morning. I'll have to improve my literacy for this new job.'

'No wonder the *Xinhua Dictionary*'s falling apart, with you looking up all those words. Why not just swallow the whole book?'

Lim Kuan grinned, and his catchphrase came easily to his lips.

'It's all in the line of work.'

HILLSIDE RAIN

No one had thought it would rain.

The weather had been so pleasant, the sky above the crop fields a clear blue expanse. The sun was a fireball bestowing unceasing light and heat on all living things. Warmth rose from the newly turned soil, and the cropland was enveloped in shimmering light. Brushing away their sweat, the comrades ran to-and-fro, some scattering fertiliser, some watering crops, some tilling the ground, some setting up trellises, and others still weeding the fruit orchard. This was the best time to work, or it was until the rain arrived unexpectedly!

And that was that. We had no choice but to run for shelter with our tools. Rain came pelting down from the borderless sky like a storm of arrows, dense and unrelenting, *pik pak pik pak*.

A few of us huddled in the shelter and immediately started grumbling.

'Stupid sky. Suddenly starts bawling like a baby.' Hands on hips, Young Li huffed as he glared at the sheet of rain. 'Pah! So much for the fertiliser. We *just* put it down!' Every time he moved, the faint whiff of shit came off him.

'The shoots are in trouble. With rain this heavy... I don't think we'll be able to transplant anything today.'

'You wait and see. Tomorrow the field will be rotting and mouldy.' Leader, a talkative and frequently agitated man, couldn't keep his words in. His thick brows lifted and his large eyes widened, and his voice went up like he was arguing with someone. 'What the hell, it's barely stopped raining this whole month.'

'I heard it's going to be like this for quite a few years.'

'They said on *The Science Show* that a volcano erupted in Mexico, and the ash cloud is changing weather around the world.' Four-eyed Wang Xin regularly listened to the radio, and knew everything about everything.

'What are we going to eat now? What kind of vegetables can we grow?' Leader rubbed his hair, which was prematurely streaked with white although he'd just turned forty. His large hands dislodged a cascade of water droplets. 'Oh, I almost forgot.' He smacked his thigh and stood up. 'The tap for the watercress needs turning off.' He clumsily shrugged off his shirt, rolled up his trousers, grabbed a sheet of plastic to hold over his head, and set off in a squelching jog.

'Hey, has anyone seen Donghua?'

'She was in the old field weeding.'

★

It was strange how long the deluge kept going. After more than half an hour, the raindrops finally slackened, like a drumbeat abruptly slowing down.

The sky remained dull, dark clouds flung across it like cotton stuffing leaking from a padded jacket. Wind gusted through the rainforest as if chasing after something, and the rain threatened to return. Leader pondered the situation, and finally waved a hand in defeat. 'Pack up for the day.'

Sure enough, the comrades had no sooner reached the rainforest camp next to the cropland when the downpour started up again, and kept going with only a few breaks.

'Where's Donghua?' During roll call, Leader realised we were short one person.

'Wasn't she at the old field? Maybe she didn't hear the call to stop work.'

'How could she still be working in weather like this? Even if she missed the order, she should take some initiative.' Leader shook his head, annoyed.

The storm continued in infuriating bursts. Dusk came early to the clouded forest. The comrades cleaning their rifles had already lit their oil lamps. It looked like the end of any normal workday, except Donghua was nowhere to be seen.

'What's going on? Still no sign?' Leader couldn't stay still. He tossed his mess tin onto a shelf, and ran outside *tseng tseng* back the way we'd come along the slope.

'Maybe she can't get across the river? The stepping stones are probably submerged by now, and you know she's scared of floods.' Wang Xin had dashed out too.

'Huh, all the more reason to stop work early! No need to be so stubborn—she's not a three-year-old.' Leader was pacing around muttering. Although we were still worried about Donghua, it was him we gathered around in our alarm. 'There'll always be work to do on the field. So she manages to pull a few more weeds. What if she falls into the river? What then?'

'That's how she is, always taking on more burdens,' said Wang Xin thoughtfully.

'Right? Remember when she got sick but insisted on staying out until finally someone had to carry her back?' Wang

Lan grumpily recollected. 'Like I said, isn't that just causing everyone trouble?'

'What? Trouble?' Maybe that was going too far. Leader glared at Wang Lan, ready to snap at her, but something seemed to slip in his tone, and he muttered, 'Haven't I said all along? The unit has all these young men and women, we could have sent the very best, but instead *she* had to come! Getting sick every two or three days. What a headache.'

'Right? She can't carry anything. Even a twenty-pound basket of yams—she was grunting and stumbling all the way back.' Seeing someone agreeing with her, Wang Lan warmed to her theme.

'She eats slowly too. More than ten minutes to get through just a few pieces of yam. Everyone has to wait for her before we can set off,' someone else interjected.

'It's not healthy to eat too fast,' said Wang Xin. 'Besides, she has stomach issues.'

'What's more important, health or warfare?' Leader was an impatient man by nature, particularly when leading a squad, and Donghua had filled his belly with rage. Without realising it, he was getting angry now, and his voice got louder. 'Now look. What time is it? And still no sign of her? The sentries have stepped down by now. What if something happens?' He turned away, spreading his large palms. 'Do we have a choice? We have to go search for her.' With that, he slung his rifle onto his back and, ignoring the people trying to stop him, stomped off downhill through the mud.

Up in the hills, heavy rain made every river swell, gushing down full of fallen leaves and withered branches, engulfing the boulders that normally rose from the riverbed, leaving only uninterrupted murky yellow, churning and roaring, impossible to tell how deep. Everyone who lived in the hills was familiar with this, and of course Donghua must have known too—although even after more than a decade in the rainforest, all kinds of things remained unfamiliar to her. But then who would expect a pampered girl from a middle-class city family like her to join the guerrillas! If Donghua hadn't known Yunhua, she might not have believed herself capable of it. There were truly times when she barely recognised herself. Her limbs were still smooth and slender as a little girl's, and her comrades were always teasing her for having 'deer' legs. If not for Yunhua, how would she have survived in the wilderness? Some things were harder to change, though. Whenever Donghua saw a large expanse of water, all the weight in her body would fall away and she'd grow dizzy—a persistent problem. Earlier, during a pause in the rain, she'd left the shelter intending to return to camp. But then she walked past the area she'd just hoed, and noticed the goosegrass, dandelions, and keremak flowers, poking their heads out after getting drenched by the rain, vibrantly green and stubbornly brimming with life; then there was another patch to one side she hadn't weeded yet, where the withered brown stalks of grass were trembling in the wind. She could sort this all out in an hour or two. At the thought, she stopped walking and gazed up: wide open sky, heavy clouds scudding by in the wind, impenetrably dim. Water trickled off a banana leaf and onto her hair; she raised a hand and wiped it off. There's still time, she thought. Might as well finish the job and turn over the soil I've hoed, otherwise I'll have wasted my effort.

As her hoe sunk again and again into the soil, soft and loose now that it had absorbed its fill of rainwater, the sky blushed a pale rose pink. Like the weather, her mood lightened. What a good thing she hadn't hurried back to camp, she thought. To be honest, though, she really wasn't feeling well. A little over ten minutes of work, and sweat was already appearing on her forehead, while her breath was growing ragged. And still she was exhilarated, having spent the whole of the last week ill in bed, forbidden to come to the cropland though she'd asked a few times. At least now she'd been declared 'fit for work'. The comrades were always saying how if you fell ill while farming, you couldn't help but worry—for the vegetables, for the shoots, for the grass, for the ground... In short, any work you left half done would tug at your heart. She wasn't an essential farmworker, but her sweat had spilled onto this soil too, and her emotions connected her to everyone else here! Yet, she'd heard someone say her illness meant her heart was burdened. There was another layer of meaning here, one she guessed as soon as she thought about it. This had caused a wash of red to rise from the greenish pallor of her face as she recalled how, more than half a year ago, she'd returned from the cropland after her performance was judged insufficiently enthusiastic, and the other comrades in her unit shot her looks of mingled suspicion and concern. The few who were closer to her had tugged at her sleeve and whispered, 'What happened? Why didn't you pass?' Even before this expedition, Leader had taken her aside and made quite a speech of encouragement. For some reason, the resentment usually buried deep in her heart came surging to the surface all at once. She hesitated, stammered, blushed furiously, but somehow couldn't bring herself to speak. Leader smiled, apparently seeing right through her thoughts, and said in a voice full of empathy, 'Yes, it's true, of course enthusiastic workers are chosen on the basis of performance, and although you've given this your all, comparisons still need to be made with other comrades to see who's contributed the most.' Why did she have to be a frail and sickly woman, pushed to the brink at her time of the month? The doctor said to keep a calm, relaxed state of mind. But no matter what she did, she couldn't escape the weight of melancholy. She rebuked herself sharply, 'Are you really labouring only for the sake of being recognised as an enthusiastic worker? So you didn't pass. Now you're grumpy and sulking?' 'No! That's not it!' her rational mind loudly protested. 'I've never thought that. Back when I first began the work of the Revolution, no one was getting evaluated like that.' In that case, what was the source of this resentment? Why this unhappiness? She grew fearful and panicky, falling into a pit of sorrow and confusion she couldn't extricate herself from.

Why had she given herself the name Donghua, Winter Flower? Not six months after she and Yunhua joined up, Yunhua was martyred during an Enemy engagement. Twenty-seven years of life, snuffed out just like that. Mist in the rainforest can vanish in an instant, even as it leaves a faint layer of moisture on your hair and face. For a very long time, she couldn't accept what had happened. She only burst out sobbing once, rending her heart and lungs, her desolate cries making the rainforest itself tremble. Then she said nothing for quite a while, grieving in silence, absorbing every detail of Yunhua into her own flesh. Finally, she was deployed back to the border zone, and took the name Donghua.

She'd crossed the wide gulf, so why were these motes still clinging to her? All she wanted from her comrades was understanding and confidence. Who wouldn't prefer to live in an environment of warmth and friendship, made up of respect, trust, and kindness?

Enough!

She kept her head down, swinging the hoe over and over, ripping up weeds by the roots, revealing the soggy blackish-brown soil beneath. From time to time, she brought up wriggling earthworms too. What beautiful, rich loam. It could have nurtured a crop of vegetables or tubers, but these weeds had ruined it.

The rain came in bursts, and she had to keep taking breaks. The roar of floodwater grew thunderous, but her fear of crossing the river was squeezed aside by concentration on her work. She'd pulled all the remaining weeds, and even gone through the morning's refuse to pick out the stubborn goosegrass and keremak stalks, which she laid out on a fallen tree trunk. The hills were full of such fallen trees; sometimes they landed across a river, conveniently making a bridge. Once, the unit had crossed the river over one of these, but she grew faint as soon as she saw the water, and only made it halfway. In the end, Yunhua had to carry her across.

Wind blew from the hills, carrying tiny raindrops like stars, brushing across her face, playing with her hair, steeped in the invigorating fragrance of wild mint and wormwood. The crops, bathed by this storm, brimmed with irrepressible life. Banana leaves spread themselves wide, vibrant and green, shedding crystalline droplets with each jolt of wind. Shouldering her hoe, Donghua walked over to where she'd been working earlier, stepping on soil she'd just loosened, feeling a sort of skin-close tenderness. Her eyes, dull for so long, were regaining a faint glimmer of delight at the labour.

Her footsteps grew steadier, and she settled into ease. Thoughts that had been tangled weeds a short while ago now seemed scraped away by her hoe.

From time to time, she bent to pick a stalk of sodden goosegrass, tossing it onto the tree trunk.

Now she stood by the roiling, howling river, and even though she'd tried to prepare herself, its rushing force petrified her, and the churning yellow filled her mind. She hastily turned her face aside. The other comrades must have already gone; she would need to conquer this herself. Her heart thudded violently, just as it had the first time Yunhua asked her out. He'd somehow known right away that her feet were only used to concrete and paved roads. Without warning, he'd pulled her onto the grass verge. She'd panicked for a moment, and stumbled a couple of paces, but Yunhua kept a firm grip on her hand, and soon she was able to walk steadily. In Yunhua's beaming eyes, she caught a glimpse of her own blushes… Thinking of Yunhua now, she felt a gush of warmth in her chest, filling her with courage like she'd never had before. She hacked off a tree branch to gauge the water's depth, then fixed her eyes on the lush, enshrouding rainforest on the far shore, and prepared to step into the water.

'Stop!' came a cry from across the river. The speaker arrived at the same moment as his voice: Leader's burly body leapt off the steep embankment, jogged a couple of steps, and plunged into the water. 'Hold on!' he panted, waving. 'Wait for me!'

MAGIC EARS

I don't deny it: I'm talkative. Go ahead and call me 'chatterbox' or 'blabbermouth'—I don't mind at all. The only people I dislike are the ones who turn a cold shoulder, the ones who're indifferent to everything. You know the sort: stone faces, giving nothing back when you try chatting with them. Like the group leader I met that time.

Here's what I think about chatting, what the comrades call 'bringing out the artillery'. After all, we're living a communal life, and comrades ought to care about one another, to create mutual understanding and share our experiences through the bridge of conversation. This is especially true in a changing environment, say a group that spends most of its time in the wild on guerrilla missions or trekking long distances. Never mind attending study sessions, as soon as you've got your gear on, all your books and documents have to be sealed in a tub and buried. Your radio's mute with no batteries—might as well bury that too. In this unnatural—yet rather common—situation, how do you pass the time between expeditions or after you've carried out your tasks for the day? Conversation, of course. It's not just my hobby, it's my obsession. Mouths aren't just for eating with, you know! Besides, talking won't cost you a cent.

On this occasion, the trekking team had successfully linked up with our brother unit, and we now had to travel together to carry out the mission our leaders had entrusted us with. Everyone was in high spirits. Even though we hadn't yet recovered from the exhaustion of the long journey, and the road ahead would be arduous and full of dangers, it was a real shot in the arm to be side by side with our comrades. In almost no time, we were getting on like a house on fire. Walking round our camp, I heard familiar greetings everywhere. 'Hey, Young Lu, just got off sentry duty?' 'Young Lu, not coming to the storytelling?' You see? It's not difficult to get along with everyone—another advantage of being talkative.

I brought up the rear when we were on the move, sweeping away our footprints with a forked stick. There were four people in the rear guard. The leader I mentioned was just ahead of me: Wu Sheng, a middle-aged man, almost 180 centimetres tall and well-built, hair prematurely streaked with white, a little hunchbacked with broad shoulders that moved unevenly when he walked—the others told me this was because he'd spent a long time doing hillside work, and carrying heavy logs had left him with one shoulder lower than the other. When I touched the raised calluses there, they were firm as pebbles. I quoted the proverb, 'It takes a lot of hammering and smelting to turn the iron into steel!' He didn't reply, just chuckled, his coarse features turning genial.

During our next break, I called out, 'Comrade Wu Sheng.' Waving the sweeping stick in my hand. 'Check this out. I've heard that one of these is on display in some museum in England.'

He'd just put down his rucksack, and now straightened up to say, 'Oh, is it?' Then he turned back to face the way we'd come, mopping sweat from his brow. The top two buttons of his shirt were undone, and he was flapping his lapels with one hand while the other fanned himself with his washcloth, trying to cool off.

'To be honest, when I first joined up, I really couldn't stand the sight of these sticks—they said the enemy is coming, but we're not going to face him, we're going to retreat. And not just retreat, but sweep the road behind us. Wouldn't it be better to use my rifle? But that… that might have been… a bit too… Anyway, I've lived through a lot, and now I can see their beauty. Everyone says we come and go without leaving a trace —all because of these sticks. It's not easy to find sticks like this. You need a fork where the arms aren't too far apart, like this one. The handle can't be too thick either, and ideally, it'll have a little curve. Look at mine, that's from an ivory tree. A few months old now and falling apart—can't quite bear to replace it yet, though.'

He listened but was clearly distracted. He kept twisting to face the path ahead, his face half turned from me as he nodded.

'A yellow bush branch wouldn't be too bad, but they're a bit too brittle…'

All of a sudden, he whistled for the unit to start moving again, cutting me off. I was a bit annoyed—it was *my* job to whistle. What was he playing at?

I turned the question over in my mind. Could he be one of those awkward bastards who didn't know how to interact with others? Or maybe he was a recluse? Well! That was a little dispiriting. Come nightfall, we'd be hanging up a tarp and slinging our hammocks side by side. If he kept this up, nodding and grunting at everything I said, this whole journey was going to be too boring for words.

When we stopped that day, it was my turn to go on patrol. The light was murky by the time I returned, and I headed to the sleeping place, thinking he might have set up my hammock for me. Instead, I found my bundle still lying on the ground, and Wu Sheng nowhere to be seen. What could he be up to? Taking my pack in one hand, I went looking for him.

'Hey, Young Lu!' Someone leant out of the tent by the big tree—Ah Heng, from the rear guard. He seemed to guess what I was thinking. 'Looking for Wu Sheng? He's round the back. Don't bother going over there, though—he keeps to himself. Always has.'

Ah, so he was the solitary type. He preferred picking a random tree near the sentry post for his hammock. Whenever we stopped, he'd carry out his tasks—patrolling, fetching water and firewood, helping with the cooking—but otherwise he kept close to the tree like an old monk meditating, or an additional sentry.

Instead, I threw my lot in with Ah Heng's 'household'. There were three of us: Ah Heng, me, and shorty Wang Hai. Needless to say, it was harder to find a spot large enough for three hammocks, and we jostled each other getting in and out. Cleaning up in the morning was more work too. Still, the rainy season was coming on, and each night brought a downpour. A single plastic sheet couldn't keep a person dry, so they warmly invited me to join them. The three of us, all chaps in our twenties, never ran out of things to say, from north to south, wide as the oceans and sky. Sometimes, taking advantage of the raging storm, we'd belt out in our raspy voices, 'How Joyful to be Young.' Proper fun.

Another rainy evening. It came spattering down in dribs and drabs, like someone droning on with a dull, outdated story.

'It's really hard camping alone in the rainy season. Even finding somewhere to stash your backpack is an ordeal. Wu Sheng really is a bit too, y'know.' Wang Hai spoke frankly, and quick as a machine gun—each sentence left his mouth hot on the heels of the previous one. 'Look, see how he's all flustered, standing one moment and squatting the next? He's in the disaster zone.' I sat up in my hammock, and there was Wu Sheng crouching in his little shelter beneath a four-by-ten-foot plastic sheet, hacking a ditch into the soil with his knife. He was on a slope, and murky water filled with twigs and leaves was gushing down towards him, leaving not one scrap of dry ground. His feet were inch-deep in mud.

'Hey, leave your pack here with us,' called Ah Heng through the rain.

Wu Sheng looked up to call, 'No need,' then bent to his digging again.

I suddenly remembered the other day, when I was making my report to him after sentry duty, and off-handedly remarked, 'Camping alone does have its advantages. It's quieter.'

'Heh.'

'Annoying when it rains, though,' I'd added, then got to my main point. 'Look, if you hang your ground sheet high, it sprays water all over your bedding. Hang it low, and you have trouble getting under it. You're looking a bit hunchbacked, actually.'

'That's all true, but—' For once, he smiled, and ruffled his short white hair. 'It's fine once you get used to it.'

At the time, I'd just thought, Oh please! Are you really saying we need to get used to any old crap that comes our way? Just make better choices! Why make things harder for yourself?

'Look, I shouldn't say anything.' I sat up, hesitating a little. 'But… but don't you think he's a little odd?'

'Odd!' Ah Heng glanced at me, then turned to look at Wang Hai. He was very short-sighted, but because we couldn't get glasses out here, all he could do was squint hard, which made him appear more observant than other people.

'He is a little odd,' said Wang Hai thoughtfully.

'I do like being on the move with him, he makes me feel safe,' said Ah Heng. 'He's really good at noticing what's going on. Those ears of his—they're magic.'

'True, true,' Wang Hai quickly agreed, smacking me on the back. 'If I have to find fault, it's that during classes he kept going fishing…'

'Huh?' My eyes popped wide open.

Ah Heng chuckled. 'He couldn't stop dozing off. We called it "going fishing".' He demonstrated, bobbing his head up and down like a chicken pecking at grain.

'In the field, though, he's completely different—no one's more alert than him.' Wang Hai picked up the thread. 'We see with our eyes, but he relies on his ears. In all the great big rainforest, no sound escapes him. I once heard him say, "The scrub and undergrowth block your sight, but nothing gets in the way of my ears." And we got lucky that time at the Orang Asli cassava field, thanks to him.'

'What happened?' My curiosity had been aroused.

'Oh, it was all because of these cassava chips we're eating now. Wu Sheng led a small group, five of us, to dry some out at the Orang Asli field.' Ah Heng squinted through the rain in Wu Sheng's direction. 'You know how it is, there are some bastards who believe too much in freedom, when work gets busy, they say there's no need for a sentry, we can keep watch as we do our jobs. The hell we will! Everyone got so absorbed we lost track of everything else. Malay soldiers were creeping closer and closer, while some of us were still sitting around the fire shirtless, chatting away. He quietly knelt down and took aim. We didn't have our guns with us. Worse, I had a list of names in my pocket—everyone in the community who'd donated to us!'

'Oh no!'

'Their rifles were about to go off when all of a sudden, Wu Sheng stopped what he was doing and tilted his head to one side—that tiny bit of sound, *chassh chassh*, had caught his attention over the crackling of the fire. Like a little deer treading on fallen leaves—but it was actually the Enemy crawling through a ditch! Without even stopping to put on his shirt, Wu Sheng grabbed his gun and made for a jackfruit tree. But wouldn't you know it? The Enemy's advance scout had arrived and went for the same tree. We all heard it. The Enemy used too much force and went crashing into one of the roots— *pak*. Wu Sheng didn't give him a chance to find his feet again, swung his rifle around the tree trunk and *pngg*, that was the end of him. By this time, we'd taken our positions too, and frantically opened fire on the Enemy as they crawled. *Pngg lngg pah lanng*, such a racket my ears went numb.'

Ah Heng was so animated, he must have been recalling the exhilaration of firing his rifle. His eyes gleamed and he smacked his thigh. 'Hey, guess how many shots my Guite submachine gun could get off? It was a good one, seven or eight per clip. A couple of bursts and I was ready to change my magazine. Luckily Wu Sheng called out, "Oi! Hold fire! Hold fire!" To think he could hear me through all those gunshots.'

In the midst of this story, a figure loomed towards us, not wearing a waterproof, just a carelessly draped sarong. His hair was wet, and raindrops were spattered across his forehead. Wasn't that Wu Sheng? Hunched over, he called to me, 'Comrade Lu, you're late for sentry duty.'

'Oh!' I'd been so absorbed that I'd completely lost track of time. Now I hastily glanced at my watch: six o'clock.

'Go, quick! You'll just make it.' Wang Hai tossed me a waterproof.

'He's five minutes late,' Wu Sheng corrected, urging me along.

I was well-known for turning up late after bringing out the artillery, which weighed on my heart the more it got talked about. At least it was right on the dot now. I bent down to put on my shoes, remaining silent but defending myself in my heart.

'How is he late? It's exactly six,' Ah Heng spoke up for me, thrusting his arm out. 'Look if you don't believe me, I have a digital watch.'

Wu Sheng looked solemnly at his own watch, and said evenly, 'I have six minutes past.'

As I sprinted out into the rain, Wu Sheng's words were swallowed by my splashing steps. 'Mine is fast, it's for military use.'

In the wind and rain, the sentry post was a spot of calm chaos. The insistent rain swaddled sky and earth in a muffled fog, but my thoughts were racing like a magic lantern show. It flashed into my brain: Could Wu Sheng be so insistent on sleeping alone because he was afraid other people would jar his sensitive ears? Was I too chatty for him? I turned back, and saw he'd already gotten back into his hammock, facing the storm-tossed rainforest, completely absorbed. What was he thinking about?

Every trekker knew things were easier for us in the belly of the rainforest, where hills were high and trees grew densely. Guerrillas like us took to these places like fish to water, like birds to the woods. The older comrades had a saying: 'Thunder god rules the sky, but trekkers own the earth.' Such freedom! Then again, if our route took us past an Enemy stronghold, if we had to cross the great river, if we had to breach the east-west road, that was another story.

Our route this time not only required us to get across a public road, we also needed to pass through a narrow strip of secondary rainforest, patchily growing back after being cleared by timber merchants. Pathways from all directions crossed here. Vine-gathering Orang Asli or hunting tribes might come crashing in at any moment. We'd only been on the move a couple of days, and already we'd come across several wild boar snares left by others. In a place like this, you can imagine the danger we'd be in if we were to leave any trace of our presence. The closer we got to the paved road, the warier everyone grew, and the more anxiety nagged at us. We'd already had several whole-group meetings, with warnings and orders that amounted to: keep a tight lid on noise, firelight, footsteps. Wu Sheng spoke more at these sessions than he ever had before. At one, he said, 'Comrades ought to speak less. Nothing wrong with talking, but there's a time and place. Talk too much and you lose focus, stop hearing what's around you. Make too much noise, and someone might hear. Better to say less.' That seemed aimed at the three of us. Later, he got even more specific. 'The rear guard ought to think more about their duties. Firstly, let's not get caught by the tail. Second, if the Enemy is following us, you should be the first to notice and eliminate them!'

Although I felt unsettled by his words, I still had faith in myself. When the decisive moment came, I would be able to restrain myself.

Crossing the public road was no easy matter. This stretch of tarmac, more than twenty feet wide, coiled through the hills like a dark snake, and vehicles passed along it constantly. To the south, Malay kampongs lined the river, a running stitch of stilt houses. Even at this distance, we could hear their chickens and goats. North of the road was a steep hill ridge. The road was cut into its slope, a forbidding cliff face to one side, a sharp drop to the other. With inhospitable territory north and south, the only place we could pass was a mile-long stretch in the middle where the road looped and the ground levelled out. Although this area had been cleared and turned into rubber plantations, the trees reached right up to the rolling hills, and our brother units had breached the road several times here. The Enemy had apparently taken note, and removed all the trees and shrubs for a hundred yards on both sides of the road, leaving wide open ground with no cover. They also built a look-out post right at the bend, and we'd heard a patrol car would leave this post once an hour, all through the night.

Even so, we would try to cross here. Come dusk, we approached the road, and sent a surveillance team to choose a junction. When it had grown dark and still, we would make our move.

We concealed ourselves in a patch of shrubbery, just beyond the area razed by the Enemy. Enough time had passed since the clearance that the ground ahead was sprouting, a lush green carpet in the twilight, rising and falling in the gloom. The road made a turn to the right, where atop a jutting dragon's-mouth hill was the Enemy camp. As darkness descended, the campsite lit up, and a guitar's *plik plik plok plok* streamed from a radio. From time to time, raucous laughter reached our eardrums. Occasionally, we even saw wavering torchlight as the Enemy walked by.

We crouched by our backpacks, not moving an inch. The dingy greenery around us felt like a dead world. No signs of life but the *chrr chrr* of nocturnal insects I didn't know the names of. Around us were camphor trees which gave off a cool, calming fragrance as darkness fell, as if trying to numb our distress. I'd experienced the impatience of pacing by a maildrop waiting for a message, as well as the agitation of lying in wait at an ambush, but at this moment, what came to mind was a description of life I'd once heard: Ten thousand arrows lurking in the dark, waiting for your attention to lapse momentarily!

Vehicles zoomed by from time to time, headlights shooting through the thin fog shrouding the road, like white wave crests atop the night-time ocean, appearing briefly then vanishing into the distance.

After an agonising wait, the lights finally went out in the Enemy camp, and the hum of traffic faded away. Leader gave the order: Get ready to cross. Stay quiet! No lights! Don't drop anything! No pissing or shitting! Shoes off!

We swiftly entered the cleared area. Going last, I used my sweeping stick to ruffle the grass flattened by our footsteps. It was pitch black, and I couldn't see where the unit was going. A few yards away, Wu Sheng's brawny body kept flickering into view—he was stopping every few paces, watching out for me.

A short while later, we abruptly stopped advancing. After waiting a long time in a grove of shoulder-high grass and seeing no movement, I couldn't stop myself tugging at Wu Sheng and murmuring, 'What's happening?'

He didn't reply.

More time passed. A *shrr shrr* up ahead. The unit had turned around. Wu Sheng brought his lips close to my ear, 'There's a situation in front, we're pulling back. We'll cross to the southwest. You're the advance scout.'

Just like that. I froze for a second, but there was no time for hesitation, despite doubt after doubt. I swung around, determined. Pulled out my compass. Luminous needle. Due southwest.

I never expected to be pulling the unit into a tighter spot than ever. After ten minutes of walking in total darkness, thorny vines attacked me all over, hooking every inch of exposed skin. Blazing agony. Unrelenting grip on my clothes. Free one scrap of cloth and another got caught. A few more steps. Neck, hands, cheeks, ears scratched. Torn uniforms. Pressing on. Vines growing denser. Setting a trap for us. Palms scraped raw. Unrelenting thorns, too many to unhook. Tearing tearing tearing at them. All around me, in the dark, the *szzxx* of clothes ripping, the stench of gore. Filled with frustration, dripping with sweat, struggling forward.

A car sped past, and in the momentary burst of light, I saw that we were still some distance from the road. At this rate, how long would it take us to get there? A suffocating feeling. Something snapped. I pulled out my knife and hacked away, avenging myself on the endless vegetation, mindlessly slashing. *Kaa-shaa ka-shaa*, vines fell before me.

Almost right away, a hefty hand caught hold of my rash arm with a grip like steel. I was breathing hard, and even in the pitch dark I could feel Wu Sheng's blazing eyes on me.

He brushed past me, smacking me on the shoulder, and I thought I heard a sigh deep in his throat. A susurrus whispered through the borderless undergrowth as the troop resumed its snail-like progress.

Several times I attempted to stride ahead and retake my place in front, but he held me back. With a start, I realised he was facing backwards so the metal tub on his shoulders could take the brunt of the thorns, painstakingly clearing a path for the rest of us.

Finally, we made it across the road. Over three hours crossing a few hundred metres of rainforest. As my bare feet reached the chilly tarmac, I glanced at my watch: ten past three in the morning!

We passed through the rubber plantation to the rainforest, stopping by an abandoned timber road. As soon as I heard the word 'bivouac' I collapsed, sitting down heavily, unwilling to move another inch. My body felt utterly hollowed out, as if someone had come along and stolen all my energy, leaving behind an empty shell.

Next to me, Wu Sheng leaned against a tree panting a little. Even though I was much younger, forging through the foliage had completely worn me out, and I could only imagine his exhaustion. I wanted to ask how he was doing, but couldn't even move my mouth. My eyes began to glaze over. I thought I heard someone urging him to sleep: 'You have high blood pressure, you ought to...'

Now that we were past the road, my heart felt much lighter. We hadn't completed our mission yet, but I felt a sort of jubilation akin to Chairman Mao's poem, 'Beyond Huangyangjie Pass, no perils can touch us'. The weather grew more pleasant, lifting our spirits and quickening our footsteps.

After climbing into our hammocks at night, the three of us would chatter away endlessly, until we inevitably attracted Wu Sheng's attention. He'd come over and lightly rap at one end of my perch: 'Hey, don't use up all your conversation at once, save some for later.'

Then we arrived at a river—not a particularly large one, its banks gently undulating, an unusual sight in this landscape. The vegetation was different too: bamboo groves, rows of trees, dense clusters of shrubs. The hilltop winds seemed imprisoned by this broad and dense green prison, trapped between one leaf and another, filling the air with damp fog. Although we were walking on level ground, the strange warmth had sweat trickling down our backs. All around I saw plants I couldn't name, vivid explosions of yellow flowers, emanating heavy, dark scents. A comrade picked one to stick in the side pocket of her backpack.

From time to time, as we passed among the broad-leaved shrubs, rainforest crabs (that is, leeches) would attach themselves to our clothes, then their dull brown bodies would crawl in a swift, looping motion towards exposed skin. We'd scoop them up so they stuck to our fingers instead, then wrench our hands apart, tearing them in two. Or else we'd stretch them long and tie them in a knot, then toss them aside. The mud beneath our feet was soft and spongy as a steamed bun. Each step left a deep imprint, and it cost me a lot of effort to erase our footprints. Scattered around, I noticed, were a variety of animal tracks.

As noon approached, we stumbled upon a 'hog hollow': a four- or five-foot mound of gnawed-off shrubs, a jumbled pile of stems and leaves reaching waist height. The leaves were still bright green and showed no sign of withering. I thought to myself: a wild boar must have spent last night here.

We paused for a break after lunch. Ah Heng went off to one side to relieve himself, but no sooner had he disappeared from view when I heard him exclaim 'Aiyah!' in a strange voice. Wu Sheng and I exchanged glances, and headed in his direction. Ah Heng was on the ground, clasping his right calf with both hands, pale face twitching. 'S–snake...' he stuttered. 'Snakebite!'

We quickly pulled off his boot. At the thickest part of his calf, two puncture marks the size of rice grains, about a half-inch apart, were oozing dull red blood.

'Venomous,' said Wu Sheng in a heavy voice. He shouted to the medic for help while unwinding Ah Heng's puttee and binding it around the wound. Fang Li, the petite medic, hurried towards us, face pale with uncertainty. This was her first encounter with a snakebite.

'I'll let some blood out. You get ready to apply the antidote and bandage him up.' As he spoke, Wu Sheng passed his blade through the flame of his lighter, and once it was sterilised, lifted Ah Heng's leg and decisively slashed a cross through the bite.

'Agh—' Ah Heng clenched his teeth, biting off his grunt of pain. Blood gushed from the cut. Wu Sheng got me to pour boiled water from the flask over it to speed up the bleeding. Soon, though, the flow had slowed, and even squeezing the wound only forced out a few more drops. Ah Heng's face was pallid, his eyes were rolling back in his head, and he was breaking out in a cold sweat.

All of a sudden, Wu Sheng bent over Ah Heng's legs, pressed his mouth to the wound, and began sucking. He spat out each mouthful of poisoned blood, then went back for more.

I'd never had to deal with anything like this. To tell the truth, as I watched Wu Sheng's unhesitating actions, my heart hammered and my palms prickled with sweat. My skin crawled as he wielded the knife, as if I shared Ah Heng's pain. How had Wu Sheng learnt to be so steely nerved? When he bent to suck on the wound, balding head bobbing up and down, I wondered how this gruff, strapping man could be so tender.

By the time Fang Li bandaged him up, Ah Heng's leg was badly swollen, and he couldn't get his boot back on. At least he was in less pain than before, and his urgent breathing had slowed.

Png! A gunshot from where we'd left the advance troops! Right away we were prone on the ground. Amid the confusion, I dragged Ah Heng behind a tree. What bad luck, I thought, having a casualty before the fighting even started. It wouldn't be easy to retreat to safety on this terrain!

Then word came from up ahead: the advance scout had shot a boar!

It turned out that while we'd been dealing with Ah Heng's wound, a pack of wild boar had blundered through the mud into our line of fire, and now a hog weighing over eighty kilograms lay dead a few paces away.

Terror followed by joy, one unexpected event coming so quick on the heels of the other—none of us knew how to respond, so we just stared awkwardly at each other.

Ah Heng's injury didn't look too bad; he'd probably only be laid up for two or three days. Then there was the pig to deal with. We'd been on strict rations for the whole expedition so far, and now we could break our fast, so to speak. Our mouths watered as if we could already smell the stewing pork. Leader called an impromptu meeting, and we agreed to find better terrain nearby where we could set up camp and rest a few days, so Ah Heng could recover as quickly as possible while the rest of us built up strength for the trek ahead. As soon as we found a suitable spot and settled down, everyone got busy: fetching water, patrolling the area, gathering firewood, boiling water, sawing boards, sharpening knives… a joyous clamour.

It was after four by the time the pork went into the pot. Grabbing some clean clothes, I was about to set off for the river to bathe when a thundering boom went off—the iron sentry we'd placed in the approach had been tripped, and explosive waves were echoing through the valley!

It had been Wu Sheng's idea to set the mine. We had a lot to do, he argued, and would be producing a lot of noise. The landmine would keep watch for us.

I knew instantly this was the Enemy. Had our gunshots revealed our location? They'd have come after us, only to set off the landmine. If that's what had happened, then the explosion would surely be followed by a burst of gunfire in all directions—that's how the Enemy usually reacted. I pricked my ears and listened carefully.

Instead, the hillside forest resumed its tranquillity. Gentle breeze wafted by, carrying only the gurgle of the river brushing against the rocky shoreline.

'Could it be another boar?' I wondered. As we were placing the mine, I'd had the thought that wild animals frequently passed along the riverside path, and the fruiting trees would surely attract herds of pigs—might one of them trip the mine? That would be ideal, giving us extra meat we could turn into jerky. To think it had actually happened!

Wang Hai came over and said quietly, 'It's very likely just an animal.'

'It must be, otherwise why aren't we hearing gunshots?' Excited that someone else was echoing my thoughts, I continued with my reasoning. 'The Enemy is scared of death. When they set off a landmine, don't they always start firing to give themselves courage?'

The comrades around us began sharing their opinions animatedly.

Leader and a few of the deputies got together for a quick discussion, and decided that Wang Hai and I would go investigate. This was exactly what I wanted, so without another word, I strapped on my utility belt and told Wang Hai to get his rifle.

'Hang on.' Wu Sheng shot us a look and held out an arm to stop us.

'What?' I remembered Ah Heng mentioning Wu Sheng's sensitive ears. Could it be that... I couldn't help glancing at those magical ears, which looked just like everyone else's. 'Did you hear something?'

'I want to come along.'

'No need, the two of us can carry it. Wang Hai's a strongman, you know!' I chuckled and pummelled Wang Hai's shoulders.

'No.' Wu Sheng looked serious, but then he always did. I couldn't guess what was going on inside his head. 'I'll go with you, and Wang Hai can stay here. I've already told Leader.'

I had to do as he said, of course, but I resented his stubbornness. I walked ahead, wondering how he'd managed to get Leader to change his mind. Did he think I wouldn't do a good job? I'd been a soldier for a full decade now. Why did they think... The more I turned it over in my mind, the more unhappy I grew, and without realising it I was walking faster.

'Wait! Where are you going?' Wu Sheng caught hold of me.

'To investigate!' I snapped.

'Back the way we came? No, we need to cut a new path.' His voice was firm.

He was starting to annoy me. So what if your ears are sharp, I thought, that doesn't mean your mind is sharp too. Why make a straightforward matter so complicated? It would take forever to hack a new path through the scrub—what if the wild boar got away in the meantime? And we didn't even have a hunting rifle with us. I didn't say any of this out loud. Reality would speak for me, and the results would teach him regret.

What should have taken no more than twenty minutes became over an hour of forging through the rainforest, and all that time there wasn't a single movement to be heard. By the time we were approaching the landmine, the sun was beginning to dip beneath the hills, and the woods grew murky, the wind rustling *hrr shrr shrr* through the trees. My mind on the wild boar, I would have rushed ahead if Wu Sheng hadn't caught hold of me. Touching one finger to his ear, he indicated I should hide behind a tree and listen.

A minute passed, then two, then five, then ten. My ears filled with the *ynng ynng wnng* of mosquitoes, but nothing else. I couldn't stand it any longer. Shooting a look at Wu Sheng, I indicated that I wanted to move on.

Out of nowhere—*anggkwnng*. The sound slashed through the silence. Then—

'What the hell do you think you're doing?'

'Having a drink of water. I'm starving. Babi, why aren't those commies here yet?'

'Relax, they'll come looking for the wild boar. Don't turn into a pig yourself!' Movement a few dozen paces away.

Through the dense scrub, I could see the tiger stripes of an army uniform.

I held my breath and felt my scalp go numb. My heart was beating so hard, I thought it might jump out of my chest. My god. Heat rose from my throat to the tips of my ears. If I'd charged ahead, I'd have run straight into the Enemy's sightlines!

How fortunate Wu Sheng was here! I turned to look at him, full of respect, and his gun was already on his shoulder. His face, pressed against the stock, was angled slightly towards me, and his cold eyes were giving me the command to open fire.

PREY

1. BARKING DEER

Barking deer, muntiacus muntjak, the largest of the muntjacs at a metre long and twenty-five to thirty kilograms in weight. Yellow all over, fine glossy fur, two antlers, long-limbed.

Inhabits hilly regions, generally active in lallang groves and among thorny shrubs. Solitary, timid and cautious. Seeks food at night, dawn, or dusk. Shelters concealed by plant growth by day. Mainly lives on grass and tender leaves, typical herbivore. Highly reproductive. Populations found in China, Brunei, Indonesia, Malaysia, and Thailand.

Anah was the best snare-setter in the unit.

This wasn't a rare skill, because most of our meat came from trapping, and most male comrades had some experience with snares. Keding himself had a couple of tricks up his sleeve.

He'd believed, though, that setting a snare wasn't just about technique. It also required… 'acumen', a word he'd once come across in a book. Whenever he and Anah set forth together, this seemed like the only term that sort of described Anah's ideas, judgements, and decisions.

For instance, where to set the snare. In the borderless rainforest, how could anyone know where wild pigs or barking deer would pass by? You had to understand the habits of all these different species, deduce which routes they would take, learn to recognise their tracks and even in what circumstances these tracks had been made.

One time, Keding and Anah set off on their rounds and found fresh boar prints by the river gully, the dug-up soil on the banks still moist, not yet dried by the wind. Exhilarated, Keding thought they should have a few snares here—

Anah stuck out an arm and shook his dark head. 'No good.'

He made Keding squat down for a closer look. 'Many prints, but far apart. Pigs running, not searching for food. Why would they come back?'

Keding had nodded, but as much as he stared at the tracks, he couldn't make head nor tail of them. How were you supposed to tell whether hoofprints were close together or far apart?

Ying Yang once told him that he'd been with old Tatak, an Orang Asli tribal elder, when Tatak had set a single snare in a bare patch of land with no tracks at all. At the time, Ying Yang had thought to himself, If this actually works, you can use my back as a chopping board. Good thing he didn't say those words out loud, because not long after that, they caught a boar weighing a whole hundred kilograms!

How had this happened?

He later worked it out: To the Orang Asli, fishing and hunting weren't just survival skills, but a sort of talent they were born with.

There were always new things to be learnt from our indigenous comrades.

Of course, snare-setting involved hunting too. In their few hours away from camp, they came upon a pack of macaques. Anah handed the rifle to Keding, who quickly pressed himself against a tree, barrel against the trunk, holding his breath, taking aim—

Pnng! The monkeys scattered.

With a rustle of leaves and branches, a macaque tumbled through the air.

Anah darted forward, knife at the ready, but no need—the macaque was dead.

He turned and gave Keding the thumbs-up.

A successful shot. A happy event, first thing in the morning. Keding's heart beat wildly with joy, and he blinked rapidly, unable to gather himself.

This male macaque must have weighed eleven or twelve kilograms. A waste of time carrying it back to camp now, but bringing the carcass on their rounds would slow them down. Keding looked to Anah.

Without a word, Anah selected a patch of ground and began digging. After a moment, he called out for Keding to go cut some wild yam, duck greens, or other large leaves.

By the time Keding returned, Anah had dug a pit two feet deep. He lined it with wild yam leaves and dropped the monkey in.

'Hey! Are we burying it?'

'That's right!' Anah grinned, baring his gleaming white teeth, something mysterious and cunning in his eyes. 'Best put it in the earth. Leave it in the open, it might go bad, or other animals might drag it away to eat.'

Keding still looked confused, so Anah added, 'Underground is clean. Not many insects, and it's colder. We can dig it up on our way back.'

'Oh! It's a primitive fridge!'

Now it was Keding's turn to give Anah the thumbs-up.

It was dry season, and so as not to startle their prey, they moved against the wind.

Hillside breezes dispersed any dampness lingering from the rainy season, redolent with the sprouting of new life, lush and fragrant. The trees had shaken off their old, yellowing leaves, and fragile, translucent new ones were sieving the warm dawn light, making the forest luminous.

The vines encircling the tree trunks and the wild mushrooms sprouting from their roots silently looked on.

All around were grasses and shrubs Keding didn't know the names of, decorated with starbursts of tiny flowers, wishes scattered across the wilderness. The tender petals of ashoka blossoms drooped from the branches, fuzzy and softer than the softest towel.

In the distance, a phoenix-chicken let out its cry of *woh-huh-woh-huh*.

Anah glanced in that direction. 'We'll get that later if we have time.'

Having bagged his prey first thing that morning, Keding's footsteps were light, and his heart quivering with accomplishment.

As Anah walked, he plucked wildflowers which he tucked into the curly hair around his ears.

Now and then he'd pick a couple of pink leaves, hand one to Keding, and pop the other into his mouth. Mimicking Anah, Keding chewed on the leaf, releasing a fresh, faintly sour aroma that made him salivate.

'Hey! This is better than water, isn't it?' Anah jerked his stubby, swarthy chin. 'Be careful. The sour ones are safe to eat, but stay away from the sweet or bitter ones.'

He stopped abruptly, sniffing the air.

They'd placed three or four snares by a small cave up ahead. Keding crept forward and heard a faint *xrrr shrr*. Anah gestured for him to move stealthily.

They peered out from behind a tree. The snare a dozen metres away, fixed to a wooden pole about the thickness of an arm, was bent in a large arc; at the other end, caught in the steel loop, was a yellow-brown barking deer, one foreleg raised in the air, revealing its rice-white underbelly.

Seeing humans, the deer let out a cry and struggled all the more wildly, shaking the steel wire. Despite its efforts, its leg was raised too high for it to get enough leverage, and its rear legs sent dirt spurting into the air as they scrabbled.

'Caught it alive!' Anah cheered.

Keding understood. The deer was a docile herbivore, and they should be able to subdue it with no problem. Tonight the unit would feast on fresh venison stir-fried with ginger, and a big pot of deer blood soup.

This was a young buck, antlers just sprouting.

Excited, Keding began untying the rope he was carrying—

Then *pah!* A yellow blur. The deer had broken free. The snare pointed straight at the sky, still quivering.

Metres away, shrubs went *shrr lah*. By the time the men had recovered from their shock, they were still again.

They examined the snare. Still intact. Hanging from the loop, tightly encircled, was a ten-inch deer leg.

Keding had heard of wild animals losing a limb to escape with their lives, but this was the first time he'd witnessed it.

Such a gentle creature too!

Unwilling to let this delicious meat escape the cooking pot, Keding snapped, 'Come on, let's go after it! It won't get far on three legs. We can follow the trail of blood.'

Anah said nothing, just released the severed leg and turned it over in his hands. Fine golden-yellow fur, a shattered white bone, trailing tendons smeared with blood.

'Quick!' said Keding.

'No good.' Anah waved away the idea. 'Danger!'

'Huh?'

'I'm serious. My brother chased a porcupine one time. Got close, and you know what he saw?'

He stood still, a mystical look in his eyes, and sighed. 'My brother saw a nangka' (that is, jackfruit) 'with three porcupine quills sticking out of it. It must have shot them like arrows! Tatak told us that when wild animals are in danger, they have secret weapons.'

He held up the leg. 'The deer surely does too.'

Keding didn't know whether or not to believe him, but Anah looked genuinely terrified, his cunning gone. It seemed there was no choice but to trust him.

Anah cut a broad leaf from a wild cabbage, wrapped the foreleg, and ceremonially placed it in his backpack.

Keding felt something lurch in his heart, a strange feeling diffusing through him. He couldn't stop staring, lost in thought, in the direction the barking deer had disappeared.

2. BLACK BEAR

Black bear, ursus thibetanus, 150–170 centimetres, about 150 kilograms. Glossy, long black fur, with a white patch beneath the chin and a white V-shaped stripe on the chest. Round head, large ears, small eyes, short, sharp snout like a dog's muzzle, hence the alternate name 'dog-bear'. Thick footpads, five toes on front and rear paws, non-retractable claws. Inhabits hilly forested regions. Sturdy torso, skilled at climbing trees and swimming. Poor eyesight, sensitive smell and heari-

ng. Mostly subsists on leaves, shoots, fruits, and seeds, though occasion-ally will also eat insects, bird eggs, and small animals. Gestation period of seven months, three cubs in each litter. Habitat includes East Asia, particularly the forested areas of Taiwan and Japan.

Even Yanhua sensed something was wrong.

Female comrades rarely got a chance to check the snares, because there weren't many people suitable to lead a squad. For Yanhua, this was a rare opportunity.

Before she left that morning, the medic Suxin asked her to bring back some wild banana vines to brew a cooling tea, because it was so easy to get overheated working all day in the sun on farming duty. She remembered having seen some by the ditch.

At this moment, though, her attention was not at her feet!

Past this stretch of steep cliffs, down a few stone terraces, was the gully, with an assortment of trees and shrubs in the way. They'd been green and glossy before, but what met her eyes now was a different glow.

She turned to glance at Danxiu, who was leading the squad. Understanding each other, a jolt of excitement surged through their veins.

Then a *hwuh luh* as the vines and leafy branches began to sway.

Danxiu hurried past her and climbed the side of the cliff, peeping through a gap in the rock.

On the far side of the gully, by a petai tree, caught in a snare made from a bent ivory tree trunk, was an ink-black creature. It seemed to sense something was amiss, crying out *aoooo aoooo*. A clumsy forepaw flailed around. A large thicket of scarlet vines had collapsed, probably from a strong wind, and now lay in a tangle over the beast.

'We caught a dog-bear!' Danxiu cried. With a *ka-tschaa*, she lifted her carbine to her chest.

There was no way they could take the bear alive. The greater worry was that, seeing humans, it would struggle more violently and snap the steel wire.

Luckily the ivory tree was firmly rooted.

Still, Danxiu pressed her rifle steady against a tree trunk, held her breath, and took aim at one of its forelegs.

Pnng! Pnng!

Black bears were loathsome, destroying so many of our ration stores. They were regarded by the comrades as Enemy Number Two.

With a desolate *aooooo*, the massive body spasmed, gasping violently like a quivering anthill.

Pnng! Without hesitation, Danxiu fired again.

In an instant, the agitated rainforest resumed its calm, with only a wisp of gunfire smoke twisting in the wind.

After studying the scene for a moment, Danxiu climbed back down and, rifle still in her hand, descended into the gully.

Her right leg had been injured at the Keruh ambush, and even after treatment it still curved outwards, barrel-like. She sometimes limped a little, but her footsteps were just as nimble as ever.

Yanhua followed behind, heart still thumping from the sharp gunshot sounds. Watching Danxiu walk ahead, she gradually returned to herself.

She and Danxiu had met when they were both in the trekking unit.

She'd respected this deputy squad leader, a 'half-new' comrade (that is, one who'd joined up after the Malayan Communist Party resumed battle footing after 1961; like many in her cohort, she'd come from the region near the Thai-Malaysia border). Yanhua respected her and understood her temperament, yet Danxiu's endurance seemed a bit mystical to her.

They were about the same age. Danxiu was a classic Guangxi girl, petite with delicate features, almost a head shorter than Yanhua, and yet she was far stronger. During a mass ration transportation, Danxiu—who weighed less than fifty kilograms—could carry over sixty kilos on her back. When they stopped to rest, she doubled back to help the weaker comrades.

Yanhua had been a rubber tapper back in the kampong, so at least she'd been familiar with hill roads. Now that she was in the rainforest, though, she had to learn everything from scratch.

When the wild fruits ripened, she followed Danxiu out to harvest them. In the vast ocean of the rainforest, Danxiu had only to stand on higher ground or climb a tree, and she'd be able to call out the locations of everything. *Tampoi! Lala! Nangka! Rouge plums! Mangoes!* Nothing in that sea of green escaped her eyes.

'You're amazing!' Yanhua once said to her, and she meant it. They'd saved so much time and energy not having to search.

Danxiu's pale face flushed red. 'This is nothing!'

Yanhua wanted to learn to do the same thing, so she asked Danxiu what her secret was. Danxiu pursed her lips and smiled awkwardly. 'You just need to recognise the leaves. Different trees have different shapes and sizes. Different shades of green too.' Then she added, 'You'll know when you've been here long enough!'

Back in the present, the black bear had stopped breathing. Yanhua began cutting away the scarlet vines, while Danxiu walked around inspecting the ground, bending from time to time to examine a track.

'Another one got away.' Danxiu pulled a coil of steel wire from her backpack. 'This one is just a cub. The mother bear must have scented us and run away.'

Looking closely at the bow made from the bent ivory tree trunk, she fitted a new steel wire to it. Clutching the slender trunk firmly and giving it a shake, she said, 'This tree is sturdy enough. We can set a new trap here.'

The scene was chaotic. All that trampling had churned up the soil, and a muddy reek filled the air, mixed with the stench of bear piss. Then there was the tangle of fallen scarlet vines and bloodstained, rotting leaves gathering in the trough.

Yanhua looked up from where she was squatting, eyes wide with surprise and doubt. 'Here?'

'The mother bear is sure to come back.' A leech was shrugging its way along Danxiu's wide-legged trousers. Without so much as a glance at it, she snatched it up and pulled it in two between her fingers, then flicked it into the mud. 'Tomorrow or the day after, she'll be back looking for her cub. For certain!'

This seemed to amuse her; her smirk spread into a grin, and her dark eyes sparkled, lighting up her whole face. 'There are eight people in our farming group, right? Two bears is eight paws, one each.'

Yanhua helped her set the snare, but her mind was full of uncertainty. Would this work?

The next day, Yanhua was assigned sentry duty.

She wanted very badly to go check the snares with Danxiu, to answer the riddle in her heart.

But sentry duty was unavoidable. She had no excuse to turn it down.

The eight of them were in charge of Field Number Three. For eight months now, they'd been growing cassava on the slopes of this dragon ridge, dense waves of lush green beneath the blazing sun. Soon they would be ready to be dug up to feed the troops.

At the foot of the hill, at the dragon's mouth, Octopus River glistened in the sun. The fertile soil it dredged up, about as wide as a football field, was where the comrades toiled raising vegetables.

The sentry post was on the dragon's back, where the cassava field met the rainforest. There were two shifts, morning and afternoon, one person looking out for the safety of the comrades hard at work tending the crops.

In the early morning, the woods were still shrouded in grey-blue mist, and the winds occasionally carried with them the long cries of macaques and pheasants. A couple of branches fell with a crash, and the breeze made tree leaves go *hwaalh hwallh*, rendering the ancient hillside forest all the more desolate.

Her duties were only to observe and listen. Inevitably, along with keeping her ears trained on the heavy silence of her surroundings, Yanhua heard the unrest within herself. Memories lay curled on the ground like yellowing leaves, withering and rotting away, becoming the humus from which new life sprouted. The wriggling of a nameless insect turned over past events in her mind—

She'd been wearing this dark green uniform for ten years now!

Her beloved had been martyred during the twenty-month encirclement campaign by the combined Thai and Malaysian forces. That was five years ago. How many storms had there been in the rainforest since then? She didn't have a single photograph of him, but his handsome, youthful figure lingered in her memory.

Then there were the attachments she couldn't track down. She'd been pregnant back then, when she and her husband managed to break through the cordon and join up. Finally, they had a baby! But how could they possibly raise a child in the midst of battle? The next day, he'd been sent to the farming village to be brought up by the People. He would be ten years old by now. Where was he? What did he look like? All she had in her mind was his ruddy baby face, the mingled sorrow and joy of his howling. Was he in school? Was he doing well at his studies? Would she, one day, be able to tell him all about his father?

And his grandparents—the father and mother who'd raised her. They must be old now. Were they healthy? Were they doing well? She'd departed without even saying goodbye—that must have devastated them.

Two years ago, someone from her village joined up, and brought news that her family had moved out of the New Village. His father had posted a change of address notice in the paper five days in a row.

Did he know where the relatives he wanted to inform were? Was he hoping that someday his sons and daughters would descend from the sky before his weeping eyes? Or were his words destined to go unanswered forever and ever?

Ahhhh. Yanhua heard her heart let out a lengthy sigh.

She stood from her wooden bench in the shade of a tree, blinking.

Walking towards the cassava field, she resolved to look out over Octopus River, which flowed from high in the hills to the kampongs. All that water gushing over countless rocks. What messages might it carry? But also, what news of the Enemy?

She stared out over the fields filled with greens, long beans, amaranth, choy sum, and mugwort. It was just as Danxiu said —there were so many shades of green carving up the land, clump by clump, patch by patch.

From across the river, in the gully where they'd been the day before, she heard a gunshot.

A carbine! Two *pnngs*, and then another *pnng*.

The howl of a ferocious beast, carried faintly on the wind.

Danxiu had been right. The mother bear had come back for her cub.

Unexpectedly, a shiver went through Yanhua's heart.

Back at camp, she brought Suxin the wild banana vines and elephant's foot she'd plucked along the way.

The medic looked elated. 'Did you hear? We're getting a bear's paw each. They're butchering them now.' Before Yanhua could reply, she went on, 'Do you want yours stewed in lingzhi fungus or daliwang herbs? I've got both.' She was so thrilled, a faint sheen of perspiration appeared on her nose.

It was true. A bear's paw each. How many people had such good fortune?

'I don't think I want mine,' Yanhua heard herself say. 'Let everyone share it. Or you have it.'

'Huh?' Suxin gaped at her. 'What's wrong with you?'

3. MOUSE-DEER

Mouse-deer, tragulus javanicus. The smallest ungulate mammal in the world, about forty-seven centimetres long and twenty kilograms. No antlers. Males have elongated canines. Slender, long limbs with narrow hooves. Yellow-brown fur on back and legs, white belly.

Inhabits tropical secondary forest, shrubbery, grass slopes. Solitary in nature, skilled at camouflage, agile movements, does not roam far. Mostly active at dawn and dusk. Herbivore, feeds on tender leaves, stems, and berries. Reproduces year-round, lifespan of about twelve years.

Populations in Malaysia, Indonesia, and South Asia.

'Aiyue caught a pelanduk!'

Someone misheard and asked, frowning, 'A Panadol? Does she have a fever again?'

'No, no, a pelanduk! A mouse-deer!'

'Oh, a mouse-deer! Aren't they also called hundred spirit deer?'

'I've heard that. They're the little spirits of the rainforest. But hardly anyone ever sees one.'

'And Aiyue trapped one! Unbelievable.'

Everyone came crowding round.

Not that long ago, all Aiyue brought the comrades was annoyance, confusion, and rage. Now this was a surprise!

Everyone stared at the tiny yellow-brown deer, no larger than a rabbit, and gabbled all at once:

'Whoa. So small. Like a stuffed toy.'

'What a pointy snout!'

'Its eyes are so black.'

Someone pointed at its legs, bound with string. 'Aiyoh! They're thin as ball-point pens.'

Aiyue squatted on the ground, stroking the mouse-deer's soft fur, not saying a word.

'How did you manage to catch such a cunning animal? I guess even a blind chicken can find a grain of rice,' said someone in a tone of disbelief and resentment.

'That's not true,' someone else retorted. 'Aiyue placed her snare under a wild olive tree. Mouse-deer love wild olives. This wasn't just luck.'

Aiyue didn't look up, but she recognised Lin Mang's sombre voice. Her heart trembled.

She hadn't actually had much confidence when she'd set the trap a day ago.

One of the older comrades had mentioned in a class on revolutionary traditions that mouse-deer loved eating wild olives. She'd made a note of it at the time. Then on this expedition, there happened to be a lush tree not far from where they set up camp, bright green wild olives about the size of her thumb scattered beneath it.

She'd picked one up and bitten into it. It filled her mouth with sour astringency.

And somehow the thought came to her: set a snare here. Now the mouse-deer was in her arms.

What an intelligent creature! She remembered a tale: The crocodile knew the mouse-deer loved eating fruit, so it quietly lay waiting in ambush by a fruit tree. The mouse-deer came along, but stopped some distance away and called out, 'I wonder if there are any crocodiles nearby? Let me know if there aren't!' And the crocodile shouted, 'No crocodiles here!' In the blink of an eye, the mouse-deer had sprung far, far away.

Had it forgotten to ask the question this time? Aiyue thought about how humans are a much more formidable adversary than crocodiles!

Aiyue was very thin, her pale face like a wild olive that had begun to shrivel. She was afraid of the cold—she constantly wore a pha khao ma around her neck and went around all huddled up, making her look hunchbacked. Her lazy eye made her give everyone sidelong looks, as if she were perpetually rolling her eyes at them.

She was only in her early forties, not even one of the oldest comrades, so she didn't get respect on account of her age. Newer recruits referred to her as an 'old revolutionary', but her feebleness and sickliness weren't assets to the unit, while her stubbornness and eccentricities, the odd things she insisted upon, made some refer to her as 'weirdo' behind her back.

That lazy eye was particularly aggravating. It made her look as if she took nothing seriously, as if she believed in nothing.

She rarely went on expeditions, because she couldn't carry much and her stomach issues meant she had to chew each mouthful of mixed-grain rice for ages, driving everyone wild with impatience as they waited for her to finish. Whenever her name appeared on a manifest, the leader would invariably request a swap.

A while back, she'd been deployed to the sewing room, only to fall out with the comrade in charge.

She'd shown up with a pair of uniform trousers. The crotch, seat, and knees were all worn through, and their wearer had requested mending.

This wasn't the first such request she'd received, and many times she'd raised the same objection: it wasn't worth it to patch something so tattered, why not just issue a new garment? She even painstakingly counted the patches that overlaid the crotch. 'Twelve layers. This has already been mended more than ten times.'

The supervising comrade refused to budge. This was exactly in keeping with their spirit of frugality! 'Or are you saying you want extravagance and waste?'

Aiyue didn't reply, just threw down the trousers and walked away.

She didn't get on with the comrades of the women's squad either. Being obsessed with cleanliness, she wouldn't allow anyone else to touch her things. At night, she couldn't stop coughing, which kept everyone up—herself included.

'Can't you let us sleep? We're not like you; we have to go out and carry rations tomorrow,' someone grumbled. Curled up in a corner, Aiyue felt herself cast into bottomless darkness.

She became more and more solitary, more and more silent, suppressing all her feelings.

This had been her first expedition since the incident. She'd felt a little happier, then this unexpected windfall arrived—a consolation of sorts.

She'd never actually seen a mouse-deer before, let alone gotten this close to one.

Her hand gently stroked its back, warm and smooth. For some reason, she felt a twinge in her heart.

'Aiyue's missing!'

'She's made a run for it!'

When the news broke out, all the comrades—whether they believed it or not—felt righteous along with their shock.

Several squads immediately formed a cordon.

Lin Mang took Xiaocheng to clear a path and liaise with the Minyun (People's Movement), across the minefield they were in charge of. Aiyue could only leave the farming villages via the great dragon path because she didn't know the hillside roads at all, so how could she possibly avoid the landmines?

Lin Mang was anxious for her, worrying he would hear an explosion at any moment.

HQ's instructions were naturally to counsel her to return, but because Aiyue was armed, they were also to proceed with caution. As leader, Lin Mang would use his discretion.

Less than half an hour into their trek, Xiaocheng was just about to step onto a pheasant plain when he abruptly knelt. Following his lead, Lin Mang quickly huddled against a petaling tree.

Xiaocheng had positioned himself behind a termite mound, M16 at his shoulder. He turned and shot Lin Mang a signal with his eyes.

This was one of their designated resting points on ration runs. There were no large trees around here, but several rocks protruded two or three feet above the ground, rubbed smooth by all the sacks of food that had leaned against them.

Aiyue sat there, arms folded across her knees, cradling her head. Her slender body quivered like a leaf in the wind.

She couldn't remember how long she'd been here. It felt as if half her life had been wafted away by the breeze.

As a teenager, she'd followed her older brother and sister down the path of Revolution. She dropped out of school, went undercover, moved around... a life of underground resistance that left her silent and permanently alert. On the island to the south, the colonial government was carrying out sweeps of arrests across the land. Aiyue worked tirelessly to help many cadres escape to Indonesia, ferrying messages, putting herself at great risk. She also scrimped as much as possible, sending every spare cent to support the Organisation.

All these hardships had left her with a ruined body full of pain and illness.

When she was finally deployed to the Revolutionary border and she saw the leaders, she burst into tears. So many of her comrades-in-arms had been martyred or were locked up in prison. The years had rushed by, and her youth was gone. There were steep cliffs in all directions, and she couldn't shake off the fear that each day might be her last. She felt as if she'd finally come home now, and all her torment melted away with her tears.

This revolutionary party had been her spiritual support. So why did it seem to misunderstand her, to despise her? She was wearing the uniform but couldn't appear dashing and upstanding.

She knew she was prone to illness and couldn't carry heavy loads. She didn't know the terrain and couldn't even navigate the mountain tracks. She wasn't suited to guerrilla life, which caused her comrades all kinds of trouble. Yet hadn't she done a lot of good underground? The leader comrades had passed on the appreciation and respect from the higher-ups.

Naturally, for security reasons, she wasn't allowed to breathe a word of what she'd done.

So to these comrades, she was just an old, feeble carcass with a sharp temper!

The Revolutionary collective was a crucible, but could it accommodate a unique individual like her? How could she settle her fragile body and soul in this place?

She stared at the vines wrapped around the enormous tree trunk, like a dark green waterfall, so tangled and entwined you could never separate them.

Her withered fingers clutched at her short, greying hair.

Her .38 revolver with the wooden grip remained in her other hand, leaning against the rock.

'Aiyue!' called Lin Mang.

She dropped her hand and looked towards the sound, not moving, just staring.

Lin Mang came towards her with his gun behind his back. 'What do you think you're doing? Let's go back. Aren't you afraid of stepping on a landmine?'

'Why did you come looking for me?' It was almost as if she were talking to herself. 'I just wanted to be alone.'

'Don't be silly.' Lin Mang grew stern, raising his voice. 'You left camp without permission. What are you going to do?'

'I needed some time by myself, to be quiet. Why can't I do anything right?'

'That's not true, you're capable of doing sentry duty or helping with the cooking. This shirt I'm wearing? You mended the sleeve. Look how fine and strong the stitches are.' He leaned over and took the revolver from her. 'But you can't just leave whenever you want. Come back with us.'

Xiaocheng walked over, holding his rifle. 'Yes, come back!'

Aiyue stood up, looking blank. The wind hit her and she shivered.

She spoke less and less after this. The other comrades had no idea what she was thinking, and thought she was just being guk (that is, sulking).

As punishment for going AWOL, she lost the right to carry arms. More despair. The Organisation ordered her comrades in the squad to show her more compassion.

At least on this last expedition, she'd been able to exchange a few words with her comrades. And at this moment, sitting there stroking the mouse-deer, a rare look of adoration and care appeared on her face.

She slowly stood up, one hand cradling the deer by its belly, the other stroking its head. The deer sensed her tenderness, and turned to look at her with its dark eyes, docile and placid.

Aiyue walked over to her hammock and sat on a raised tree root. Reaching into her backpack, she pulled out a bright green wild olive, took a bite herself, and offered the rest to the deer.

The sour, astringent flavour permeated her mouth, and a sensation she couldn't put into words surged in her heart. She chewed and swallowed.

Lowering her head, she began to untie the string binding the mouse-deer.

SPELL

If Tatak were here right now, what would he say? Or would he just chant another spell?

Looking past the tree with its aerial roots, the trio were stunned by the sight awaiting them.

It was just half a month ago that Ying Yang and the snare-setting team were last here on this plain with its large trees, clumps of wild bamboo, and dense groves of ashoka with orange-yellow flowers. The pale leaves drooped in clusters, like a white scarf around a woman's neck.

All of a sudden, Tatak stopped and bent to pick dried leaves off the ground. Apparently, they were going to set a snare there.

No one understood why.

Sure, this was a piece of level ground by the river, but there were no wild fruits or loose earth, and scarcely any animal tracks to be seen. Why here?

A leech shrugged its way up his calf. Ying Yang grabbed it between his fingers and ripped it in half, then tossed the two bits aside.

'Tatak!' he yelled.

Tatak was an Orang Asli tribal leader, as well as their comrade. Scrawny and dark, he was about the height of a twelve-year-old. They weren't sure of his age, but white was starting to show in his curly hair. 'Tatak' was a term of respect for Orang Asli elders, in their language. He had an actual name, of course, but the comrades took their lead from the Orang Asli and just called him Tatak.

Tatak squatted, eyes narrowed as he ran his hands through the dry leaves, studying their surroundings carefully, sniffing, and muttering a spell. Then he drew the knife he kept at his waist.

This was the same spell he'd chanted as soon as they'd reached the trapping zone that morning. Next, he'd picked up a handful of dried leaves, ripped them to shreds, and scattered them over the ground. Everyone exchanged glances and went along with whatever he was doing.

They hadn't understood what he was saying. All Ying Yang could remember was his proud bearing. Shaochuan was there too, grinning broadly, though it was unclear at what.

As Tatak brushed past them, he muttered in Malay, 'Boleh lah.' *It's okay.*

He pranced away with his unusual gait: only his toes touching the ground, more a jog than a walk. Soon, he was back with a long, sturdy wild boar snare, about the girth of a human wrist.

No one else had thought this was a good spot. They normally set multiple traps in one place, so any animal that wandered in would find it hard to get out unscathed. But on this occasion, they all stood aside, and Ying Yang was the only one who helped Tatak with his snare.

And now, two weeks later, it was this very snare, its tripwire low to the ground, that held the rear leg of a huge wild boar firmly in its noose, trapping it against the thigh-thick ashoka trunk. It was panting hard, its breath heavy with musk.

'My god, what a hog!' Shaochuan exclaimed.

Kong Wu's eyes flashed. Acting on instinct, he planted his feet firmly and held the other two back. As the unit's quartermaster, he seldom went on these trapping expeditions— maybe less than once a year. Yet today, he'd been lucky enough to find this huge wild boar waiting for him.

'Tatak's amazing!' said Ying Yang, face glowing. Helping Tatak set the snare that day, he'd grumbled to himself, 'If this actually works, you can use my back as a chopping board.' Luckily he hadn't said this out loud!

Thinking back to Tatak's demeanour, Ying Yang couldn't help wondering: What did spells have to do with hunting?

He'd visited the Orang Asli village before. As bamboo instruments clopped rhythmically, the comrades joined in the tribal dance, waving their arms and legs, throwing their heads back. After a while, some Orang Asli youths invariably went into a trance, writhing and convulsing uncontrollably. That's when Tatak would be brought out to whisper a spell in their ears, to summon their souls back.

The spell didn't work on one of them. The unit's medic came forward and waved some ammonia under his nose, which brought the young man back to full consciousness instantly.

'What should we do?' said Shaochuan to Kong Wu, snapping Ying Yang out of his reverie. Shaochuan glanced at the wild boar and slung his hunting rifle from his shoulder. 'Should we kill it?'

The wild boar tried to get to its feet, but its rear leg was too hopelessly tangled, and the most it could do was raise its front legs a little. Its vast head shook, and a huffing sound issued from its mouth. Its eyes gleamed viciously, and its perked-up ears trembled faintly. Its bristles stood on end as it grunted. A thread of drool dripped from one of the tusks protruding from its mouth. The ground beneath its hooves had been churned into mud.

'It's too close to the tree trunk to move, and it can't get its leg free. We've caught it alive!' As quartermaster, Kong Wu's job was to make sure they had enough rations, so naturally he was making some calculations now. 'If we kill it, we'd lose a whole lot of pig blood.'

'It's enormous! A hundred kilograms, maybe. How are we going to carry it back?' Shaochuan, the scrawniest of the group, was concerned.

'We'll take it in turns, between the three of us,' said Kong Wu, looking at Ying Yang, then Shaochuan. 'How long has it been since we tasted pig blood soup, comrades?'

Kong Wu was a generation older than the other two, and had suffered from diabetes for many years. If he was willing, how could they say no?

It was normal for them to haul sacks of grain weighing fifty or sixty kilos. A few years ago, during the encirclement campaign, Ying Yang carried a ninety-six kilogram drum of cooking oil all by himself. That night, he was so exhausted he showered sitting down, but the next morning was as full of energy as ever.

He'd never tried lifting a hundred-kilo boar. How could he say it wasn't possible, if he'd never tried? He welcomed the challenge.

Shaochuan hacked off a sturdy branch about a metre long and the thickness of a big toe. He tied a nylon rope firmly to one end.

He shot a quick glance at Ying Yang, and the pair slowly approached the wild boar from either side.

The boar was struggling hard and its squeals grew more intense. The tree shook violently, as if it was about to fall.

Shaochuan lunged forward and thrust the wooden pole lengthwise into the pig's mouth. With a dull crunch, the creature chomped down on it.

With his other hand, he quickly tossed the rest of the rope over the boar's muzzle, making a loop around the other end of the stick. Ying Yang caught it and threw it back under the boar's chin. Shaochuan made another loop around his end of the stick. They flung it back and forth, over and under, binding the beast's mouth shut in the blink of an eye. Sensing danger, it lashed out with a front trotter. Ying Yang wasn't able to duck aside in time and got hit on the leg.

Kong Wu bent his knee and leaned forward with his entire weight on the boar's belly, holding it immobile against the tree. All it could do was scrabble with its rear legs, throwing clods of soil into the air. No longer able to squeal, it emitted low moans from deep in its throat.

The three men let out long sighs of relief, their foreheads glimmering with sweat.

None of them had forgotten their old comrade Li Jian, whose right hand was missing below the wrist where a wild boar crunched through the bones and swallowed it whole.

A light breeze drifted by, carrying a faint floral scent through the muggy air, along with the foul smell of hog. That's when they noticed the orange-yellow blossoms at their feet, most of which had been trodden into the mud.

Working together, Ying Yang and Kong Wu tied the boar's front and rear legs together. Now that it had been vanquished, its ferocity disappeared without a trace. It lay there like a brownish-grey mound of earth. One eye swivelled on the upturned side of its face, defeated and pitiful.

Shaochuan split bamboo stems and lashed them together with rattan vines, to make a simple carrying pole. They could tie the boar to this, the better to lift it onto their shoulders.

He prodded the creature's balls with the tip of his shoe. 'Wow! They're like a couple of mangoes.' He winked at Ying Yang. 'Do you think Quartermaster here would let us brew these up as a tonic?' He turned to Kong Wu. 'Ying Yang just got married! The Party should take care of him, right?'

Whenever they caught a male animal, say a water buffalo or a deer, the kitchen didn't cook the penis or testicles. These were left out for anyone who wanted them.

'Can you stop your nonsense for one minute?' snapped Ying Yang, flushing red.

'No problem! They're delicious. And you've spent so much energy today.' Kong Wu grinned, narrowing his eyes into a squint. 'It'll do your body good.'

Kong Wu had been living with diabetes for quite a while now. They detected it while he was still working as a fisherman —apparently it was hereditary. Since entering the rainforest, he'd had to inject himself with insulin daily. His arms and thighs were full of holes. His skin took a long time to heal, and the arms protruding from his army jacket were shrivelled and dried up, like branches whose cracked bark was ready to fall off at any moment.

When he couldn't get hold of insulin, all the energy drained out of him. Yet he never let this show, and whenever it was his turn at a task, he raced ahead to get there first. One time, they shot an elephant, and he went along eagerly with his comrades to fetch the carcass. On the way back, he felt so weak he had to gnaw on the raw meat to keep going.

He was fond of saying, 'When it comes to Revolution, if you're not afraid to make sacrifices, nothing is impossible!'

Now he insisted on being the first to carry the wild boar.

Nose to tail, it was about the height of a man's chest, and god knows how much that bulging body weighed. Its curved rump was planted in the ground, like a tree stump. Kong Wu bent at the waist and tugged with all his might, but couldn't get it off the ground.

Ying Yang and Shaochuan stood on either side, heaving and lifting, until they'd finally managed to get it onto Kong Wu's back. He staggered ahead, wreaking carnage on the thin tree trunks to either side.

After a dozen paces, his legs buckled and the boar slid off his back, landing with a thud. Kong Wu took a tumble too, and sat down hard on his rump. From the boar's bound mouth came a string of muffled squeals.

Ying Yang's turn. It felt heavier than a ninety-six-kilo oil drum, and he couldn't get it on his back without the other two helping. The curved mound of flesh was much heavier than him, and even the slightest wobble made chaos of his footsteps. It was like a giant hand pushing him down. Impossible to walk steadily. He struggled ahead for twenty-odd paces before stopping. Suddenly, as if gravity had given the animal an extra-strong tug, it dragged him down onto his back.

They smelled something foul. Murky green shit was streaming from the creature's anus.

After a few rounds, all three were soaked with sweat. Kong Wu's face was so slick his black-rimmed glasses slid right off his nose.

They each cut a length of wood and held it like an oar, steadying themselves with every step. Even so, their legs wouldn't stop trembling as their burden shoved the rack down hard on their shoulders. Their arms glistened purplish-red, veins protruding like they might burst through the skin.

Now they were going uphill. Shaochuan leaned the boar against a tree trunk and slipped his arms from the straps. His chest heaved and he murmured, 'I… I can't, that's enough! It's heavier than we are. How long will it take to carry it home?'

'Let's slaughter it. If we cut it up, we'd only have to carry thirty or forty kilos.' Ying Yang looked at Kong Wu through a haze of perspiration.

'I thought of that,' said Kong Wu, his face almost black. 'But we'd lose the blood. Better the three of us suffer now, than the whole platoon miss out on this nourishing broth.'

'I… I don't know if I'll be able to get it home. If… if we aren't careful, we'll injure ourselves. What if one of us twists an ankle?' Shaochuan's voice was low, mingled with panting.

'How many things have we done that looked impossible? See how long the struggle has been! We aren't just tested on the battlefield but also our fighting spirit and willingness to suffer in ordinary times!' Kong Wu looked meaningfully at Shaochuan.

Shaochuan was in the process of applying for Party membership. His mouth hung open as he struggled for breath.

He'd joined the unit fifteen years ago, and had been through quite a few harrowing experiences in the assault force. Those of his comrades who'd enrolled at the same time as him had all been accepted into the Party by now—if they hadn't been martyred. But he was too outspoken, and his big mouth kept getting in the way.

When he was transferred earlier this year from the assault force to the border zone, he had to hand over all his good equipment, especially his knife, leaving him with a blade less than half a foot long, more like a toy. Six months later, there'd been no sign of a replacement, while trekkers under Central Committee typically got more than one each! He voiced his dissatisfaction at a meeting, saying something had gone awry with the principle of 'according to his need'.

Previously, during a study session when they learnt the Party's history, he'd said they'd gone down the wrong path during World War II thanks to the machinations of Lai Teck, but even if that hadn't happened, could they ever have taken power, given the calibre of Central Committee back then?

He couldn't remember which high-ranking cadre he heard this from, but Mr Tan Kah Kee himself had said the Magong were no better than children.

He spoke eloquently, but these views left everyone fuming.

Afterwards, the branch cadres counselled him more than once, solemnly urging him to study hard and build a good foundation so he could learn to place more faith in the Party.

Faith? He'd never felt he was lacking in faith. Yet one day passed after another, and he remained unable to make out the way ahead.

He was exhausted. Even at rest, his legs wouldn't stop trembling. Each time they shook, a little more energy fell away and evaporated.

He blamed himself for not being as young and strong as Ying Yang. He'd let Kong Wu down, by not having the proper spirit of suffering.

But he was about to collapse. Why hadn't he realised what his limits were?

He turned aside, spat viciously into the large clump of fan palms next to him, wrenched open his water bottle, and drained it.

Kong Wu stared into the darkness of the rainforest, shoulders slumped, waiting for his strength to return. 'There are times we need to trust in the power of our minds,' he muttered to himself.

Ying Yang was still breathing hard, brain empty. Then, for some reason, he recollected Tatak reciting his spell.

Would Tatak's chant replenish their energy?

Kong Wu climbed shakily up the slope, oozing beads of perspiration with every step. Shaochuan and Ying Yang followed close behind, sweat seeming to drip into their hearts, *tok tok tok*.

His rubber boots were drenched in sweat. As he stepped on a branch, its bark abruptly slid off, sending him skidding and tumbling forward. Like a falling boulder, the boar crashed down on him.

Shaochuan and Ying Yang rushed over and lifted the boar upright, then helped Kong Wu to his feet. One arm of his glasses had snapped in two, and was dangling from his mud-filled ear.

'Here, I'll take over.' Ying Yang stooped, ready to lift the rack from Kong Wu.

'No, I've only walked five or six steps, I'll keep going.'

'You can't! Look, you're bleeding.' Shaochuan pointed at the blood trickling from Kong Wu's temple, leaving a trail through the grime on his face. Kong Wu wiped it away with his sleeve.

'Oh no...' Ying Yang noticed something. 'The boar's eyes aren't moving.'

He rattled the rack, and his voice grew louder. 'Hey! I think it's dead.'

Shaochuan poked at its eyes and grabbed a tuft of fur. 'Yup, as a doornail. It's dead!'

The three men sat against a tree and were still for a very long time.

Hidden among the leaves were tiny magnolias no bigger than soybeans, the half-open fleshy pale-green petals like hidden smiles. Their fragrance drifted lightly through the air, barely there.

Kong Wu pressed his palm against his forehead to staunch the bleeding, and stared at his ruined glasses.

Shaochuan rolled and lit a cigarette. His eyes narrowed as he took a deep drag.

Ying Yang kicked the dead boar hard on the rump. 'Fuck! It was too heavy! Of course we dropped it. Serves it right, getting crushed to death. Shame about the pig blood soup, though.'

WILD MANGOES

1.

Yejin bit into the last slice of preserved wild mango, savouring the mouth-watering acidity and the mango fragrance that hung heavy in the morning mist. He chewed and swallowed slowly, recalling the sourness of the half-ripe fruit. The sweet-sharp flavour of wild mango encapsulated the season when fruit and flowers filled the rainforest, and he knew that once he'd swallowed, it would be harder to call to mind.

More than a year ago, he'd stumbled upon the lush wild mango trees on the chicken heart ridge between branches of Three Forks River and made a note of them.

This knowledge came in useful when Lianyi got scurvy and her face, once porcelain, took on a greenish hue like the desolate moon peeping between thick crowns of trees. The comrades in her squad said the slightest pressure left bruises on her skin from tiny blood vessels bursting. On the rare occasions she showed herself, her enormous eyes often held a startled expression beneath her high brows, the whites clearly visible in every blink and glimpse, making her look childlike and vulnerable.

In order to make sure she got the vitamin C she needed, the next time he was on patrol to check the wild boar traps, Yejin made a detour.

In the cool shade of the wild mango trees, the air around him was faintly sour sweet, everything washed clean by the hilltop's dawn mist, intoxicating as the quiet buzz of alcohol. Like being in a fairy tale. On the ground, fruit lay amid the fallen leaves, overripe flesh split open and attracting swarms of flies. The thick canopies were dark green, dense as smoke, dangling clusters of fruit the colour of jade. He clambered up a trunk, and as he brushed past the mangos they rubbed together, rustling like the golden song of summer.

That day, he brought a large sack of mangoes back for Lianyi, praying their yellow flesh would help her face regain the plump ruddiness he'd so cherished during morning calisthenics.

Sometime after that, a little jar of preserved mango made its way to him.

He held the squat, pot-bellied earthenware container that had once contained Tianjin pickles. She must have somehow gotten a message to the Minyun comrades in the village to send it along with the usual supplies. She'd even fashioned a wooden lid to seal this gift from the rainforest's summer.

When the mangoes had been eaten, should he return this nifty little container to her?

Ah! There she was, swathed in waterproof fabric, coming towards him from the clothes-airing hut. As she passed, she tilted her face a little, like the cover lifting slightly off a jar.

She never asked for her container back, so he happily kept it. Its earthenware interior retained the enchanting scent of wild mango.

Raindrops clung like pearls to the plastic sheeting of her squad's dorm. The wind stilled, and the heavy moisture that filled the air enveloped the rainforest with dingy, flickering shadows.

The rainy season had arrived.

A moment ago, he'd been in the hut too. The nightly airing of clothes was a painstaking chore during monsoon season. They were setting off on an expedition later that day, and he wanted to make sure he had a spare uniform for the road.

Lianyi was also in the expedition group. When he got to the head of the queue, he decided to pick out her clothes—she always fastidiously hung them at one end of the horizontal poles; he recognised the serial number embroidered on her trousers—and placed them by the stove to dry faster, before returning them to her usual corner.

By the light of the flickering flames, he took Lianyi's clothes from the rack and bundled them to his chest. Before returning them to their spot, he couldn't help burying his face in them. They were warm and stiff after hanging by the fire, and he felt the rebarbative lick of flame.

Though he was all alone in the airing hut, he still felt a searing blush wash over his face, just like the first time he saw her...

This was right after he'd joined the border-zone assault force, when everything was new and mysterious. In the centre of their camp was a large lecture hall, next to which was a basketball court (with a floor of flattened earth, of course), almost the same size as an actual court, surrounded on all sides by a wall of sweet bamboo reaching dozens of feet into the air.

He'd just come from the sentry post. It was almost dinner time, and an animated game was in progress. The others watched the frenzy as they waited for their meal.

Yejin inserted himself into a gap in the wall of green uniforms.

One player managed to get the ball right up to the basket. *Pah pah pahpah*—score!

As Yejin leaned forward for a better look, his arm brushed a comrade's shoulder—

The comrade abruptly pulled away.

When she turned, he realised it was a woman. Why was her hair so short?

'Sorry, sorry!' he said over and over, heat spreading from the tips of his ears to his neck.

That was Lianyi.

Afterwards, he learnt female fighters kept their hair short against the heat, and some even had crew cuts like the men.

For a long time after that, he stammered awkwardly around Lianyi, embarrassed by his clumsiness. For her part, she seemed completely at ease, and when they chatted, she would burble with laughter till he blushed bright red.

2.

The long-lived rain had been falling steadily for thirty or forty hours. Although no one expected the skies to clear, Lianyi was frustrated that it showed no sign of stopping. She stared out and muttered to herself, 'Damn this weather!' She stuffed a full water bottle and a packed lunch of ten boiled cassava pieces into her rucksack, and fastened the opening tightly. Next, she wrapped her carbine in a plastic sheet.

There was no way to stay dry in weather like this—no matter what, they would get soaked. Their rifles had to be protected, though. She stuffed a thick plastic sheet into the back of her trousers, so she could sit on it instead of the wet ground. The comrades called this a 'pheasant tail'.

An essential item, and not just because of the damp.

When the dispatch sheet was posted the previous evening, she saw she'd been allocated to the team meeting the Minyun liaison bringing their rations, which gave her pause—she was on the third day of her period. She could have asked to swap for sentry or patrol or kitchen duty instead, but she'd thought she should be done by the next day. Instead, she woke to find her flow as heavy as ever, but she couldn't drop out now—it was too late to find a replacement, and it wasn't fair to make seven people carry eight people's load, especially in this weather. She placed another wad of coarse bamboo paper in her pants, knowing this might not do any good once it got sodden. At least the pheasant tail would give her another layer of protection—or camouflage.

As she left the airing hut and passed the Third Men's Detachment, she saw Yejin staring blankly at an earthenware jar. What could he be thinking about?

How maddening the rainy season was!

In the last couple of weeks, the commander's wife Guixiang had sought her out several times for a heart-to-heart about Huang Qiang, the leader of Ninth Detachment. Lianyi agreed with many things she said: Those who'd joined the movement at a very young age got called 'old comrades' even though they weren't actually elderly because they'd given so much of their life to the struggle. These people needed a revolutionary partner, someone to support and be supported by, a helpmeet. Old comrades had many good points. They were tremendously loyal, and although they hadn't had much education, they had guerrilla knowledge instead! Huang Qiang had been the commander's personal bodyguard for several years. If their battalion were a little larger, he'd definitely be promoted to squadron commander. Most importantly, everyone shared the same revolutionary ideals and, being in the same unit, spoke a common language. A little difference in age wouldn't be a problem.

She listened in silence, head down, allowing her fringe to flop over her face so Guixiang wouldn't know how she felt.

Not that she had any idea how she felt.

Huang Qiang was well into his forties. He'd joined up after the colonial government declared a state of emergency on 20 June 1948, when he was only twelve or thirteen. The older comrades still referred to him as 'that young devil, Huang'.

Huang Qiang had taught one of the study sessions during her training. He spoke about how, back in the day, he'd been part of Old Commander Ma's team, the one that ambushed and killed High Commissioner Henry Gurney. How the new recruits' eyes shone, to hear these tales of gunfire echoing from historic times.

Like her fellow trainees, Lianyi had nothing but respect and admiration for the old comrades who'd come through battle. Everyone was hugely inspired by their display of revolutionary zeal, determined to emulate their example of fighting steadfastly and driving out the forces of imperialism.

But to be his partner? They would have to live together! She didn't think there could be true understanding between them—there was a gulf neither could leap across. She felt faint panic, mixed with a sadness she couldn't explain.

Yet Guixiang insisted men and women comrades couldn't behave like people on the outside, getting to know each other and holding hands. 'We don't need that sort of thing. Our understanding comes from political unity.'

Lianyi knew how two comrades became a couple: one wrote a letter declaring themselves and handed it to the Organisation to pass on. The other responded after carefully considering the matter. Guixiang said, 'You don't find out much about each other this way. True understanding comes only after marriage!'

Guixiang's deputy, a young woman from Guangxi whose nickname was 'Shrimpy', once told Lianyi how she and her husband cemented their relationship by exchanging letters, and not a soul knew for more than half a year, until the Organisation announced that the two of them would be moving in together that very night. The comrades were shocked! Shrimpy must have been thinking of everyone's stunned expressions as she recounted the story, because her face filled with gleeful pride.

And yet—Lianyi still felt something was missing. Being comrades was different from being husband and wife. How could she decide just like that? She couldn't talk herself into it.

She hesitated, not knowing how to answer.

Guixiang's eyes gleamed and she leaned closer. 'Unless you have feelings for someone else?'

A figure flashed across Lianyi's brain with a roar. All of a sudden, she felt dizzy and bowed her head even more.

3.

Yejin put on his rucksack and bent to get his ebony road-sweeping stick from beneath his bamboo bed.

Perhaps because he worked so patiently and carefully, everyone seemed less worried when he was the one covering up their footsteps. He couldn't remember when this started, but he was always bringing up the rear, and the comrades referred to him as General Road Sweeper.

His detachment mate Li Qun came over. 'What the hell! Three damn days of rain, and still no sign of stopping.'

It was true. He looked up at the two huge meranti trees outside the hut, glistening from the rainwater gliding noiselessly down their coarse bark. The dawn light hovered past their tall crowns, a curtain of rain cutting it off from view, leaving only a confusion of distant clouds.

'Hey, did you hear?' Li Qun cut to the chase. 'Guixiang is introducing Lianyi to an old comrade. Shouldn't you write her a letter?'

'What are you talking about?' Luckily the hut was dim enough to hide his blazing face.

'We sleep in the same bunk, you think I don't know? Don't say I didn't warn you.'

Li Qun was due to go out that morning to check the bamboo pipes that supplied their water, in case the copious rain had blocked them. As he passed by Yejin, he blurted out, 'I suppose there's no point waiting for a girl to write *you* a letter?'

Writing a letter. The first step in building a relationship with the object of one's affections.

He'd wanted to write for a long time now.

How many times had he come back from sentry duty, lit a small guerrilla light, and sat there blankly with his chin in his hands?

How should he even begin this letter?

Coming to the unit had brought him a new life, made him a new person. He'd named himself Yejin. For security reasons, only the Organisation knew his previous identity. His comrades didn't know his real name, nor anything about his past or his family.

Everything began from when he took that name, Yejin.

It was the same with everyone. He only knew about his comrades' lives after they'd acquired their new names.

This being the case, what did he know about Lianyi?

Because of that embarrassing incident when he'd mistaken her for a man, he couldn't stop thinking of her cropped hair.

Then, a couple of years ago, they'd both been on a long march along hill roads. It lasted more than two months—twenty comrades, men and women, thrown together day and night.

The two of them were rear guards. They set off into the dense rainforest, hunting and fishing along the way to replenish their supplies. All went smoothly. Night fell, and they strung up their hammocks. Lianyi and the female comrade next to her answered the chattering nocturnal insects with their own stream of conversation. They kept their voices low, but their laughter rang clear and bright, and found its way into his ears. 'Three women make a marketplace'—apparently this expression was true, even in the armed forces! He couldn't understand how the women fighters had so much to say to each other. Despite the rain, they sang 'Coral Song' and 'In Praise of Red Plums'. The tunes brought him back to the time he'd spent underground, hiding away in a wooden hut listening to cassette tapes.

Her voice was sweet and tender in the desolate chill of night. He felt warm, as if he'd managed to reach beyond the rain to the morning sunlight pouring over the hills.

They were supposed to connect with a brother unit by Sungai Perak to pick up rations, but they were attacked along the way. Some of them were injured, and they had to double back. Now they had to keep moving in order to link up with an assault force unit to the south of the east-west road, but were in danger of running out of food.

They'd come more than two-thirds of the way, and nobody wanted to turn back now. Besides, their rucksacks were full of items desperately needed by the assault force unit, who would be waiting for them. They all felt the weight of this expectation.

After telegraphing a message to get permission from HQ, they dug up one of their few buried rations, and continued with the original plan. There was much less to eat now, though.

As they drew closer to the main road, their rucksacks had grown much lighter, and their bodies were reduced too. Every fighter had shed between five and ten kilograms.

For breakfast, they got waterlogged rice—as much as they could eat. The leftovers were shared out for lunch, and when they stopped to rest around three or four in the afternoon, each person got two spoonfuls of sugar for dinner.

Yejin always gorged himself at breakfast. Soon he was having one and a half mess tins of rice rather than just one, and still he never felt full.

The male comrades exchanged uneasy looks, all thinking the same thing.

Lianyi only ever took half a mess tin of rice. Day after day.

Finally, he couldn't resist commenting, 'So little! Is that enough for you?'

'Waterlogged rice expands your stomach, which only makes you hungrier.' She smiled faintly. 'An old comrade taught me this: your stomach stretches like latex. Better to restrict yourself.'

Deep down, Yejin knew if everyone ate as much as him, there'd be nothing left for lunch!

But how could he endure this hunger?

At dinner, you dissolved your sugar ration in a scoop of water, and headed to your hammock after glugging it down, only to be woken before midnight by your swollen bladder. For the rest of the night, tormented by your gurgling stomach, you tossed and turned like a pancake on a griddle. As you drowsed, the aroma of food surrounded you, and you dreamed of snack vendors in small town alleyways, of the city's hawker centres, all wafting with delicious scents. Soon your drool was puddling on the hammock.

Breakfast seemed an eternity away. How to endure till then?

But he knew he must fulfil a young fighter's duties in these difficult times.

When the group stopped to set up camp, the most back-breaking work was fetching water. Normally this was nothing, but by late afternoon, when their legs felt like logs and their feet dragged on the path, a vine no thicker than a little finger was enough to trip them up. As soon as Leader called a halt, everyone slumped against the nearest tree, so exhausted they couldn't even focus their eyes—anything farther off was just a blur! At these moments, Yejin would drag himself upright and grab the waterskin from the cook's aluminium pot. He'd volunteered to get water every single day.

Once, when Quartermaster was handing out rations, he got a third spoonful of sugar.

His mouth gaped. Before he could say anything, Quartermaster deadpanned, 'Ask Lianyi.'

Li Qun, the head of the combat team, overheard and said, 'No need to ask. When I got back from patrolling the hills yesterday, I had an extra ration too. Lianyi said we were using so much energy while she wasn't doing much, she'd be fine with just one spoonful.'

This made Yejin blink as if grit had flown into his eyes. He turned and saw, in a grove a short distance away, slight and slender Lianyi bending to pick up a large, withered tree branch that she would drag back to camp for firewood.

Around this time, he started feeling unwell. When they stopped for a break after each leg of the march, he'd shut his eyes for a moment and doze off instantly. At lunchtime, the spoon sometimes slipped from his hand without his noticing.

Even so, he insisted on fetching water—he was the youngest person in this group. Every day, he'd go shirtless to the bottom of the gully and jog along for more than ten minutes, till he heard the flowing river.

He filled the waterskin and swung his right arm around to bring its twenty-odd kilograms onto his back. The moisture squeezed out by this manoeuvre trickled down his back, his trousers, his rubber shoes, and onto the ground. The sides of the gully were steep. Normally, he'd be able to sprint to the top with a spurt of energy, but now he had to crawl. When his right hand slackened, water slopped from the container over his shoulder, and suddenly the soil beneath his feet turned into mud. He looked up at the camp, high above him. When he raised his hand to mop the sweat from his face, stars appeared before his eyes. Just like that, his feet slipped out from under him and he was tumbling down.

He landed face up in a crevice, and instinctively reached out to steady himself. His hand landed on a pokok nibung's cluster of porcupine-like spines, and the thick thorns slashed his palm.

Covered in mud, he limped back to camp. Less than half the water remained in his container.

He held out his trembling right hand. Everyone cried out, and some of the female comrades had to turn their faces aside.

Lianyi was the assistant medic. After he'd cleaned himself up, they sat on the protruding root of a rouge plum tree and she disinfected his hand, then plucked out the thorns one by one with tweezers.

The sun began to set, and still she hadn't managed to get them all.

As dusk fell over the rainforest, a returning hornbill passed overhead and let out a squawking cry. A teardrop fell onto his hand, and the sting of its salt made Yejin grab his wrist and yelp.

Lianyi looked up, tears glistening on her cheeks. 'I'm sorry!' she cried out.

Oh, that face, like the full moon. In the days after this, he recalled from time to time how fresh and clear it had been.

Their most intimate encounter. Why did this sweet contact, skin to skin, have to be wrapped in shuddering pain?

How could he even begin to write this letter?

4.

Rain fell noiselessly.

No lightning, no thunder. Even the faint wind had stopped. Every animal was hiding in its burrow. No howls or chirps. If you listened carefully, you could just make out the faint patter of raindrops.

Yet the rainforest was awake. The drizzle had been falling day and night, stirring the leaves. They glistened with a sheen of moisture, like butterflies flapping inky green wings through damp mist.

When the rain stopped, these nameless trees would release a heart-quickening scent of newness, from their trunks, their leaves, their sap, their shards of fallen bark. For now, there was just a stagnant reek, as if someone had turned over piles of rotting leaves to expose the damp decay beneath. It pervaded the air and roiled all around them.

The rainforest was sodden. Like a reflection in a lake, it swayed blearily, both real and not real.

Soaked through, hands and feet icy, the comrades walked quickly to keep warm.

They met the Minyun comrades at a pheasant plain. Everyone's skin was slick with rain. They quickly exchanged supplies and messages, saying as little as possible, then bid goodbye and turned back the way they came.

There were eight bundles. Apart from the usual necessities, oil and rice and tinned goods, there were also two bamboo baskets of pork, more than forty kilograms each.

Yejin was on road-sweeping duty, so they gave him a bag of tins weighing more than thirty kilos. Out of the corner of his eye, he saw Lianyi squat to get one of the baskets of pork onto her back. Her face was greenish in the cold rain, and a strand of her hair—now longer than before—was plastered across her cheek, brushing her purplish lips.

Moving supplies in the rain felt very different to doing it on a hot day. The chilly water cooled their heavy burdens and overheated bodies. Even so, they were walking a couple of thousand feet through rainforest, and soon their faces were covered in sweat that mingled with the pouring rain, channelling salty liquid into their mouths.

The path beneath their feet felt more uneven than usual. Whenever they had to go up or down a slope, every step was a trap—the road was soaked from days of rain, and slick stretches lay hidden beneath fallen leaves, liable to send their feet skidding out from under them, sending them and their burdens splat into the mud.

Finally, they arrived at Cassava Farm River. Mist rose from the water and an unruly gash in the clouds allowed greyish afternoon light to pour down. The stepping stones had been washed away or submerged. The comrades found wooden sticks to probe the depth with each step as they forded the murky stream. Leader and a male comrade stationed themselves at the midway point, ready to pull anyone to safety.

Yejin swept away the confusion of footprints on the hill track, some shallow and some deep, like his mood this morning, a criss-crossing jumble that refused to be cleared away.

He glanced at Leader in the middle of the river, an old comrade, and tried not to think about what Li Qun had said that morning.

He'd heard the rumour too: Guixiang had been matchmaking Lianyi with an old comrade—Huang Qiang, apparently. This wasn't unexpected, as Huang Qiang was one of only two old comrades in their unit who were still unmarried.

Li Qun had meant well with his warning. If Yejin hadn't known, if he'd gone ahead and sent his letter, he would now be in a state of confusion, unable to be certain what lay in Lianyi's heart. All he knew was when their eyes met, something shifted in her expression. He remembered how good she was to him, and would forever taste the sweetness of those extra spoonfuls of sugar. He'd never forgotten the tears she shed for him at dusk. Besides, she'd never refused the concern and gifts he'd bestowed on her—he made sure they were always appropriate —and the fragrance of those wild mangoes gave him endless beautiful fantasies.

Feelings are just feelings, though. Lianyi was equally friendly with everyone else in the unit. Everything seemed uncertain in the mystical light that pervaded the rainforest in monsoon season. Was he waiting for a delightful surprise or disappointment? The only person he needed to face was himself.

Li Qun's well-intentioned warning reminded him of all this, and he found himself in an unexpected state of embarrassment.

He had a lot of respect for Huang Qiang. Like many old comrades, he wasn't well-educated and didn't have much to say, but his every move was full of steadfastness and resolve. These comrades had decades of guerrilla experience and all kinds of hidden abilities they could deploy at crucial moments, easily resolving any difficulty.

When Yeqin was sent from the assault force to the Thai border, it was Huang Qiang who led the dozen or so of them north. At one point, they went more than ten days without a single successful hunt and were reduced to living on foraged wild vegetables seasoned with belachan or salted black beans. The lack of protein began to chip away at their energy.

One evening, Huang Qiang brought Yejin and Li Qun fishing at a river near their camp.

The hill stream flowed clear and cold, and oddly shaped rock formations lined the banks. Some stretches were calm, while others burbled agitatedly as they snaked between patches of grass and moss-covered stones.

Yejin asked Li Qun where they could find bait. 'No need,' said Li Qun, winking. 'All you have to worry about is catching the fish. Move fast, or you won't be able to keep up!'

Huang Qiang found a thin bamboo pole, pulled a fishline strung with hooks from his bullet pouch, and tied it to the pole. Without stopping to bait the hooks, he made for the bank.

Li Qun kept a lookout, while Yejin took charge of netting the fish.

Huang Qiang reached the water's edge, and with a flick of his hand, sent the string straight at the river. As soon as it touched the surface, the line went taut and emerged with a silvery-white fish more than a foot long struggling violently, making the slender fishing rod jerk around.

It took Yejin a moment to understand what he was seeing. He opened his mouth, but before he could say, 'Wow', he realised he should lunge forward and catch the fish. He recalled something he'd once seen in a movie: a stage magician casting a fishing rod into the audience and reeling in a live fish from out of nowhere.

Huang Qiang snapped off the pliant branch of a shrub, leaving the leafy end intact, and impaled the fish: in through the gill slit, out through the mouth. The fish could no longer move, apart from its gasping mouth and the tail that wouldn't stop squirming, slapping against the fallen leaves.

Turning back to the river, Huang Qiang lunged again, and his rod twitched. Warm afternoon sunlight poured through the trees and danced off the silvery skin of the spasming fish, dazzling Yejin. Droplets of water spattered from their bodies, spraying Huang Qiang all over as he excitedly launched himself from the bank again and again.

Some of the fish weren't securely hooked, and fell onto the bank with a splat. By the time Yejin managed to grab hold of these slippery creatures, Huang Qiang had hauled another one out. It was more than one pair of hands could cope with, and as Li Qun had predicted, he wasn't able to keep up.

In less than half an hour, there were more than twenty fish on the stick!

When they stopped for a break, Yejin took the opportunity to examine Huang Qiang's fishing rod. The only thing on it was a bright red plastic bead, a little smaller than a wild cherry.

'Well? I wasn't bluffing, was I?' Li Qun stuffed his catch into his rucksack. 'It's a trick lure. The fish think it's a berry and bite. One t-tug on the rod and they're hooked.'

Yejin glanced at Huang Qiang, who was getting out his tobacco box to roll himself a cigarette. He let it dangle from his mouth, and in his narrowed eyes was a smug gleam.

Could it really be that simple? Yejin couldn't resist grabbing the rod and mimicking Haung Qiang's actions, tossing it out at the water. After almost twenty attempts, he hadn't caught a single fish.

'No, no, that won't work.' Huang Qiang stubbed out his cigarette and rose to his feet. 'The tr-trick lure only w-works once.' He had a mild stutter. 'The f-fish are clever! You have to k-keep moving. W-watch closely and be quick. See a fish m-move, and strike there. Don't drop it j-just anywhere, you'll scare away the fish!'

By dusk, they had over a hundred little fish, weighing more than twenty kilos in total—a good meal, with enough left to be dried by the fire for rations.

The image of Huang Qiang nimbly sending out his line kept playing in Yejin's mind, but he couldn't work out how to spot the right place and attack just so. A mystery to this day.

Later on, he heard that Huang Qiang picked up this skill when he was injured in a skirmish and left to recuperate in a Malay unit for more than ten years. The Malay comrades taught him this trick.

If Guixiang really was trying to matchmake Lianyi with Huang Qiang, Yejin didn't want to stand in their way. This old comrade had given more than half his life to the Revolution.

How could Yejin forgive himself for taking away his one chance at rejuvenation?

Even before writing a single word of his letter, he already felt the unease that comes from going against your conscience.

★

'Are you all right, Lianyi?' called Leader from the centre of the river. 'Quick, everyone's already crossed!'

'I'll be okay. You go ahead, I'll catch up.'

Yejin looked back and saw she'd stopped for a rest, her bamboo basket on a river rock.

'Look after her, Yejin,' said the commander. 'But don't fall too far behind!'

Yejin went over to Lianyi. 'I'll carry you across,' he said.

'No need.' She struggled to her feet. 'I can do it. No need to follow me.'

He watched as she plunged her stick into the river. The murky water rose over her ankles, her calves, her knees. When it was halfway up her thighs, she trembled and faltered.

The stick slipped from her hand and was swept away by the rushing water. She cried out.

Yejin was in the water right away, splashing over to her side.

As he handed her his road-sweeping stick, he detected the dull reek of blood, mixed with the muddy stench of the river. The tea-coloured water swirling around Lianyi's trouser legs was momentarily stained with red-brown liquid that quickly dispersed.

Right away, he understood why Lianyi had insisted on crossing alone.

Lianyi limped away from him, shaking as she reached the other bank.

5.

Lianyi walked with her head bowed, raging at herself.

Why was she so pathetic? Why did she have to embarrass herself in front of him?

Who could have guessed her flow would be so heavy this month? Between the rain, the river, and this sodden uniform, there was no way to keep it hidden. Ugh! Even she could smell the odour on herself. Her only choice was to hang back from the rest of the group.

She tried to work out from Yejin's face what he was thinking. Surely he could tell. But he sincerely wanted to help, and was stronger than her. Should she let him carry some of her load in his rucksack? Or just swap her cargo with his?

But he was sweeping the road! A tricky task, given how many footprints they were leaving.

She hadn't forgotten how, during her bout of scurvy, he'd picked all the fruit he could find while out on patrol: tampoi and other sour fruit... as well as those wild mangoes.

She'd silently accepted these gifts, thinking this was a sign, a hint, an encouragement—but the longed-for moment still hadn't arrived.

That laid-back personality. He was waiting for the right time.

Did he realise they'd reached the critical juncture? She would never give herself to Huang Qiang, but could she tell Guixiang who she actually liked?

What a dilemma! What a struggle!

The rain cooled her feverish temples, and water sluiced down her hair to her pale neck and heaving chest. The droplets kneaded her tormented heart. Why was he being so obtuse?

Leader and the other comrades were farther down the slope, disappearing into the hillside. She could only make out where they were from the slight swaying of shrubs.

She looked back. Yejin was doubled over, carefully sweeping away their tracks between the riverbank and rainforest.

Should she wait for him?

This was a rare chance the heavens had bestowed upon her! Lianyi's forehead blazed. But what would she say to him? They both got so tongue-tied, how would they navigate this? Should she hint that he ought to... write a letter?

She looked ahead. The slippery slope was now bare mud, trampled into slurry by the comrades, roots coiling through it like snakes. Rain splashed into the mud or puddled in their footprints. The shorter shrubs on either side had been uprooted by the small landslides and sprawled downhill.

Yejin had almost caught up with her.

Lianyi instinctively started moving, as if hurrying away from something,

And then—'Oh!' Yejin saw Lianyi step on a loose clod and land on her bum in the mud.

She twisted around and got back up, but before she could take a step, she cried out again, tumbled back down, and slid a few metres!

She tried to get up on her knees, but couldn't seem to find any purchase, and slipped again. The bamboo basket had almost come off one shoulder, and was spilling its contents onto the ground.

Lianyi pulled the shoulder strap back on. Instead of standing up, she began wriggling downhill on her bum, hauling the basket after her.

Like a gust of wind, Yejin rushed to her side.

He could never have imagined Lianyi, normally so fastidious, practically reclining in the mud, like a wild pig rolling in filth, smearing itself all over.

He handed her his stick and said, trying to sound casual, 'Come on, stand up! This isn't a pretty sight.'

Lianyi's whole body went limp, and tears blurred her vision. She didn't know if she should blame herself or the heavens for this predicament, but abruptly snapped, 'What do you mean not a "pretty sight"? I'm carrying supplies for the Revolution, aren't I? What could be prettier than that?'

Yejin stared. 'Um...' The thought occurred that the pork must be weighing her down. He held up her basket. 'Why don't... Why don't we swap?'

Still lost in her thoughts, she kept dragging the basket downhill. 'How could I look pretty? Soaking wet, covered in mud, you're not going to find anything pretty here!' She was no longer making sense. 'Of course I'm not a pretty sight. I'm hideous, and that's why no one's written me a letter!'

A letter! Without prompting, the words came out of her mouth! The earth and sky grew absolutely silent, and the sound of rain vanished completely.

'I... I mean, if... if no one... helps you, that... that doesn't... doesn't make our unit look too good.' Yejin actually managed to come up with words that might comfort her. He spoke with effort, rain and sweat pouring off his forehead.

Even so, at this moment, he felt light and easy, as if the weight pressing on his chest like an enormous rock had fallen away. His body was so buoyant it was floating. He just needed to turn and take a few steps out of this morass.

Lianyi's left boot had slipped off, and was filled with thick, gloopy mud. He picked it up, knocked the mud out, handed it back to her, and reached out to gently tug at her basket. 'I'll write you a letter,' he said, 'if you give me your burden.'

Her head bowed further. Her nose prickled, and she had to try hard not to cry.

SWANSONG IN THAT FARAWAY PLACE

Year end was approaching!

One night not long ago, the changing season quietly removed the moist navy-blue gauze shrouding the rainforest. The sun, asleep for so long, was finally waking up, expelling the foetid air it had held in for so long, blowing out a sea of mist that meandered through the valley.

The wind passed between tree trunks, slipped between leaves and branches, her tender caress dusting away mouldy damp from the long rainy season.

Fallen leaves capered across the ground. In the quiet afternoon, an occasional shoot sprouted, pale yellow poking through wet dark brown soil, sending a *shrrr* through withered foliage.

Translucent new leaves clung tremulously to the branches: rice-white, violet, crimson…

Crisp chirping among the trees.

Overnight, the dry season had arrived.

And with it, the celebratory *dong dong dong* of New Year singing and dancing.

The campground stirred itself, ready to bid farewell to the old and welcome the new.

The festivities were a pick-me-up, an encouragement in the face of the arduous struggle.

When the Enemy wasn't hounding us, New Year had a special meaning for the comrades in the border zone. Spouses and siblings who had been deployed to different worksites began counting down the days till they could come together again.

Around this time, Unit HQ did its best to recall all the comrades who'd been deployed elsewhere. The joy of being reunited added to the jubilation of the season.

Of course, the holiday also marked yet another year's baptism by gunfire, a celebration of the ongoing struggle.

In the farming villages, the Minyun volunteers were on the move, arriving almost every day with supplies for the festive meal. Basket after basket of nine-pound chickens passed by the sentry post, the fowl clucking away on the backs of comrades who couldn't stop grinning.

The storage shed was piled high with all manner of festive goods, with the quartermaster team busily darting around the heap.

All year round, the comrades subsisted on mixed grains with every meal, but at this festive time, they would have a few days to enjoy white rice served with delicious dishes: white-poached chicken, Guangxi stewed pork, kelah merah fish from the croplands, all kinds of fresh fruit and vegetables... As the ingredients were carried past everyone's eyes, their tongues danced with memories of delicious flavours, heightening anticipation for the holiday.

Each squad was rehearsing its contribution to the New Year Concert. In the dusk after dinner, the hills would resound with music and singing.

Ding Feng cleared his throat. As soon as the accordion was done playing the introduction, he launched into song, 'Even the highest mountain will be scaled, we the trekkers have never failed...'

The comrades loved hearing this song at the holidays, and he never disappointed them.

After the first two lines, however, his singing abruptly stopped, and so did the accordion.

A melancholy wisp of flute music drifted like smoke across the campground, winding its way out into the rainforest, silencing the joyous singing that had echoed through the hills a moment ago.

Ding Feng stood absolutely still and listened. He was a strapping man of almost forty, prematurely balding—the evening wind ruffled his few sparse hairs like wild grasses. His head tilted to one side, coarse brows frowning, eyes filled with distant thoughts.

Sure enough, the flute poured out the familiar melody, 'In that Faraway Place'.

In that faraway place is a good maiden, all who walk past her tent turn back for a lingering look. Ding Feng's lips remained shut, but the words resounded in his heart.

He turned to the accordionist. 'Ah Xiang's playing that tune again. His arrangement?'

Ah Xiang stood beneath a jackfruit tree so large it would have taken three or four people to encircle its trunk, which stretched into the darkness like a ladder reaching into the heavens. The setting sun glimmered on the shoulders of his dark green uniform. All was murky behind him, like dim memory.

He began warming up, letting out a sharp blast that startled the wild pigeons roosting on a nearby branch. Flapping their wings, they moved as a flock to a higher perch.

Nearby was a wooden block intended as a bench, but sitting down to play the flute suppressed the breath, which came more smoothly when he was standing.

His attention was on the reddish-brown bamboo flute at his lips. Six fingers moved nimbly across its length, and the notes flowed from it, delicate and unpredictable: now soaring, now gliding, now somersaulting, now wafting plaintively. As the music surged, his fingers shifted as rapidly as seagulls ducking between the waves.

Mi-so-la-laso-mi-so-la-sola-mi-so-so-fa-so—mi-so-la-somi-re-mire-do-re-mi-so-do-re-mi-redo-ti-la.
In that faraway place is a good maiden…
I wish she would take her fine leather crop and gently whip my back.

a landmine, an injured leg
'from now on, I'll be holding you back, do you regret it?'

Ah Xiang brought the bamboo flute with him when he joined up.

On that night, Chunxi came running to pass on a message from the Organisation: they would be on the move soon, and he should prepare to join them!

She'd already packed. Her words came out without pausing to draw breath. By the light of a kerosene lamp, sweat glimmered on her red face and her heart thumped wildly. With a habitual gesture, she wiped the moisture from her nose.

'On the move?' Ah Xiang's mind went blank, and for a moment he couldn't think.

'Yes!'

A cadre from their underground network had been arrested and betrayed them. Quite a few of their comrades had already been captured.

This was all happening so suddenly. Ah Xiang was thrown into confusion. It had already been a while since he left the New Village for this remote hillside settlement. Now he had to leave again. Who knew when he'd be back? He had to sort through his possessions, and give his parents some kind of explanation.

'No way!' Chunxi glared at him. 'If you go back now, you'll walk straight into their net.'

He ought to have known that, but he couldn't think straight. He moved clumsily, uncertain what to do.

In the end, Chunxi helped him to pack.

Ah Xiang held up his two flutes, ready to stuff them into his backpack, then hesitated. He'd been playing for more than a decade, and it would be hard to leave these behind. But would he have a use for them? Wouldn't they need to be silent in the rainforest?

His hand hovered in the air. Chunxi shot him a look. After a moment's thought, she said, 'Bring one of them. Warriors require music as well as the voice of Revolution. We'll need instruments. It doesn't weigh much, anyway.'

Ah Xiang discarded the long flute. The short bamboo one was better—it broke into two halves for easy packing. Besides, he had a vague sense that the anguished tones of the long flute might not be quite right for the military atmosphere!

Honestly, it would be hard to find anyone who cared as much about the bamboo flute as him and Chunxi.

During the winding journey to joining up, he spent a night at a small hotel with some trekkers. Before going to bed, one of the trekkers saw the disassembled bamboo flute and said, not trying to hide his surprise, 'What did you bring that for? Guerrillas have to stay away from noise and fire!' Then he pulled a dark grey revolver from his belt and banged it down on the bedside table. Making a fist, he said, emphasising each word, 'This—is—the—only—thing—that—counts!'

The *thunk* of the gun hitting the table lingered in Ah Xiang's heart all the way north.

Only when they arrived in the hills and had a welcome party on the first night did he put his flute back together. The new comrades were invited to perform, so he played 'Cracking the Whip, Delivering Rations on Horseback'. Everyone's eyes were gleaming in the lights of the lecture hall, and their warm applause finally pushed the *thunk* away.

Thank goodness for Chunxi. If not for her, the flute would have been left in that broken-down hut.

Long ago, Chunxi asked him why he sang 'I'd happily be a little lamb, following by her side, I wish she would take her fine leather crop and gently whip my back.'

She was twenty years old at the time, riding side-saddle on the crossbar of his bicycle, the countryside wind making her mid-length hair billow. A few strands brushed his cheeks, his eyelashes, his nose, itching them.

As he pedalled harder, he took the opportunity to breathe, breathe deep, absorbing into his memory all this air, fresh as morning mist, with a faintly milky scent.

He didn't reply. There was no need. Mischievously, he puffed warm air onto her pale shoulders.

They'd grown up together in the same New Village. Having known each other for so long, many words could go unsaid.

The next time they sang that song, it was in the unit's little hut.

This company had less than two hundred people, about two-thirds of them married couples who mostly lived apart in their squad's single-sex dorms, apart from one night every two months when it was their turn to spend the night in the little hut.

They were young—when they joined up, Chunxi was only twenty-three, and Ah Xiang twenty-six. They worked with the other comrades to transport and bury rations, to patrol the hills and set snares, to farm the croplands, to liaise with the Minyun, to trek the hill roads... There were many days ahead of them, they thought, and no rush to live together.

Even so, Chunxi took the initiative and went to Unit HQ to ask for permission to get married.

More than half a year before this, Ah Xiang had set off with a small group to an established battle zone, to take up a military position. Afterwards, Ding Feng said they'd spent their time there manoeuvring through a dragon ridge thick with wild nipah palms, checking the batteries of old landmines and setting new ones.

'I'd never seen such a big palm grove. Clump after clump of them—like a new plantation. A day and a half later, we were still wandering through. A gigantic maze.'

Ding Feng was the advance scout, stopping and starting, carefully probing the path ahead.

The large, feathery fronds of the nipah palms swayed in the noontime sun. Peering between the leaves, there were only more trees to be seen, reaching endlessly into the distance. A gentle breeze blew through the dappled light.

The chirping of cicadas covered the land.

Every now and then, they heard a hill-chicken (that is, a pheasant) squawking not far away, and sometimes one would appear, shooting lightning-fast through thick fallen leaves before burrowing into the undergrowth, or else flapping its speckled wings as it vanished among the quivering palms.

The first stretch of palm trees were all around the same height and size, making Ding Feng's thick brows furrow as he tried to navigate.

Ah Xiang stuck close to him.

Finally, they made their way along a side ridge and emerged to find a range of hills extending to the east and west, thickly covered with yet more nipah palms.

Ding Feng brushed aside the fallen leaves at the start of the path, and in a few quick steps had reached the dragon ridge. Ah Xiang remained two or three metres behind him, on high alert.

Ah Xiang noticed a shrub next to him, about shoulder height, young crimson leaves on long stems. He took a closer look, and realised with a start that these were the same leaves he'd gathered as a child to make mouth harps. Just the day before, he'd demonstrated this for the others, and one of the comrades teased, 'I guess that plant was your first music teacher!'

He looked up and found Ding Feng ten paces ahead of him, turning towards the right side of the dragon ridge.

'Stop!' yelled Ah Xiang, sprinting towards Ding Feng.

This was the very ridge where, just yesterday, they'd set a new cluster of landmines! Ding Feng had been walking obliviously towards them, drawing ever closer to death!

Ah Xiang was reaching out to prevent Ding Feng taking another step when—

Huwoong—

An explosion! Shock waves, thick smoke, scattered sand and dirt. Ding Feng was tossed in the air, landing on his rump. All the comrades behind him were thrown to the ground too.

He shook his head, feeling dizzy, trying to dislodge the soil caught in his sparse hair. Blinking rapidly, he established that he wasn't hurt. What had happened?

Still sprawled on the ground, Ding Feng brought his rifle onto his shoulder and crept forward—

Ah Xiang was slumped a few paces away, facing the sky, propping himself up with both arms. In front of him was a crater about the size of a washbasin, a tangle of exposed roots protruding from it, among them an eye-catching crimson wire, still wreathed in smoke. The air was filled with the choking stench of gunpowder.

Ah Xiang's left trouser leg flapped emptily. Everything below the knee was shattered.

'Ah Xiang stepped on a mine!' shouted Ding Feng, leaping to his feet and dashing towards Ah Xiang.

'Hang on!' Ah Xiang held up a hand, breathing hard, his voice shaking. 'This is a cluster mine—there are three of them. Fuh-first, remove the batteries. Be careful!'

A few months later, Ah Xiang had mostly recovered from his injuries and new skin was growing back millimetre by millimetre over the wound. His shaken nerves gradually calmed down too.

It was at this time that Chunxi returned to the border zone from her posting with the guerrilla support squad. Right away, she wrote a letter to Unit HQ saying: *I want to live together with Ah Xiang.*

In the little hut, she asked Ah Xiang, 'That day, you'd already shouted for him to stop; why did you need to run over there?'

'The cicadas were making so much noise, I was afraid he wouldn't hear me.'

'Ding Feng blames himself. He says it's his fault this happened to you.'

'How is it his fault? I'm the one to blame.' Ah Xiang gently stroked the shiny new skin on his stump—it felt tight, and he had to rub it to relieve the itching. 'It all happened so quickly, I ran towards him without looking where I was going. Maybe this is—fate.' He said it lightly, but the word sent a quiet tremor through his heart.

He never normally spoke like this, but he had no anxieties in front of Chunxi.

In the few years since joining up, he'd experienced a lot—so many memorial services, so many wounded comrades-in-arms, so many guerrilla friends with stories of being adrift, going hungry, getting caught in battle, losing comrades. In his mind wafted one image after another of bodies, full of life but now lost. He couldn't help thinking that one day, he would be the one in danger.

'I had a dream, actually—I saw myself sent flying by a landmine.' Ah Xiang smiled grimly, then his expression softened. 'Still, that's how we got to live together sooner.'

He took Chunxi's hand, which had been caressing his stump. Eyes full of clear, deep emotion, he said, 'From now on, I'll be holding you back. Do you regret it?'

Chunxi was silent, head lowered. Turning her face to one side, she leaned against his chest.

'I'd happily be a little lamb, following by her side, I wish she would take her fine leather crop and gently whip my back.'

She sang quietly, as if talking in her sleep. Tears quietly seeped from her eyes.

victory and despair
laugh and that's a lifetime, cry and that's a lifetime too

I have to raise a glass with her tonight, thought Ah Xiang, sitting on the edge of the bed in the little hut.

This bottle of longan liquor had been steeping for several months, from when Chunxi set off with the battalion to transport food supplies across into Malaysia. Quartermaster had brewed a few dozen bottles of rice wine, and she'd bought one for Ah Xiang. Into it went the remains of the small packet of longan flesh they'd been saving.

He gently shook it so the longans at the bottom swirled around. Plucking out the stopper, he let the alcoholic fragrance fill the hut. He placed the bottle on the bamboo bedside table.

By the table was a gun rack at shoulder height. Normally this held his revolver, but tonight it had been replaced by a particularly huge pitcher plant. A whole foot long, about the thickness of an arm, slick outer walls striped vibrant purple. The vine it grew from was twined around the rack, and the pitcher hung slantwise, its fleshy lid open, a large bouquet of wildflowers protruding: pale violet hill orchids, pink peonies, a couple of long leaves among them.

Chunxi had brought it back that afternoon, and the other comrades surrounded her to take a look. You hardly ever saw such big pitcher plants!

She was excited, her face flushed red. After more than a month of hard labour transporting rations, her round face had grown thinner. Her fringe dipped down to touch her eyelashes, quivering whenever she blinked, and her eyes blazed fiercely and she exclaimed, 'You'd never have expected it, right? All the way up there on the border dragon, so hard to reach on foot—it's covered in these kinds of plants, and all sorts of flowers!'

In front of all their comrades, she'd impetuously thrust the bouquet at him.

★

The aroma of rice wine faded, and the little hut filled with the delicate scent of wildflowers.

Chunxi's absence this time round had caused Ah Xiang much more anxiety than previous expeditions, as if his heart were hanging in mid-air.

South of the border dragon was Malaysian territory. Before losing his foot, he'd often gone with the defusing team into dense fields of Enemy landmines, their batteries long run dry. One tug and a string of them came up. In three days they'd collected several hundred.

But what if they happened to come upon a live mine?

An idea stirred in his mind, he couldn't say since when. Like a seed, it had touched the ground, started sprouting, growing daily.

Once, in the afterglow, he murmured it to Chunxi.

She gently swatted his cheek. 'No! Do you want to commit an error?' Then she hugged him tight.

Chunxi loved him so much! Perhaps if it were a fait accompli, she'd make different calculations and have different ideas.

The night was like water. The glow from the guerrilla light (a kerosene lantern), wavered in the air, casting patches of illumination like his scattered thoughts.

At long last, Chunxi was back. They poured large glasses of tea-coloured longan liquor, taking small sips as they chatted.

The home-brewed rice wine was unctuous and smooth. The aroma of longan wove through the alcohol fumes, drifting like mist through the silence of the little hut, making it feel like springtime.

Chunxi, in the flesh, sat by his side, telling him everything that had happened since they parted, yet none of this felt real to Ah Xiang, as if both yesterday, now vanished into the night winds, and this very moment were from a fantastical landscape.

Before they turned off the lights, Chunxi's eyes peered tipsily from beneath her lashes, and in a sweetly slurred voice, she whispered, 'Where is it? I'll help you put it on.'

The Organisation issued condoms to all the couples with access to the little hut, but not many—each one had to be used two or three times.

Ah Xiang smiled mysteriously. 'All done.' He leaned over and blew out the guerrilla light, *phoo*. His strained expression faded into the darkness. The tips of his ears were scalding, and his heart abruptly began beating much faster. He could hear the blood surging through his veins.

He no longer knew what night it was. Pale moonlight seeped through the green tarp that formed the roof of the little hut, and spilled onto the bamboo bed.

Chunxi's round face, shining palely from the gloom, contained all the magnetism that existed between heaven and earth. Ah Xiang drew close and kissed her at great length, inhaling deeply of the milky scent that mingled with the air, fresh as morning mist.

Then an island rose from the fog, baptised a thousand times by the jade green ocean, too beautiful to name. Snuggling against it, Ah Xiang's fondling hands encountered softness, roundness, comfort.

Chunxi reached out to gently nudge his shoulder. Understanding her meaning, he lay back. His body was a parched wilderness with smouldering lava beneath ready to erupt. Chunxi lay atop him, splaying open an incomparably fragrant, joyous paradise. He entered her and was enveloped in moist warmth. Every dry, cracked pore was penetrated by buttery rain. Deep within, vibrating, thrusting on a crest of pleasure. Trembling, he wanted to shout, but held the words back, a trembling cherry on his tongue... *Oh! Oh!* As a boy, he'd picked so many wild cherries. When he presented Chunxi with them in cupped hands, she invariably chose the biggest and popped it into his mouth. *Oh!* She pressed her lips to his as the scream threatened to rip through them. Ah Xiang's hands clutched her pale back. Two ardent flames came together with a muffled, soul-summoning explosion in the depths of the night.

Ah Xiang rolled over, pressing Chunxi tightly, tightly to the bamboo bed. He felt violently shaken, warmth flowing through him, no thoughts in his mind, just emptiness. He forgot his disability, felt nothing but Chunxi stirring gently beneath him.

Ah, beneath the moonlight, in that faraway place...

Ah Xiang lay quietly, staring at the sky beyond the tarp.

He had no idea what time it was, but pellucid moonlight spilled onto the tree branches outside with a crisp *tng tong*. He felt soft, tender motion against his body—Chunxi's affectionate fingertips. *Oh! What a beautiful night!*

He felt completely unrestrained, his limbs luxuriating, all the heat in his body ebbing away. The lingering sweetness from faint damp at his forehead and chest.

They didn't have many material things living in the hills; their daily life was harsh and spartan. Yet the deep attachment between them was like the moonlight, sparkling intoxicatingly in the gloom. After his injury, he had been redeployed to the print room, while Chunxi remained in the reserves, always getting sent out on expeditions, running around in all directions. In a whole year, they were only able to share a handful of these brief, magical nights.

Chunxi was cleaning up. He'd tried to get up and deal with it himself, but she'd gently pushed him back onto the bed. The glow of a flashlight played around his thigh like a firefly.

'Aiyah!' Chunxi cried out, keeping her voice low. 'How did this happen? The condom broke!'

Ah Xiang lay perfectly still, feeling a little guilty. This is what he'd wanted. What should he say?

'Now what? What should we do?' She turned the torch onto his face.

Screwing up his eyes, he avoided her gaze and tried to comfort her. 'Don—don't worry, it's just this one time, may—maybe nothing will happen.'

'No, we're done for!' She pummelled his thigh. 'You bastard!'

He said nothing. Chunxi loved him, and it didn't matter how she yelled at him now. Despite his words, his heart was full of joy that his plan had come off. Their exertions earlier had hurt his injured leg, but he had no regrets—he'd assumed a more effective position. Every step of his scheme was turning out the way he'd wanted. Now he hoped that in the face of this fait accompli, Chunxi would feel the same way he did.

His mind turned to the strength that would come from the eternal mothering instinct.

Right away, he was shocked and uneasy that this thought had come to him. Since when had his brain been assaulted by such reactionary, backward thinking?

Ever since losing his foot, he'd hardly gone on any expeditions, and mostly his work in the print room kept him busy. Before going to bed each night, he'd remove his metal leg and examine the stump that was shrivelling by the day, feeling as if he was observing his own life. His own experiences, his encounters in the unit, these relatively placid days—all aroused an unprecedented wave of memory.

After he first began living with Chunxi, he wrote his first letter to his ageing parents since joining up (without mentioning his leg, of course), to let them know he and Chunxi were doing well. There was no guarantee that the letter would be delivered, and the Organisation had warned him that getting a letter out would entail a lot of fuss and bother, but he'd insisted. In the depths of his mind, he could sense a traditional, conservative side of himself. Marriage was the point when a child truly left his parents' care. His parents both liked Chunxi and would be relieved to hand him over to her.

He'd never regretted his choice. When he first joined up, he'd been called to action by so many beautiful dreams and heroic ideals: storming mountain ranges in the line of duty, passionately taking part in the armed struggle. The romance of youth! The fire inside him still smouldered among the ashes, but had unavoidably been tamped down by the moments and hours, the months and years. The comrades came together in vigilance, day and night. Their hard work wasn't just focussed on survival, the struggle, defeating the Enemy's encroachment and slaughter but also on fighting against despair.

Ah Xiang was energetic and hopeful. He never spoke disheartening words or threw tantrums, and even made use of his talents by composing songs for the warriors, stirring tunes that brimmed with joy and vigour.

He could see his whole life clearly, and treasured all that he and his comrades had given up. Laugh and that's a lifetime, cry and that's a lifetime too. For the sake of their faith and ideals, their lives had to be filled with the spirit of sacrifice and nobility!

Many times he had contemplated the final moments of his life, the end of the rough road as dusk descended. Many magnificent young lives vanished without a trace in the rainforest, like the fog of night. He felt keenly the weight and unfairness of this, as well as the anguish of surrendering to fate.

In the tug-of-war between life and death, neither side would win. So how could anyone find equilibrium or hope?

Hence this idea, which brought with it conflict, contradiction, and confusion; but as it developed, also determination, stubbornness, and the urge to keep going no matter what the outcome. He wanted to leave something behind in this world: a seed, a sapling.

The seed had lodged in his heart, and its roots were spreading.

Chunxi nestled against him, breathing evenly, snoring softly.

When he shut his eyes, he found himself observing an unfamiliar self.

Would Chunxi still recognise 'him' when he woke the next day? Would she be able to accept 'him'?

> loss is such quiet anguish
> in the night she touches her chest, and imagines breastfeeding

As promised, Chunxi had a fever!

Under the instructions of Suxin, the medic, the tip of a young plant shoot was placed in her vagina. This was a sort of 'magic grass' that had no name. It would solve the problem.

Suxin had joined up at the same time as them. She knew Chunxi well, and said reassuringly, 'Don't worry. This magic grass is very effective—it's a traditional remedy from the Malay kampongs. No need for anything invasive. You'll have a fever, then a few days from now, the foetus will leave on its own.'

Chunxi remained in the dorm for a few days, on sick leave. During daylight hours, while the comrades went about their tasks, her thoughts ran wild in the empty room. She'd never experienced anything like this.

How many times in her life would she have to wait like this?

Her mind went back to when she first joined up—the confusion and uneasiness she'd felt then, the uncertainty if she was doing the right thing, but also her determination to make this choice!

How was her mother doing these days? She avoided thinking about this, because it would only add to her anxiety. Her mother was a second wife. She had to share her man with another woman, and only saw her husband on weekends. Naturally this made her more attached to her children. Chunxi had been away from home for many years now—she would get used to this sooner or later. Her mother would ultimately settle herself amid the turmoil of these shattered emotions.

So why had the cruelty of severing a family connection now rebounded on her, like a form of retribution?

Should she be upset? Should she blame Ah Xiang?

He heard she had a fever and came to see her first thing in the morning.

They looked at each other, but apart from 'how are you', neither had anything further to say. Perhaps they'd already used up all the conversation.

When she realised she'd missed her period for the second month in a row, and a test showed she was pregnant, they'd had their first blazing argument.

Ah Xiang confessed he'd done it on purpose. He wanted them to have a child.

'You're insane!' she'd raged. 'I thought you were just talking about it. But you actually—How are you going to bring up a child?'

He hung his head. 'I know it was selfish.' He looked up, biting his lip. 'This is all we'll have in this life, right? Like being stuck on a desert island in the middle of the ocean.'

'Yes, exactly! How could you bring up a child here?'

'So I thought, good thing we're in the border zone—easier to send the child away.'

Chunxi sighed. 'Then someone else will bring it up. It won't be yours.'

'We grew up and left our parents, didn't we?'

'That's different! That was for the Revolution!'

'No one knows what the world is going to be like in the future. Life has to continue—that's a responsibility of the living. Where there's a seed, there's hope.'

'How could you have so many twisted ideas?' Chunxi sighed again, shaking her head. 'How are we going to face the Organisation, or our comrades? You can't just think of yourself. Won't having a baby add to the unit's burden? You're so horribly selfish!'

Ah Xiang was silent.

'Have you forgotten? What you told me?' Chunxi suddenly yelled.

This was at year-end, when Ding Feng's lover (in the unit, married couples were referred to as 'lovers') was about to give birth. It was a cold, drizzly day, and Ding Feng had been hunting around for charcoal to keep her warm. Whenever Chunxi was on kitchen duty, Ah Xiang would remind her to grab some for Ding Feng. Later, though, Leader criticised her for it, and said she was fostering incorrect behaviour!

A baby girl arrived, squalling. Mother and daughter were safe. Bubbling over with emotion, Ding Feng reported the happy news to his comrades after morning roll call.

Chunxi hadn't been there—she was busy in the kitchens. Ah Xiang went over to Ding Feng, who was tongue-tied with excitement, and shook his hand heartily. 'Congratulations!'

Around them, however, were silent lips, expressionless faces, lowered heads. Some even turned away, mumbling, 'What's there to celebrate?'

Ah Xiang told her about this afterwards, looking indignant. 'Aren't we taking part in Revolution for a better tomorrow? Aren't all our sacrifices for the sake of the next generation? So what's wrong with having a child? Why couldn't they have wished him well?'

He felt the injustice keenly. His comrades' reactions left a deep impression on him.

'I know all about having to bear the consequences of our mistakes. Who could know that better than me?' Ah Xiang held up his leg stump. 'All injuries will eventually pass. I can face this.'

'I'm sorry, Ah Xiang.' Chunxi looked straight at him. 'Even if we could deal with the Organisation's punishment and our comrades' eyes, I wouldn't be able to face myself. Please don't blame me. I couldn't bear it.'

'Are you—are you really planning to get rid of our child?' Ah Xiang said, his face twisted with pain and disappointment.

'…'

For days after that, she turned over all kinds of thoughts in her head. Did she blame Ah Xiang? No! Over and over she asked herself if there wasn't even a shred of this way of thinking in her mind?

On this morning, before setting out on her expedition, the squad's minx Songjun made a special trip to the kitchens to pick up Chunxi's breakfast—a meal specially prepared for invalids: a bowl of oatmeal porridge and some soda crackers. Songjun was a 'guerrilla brat', having been born in the rainforest fourteen years ago, then sent to the farming village to be raised by the People. She'd joined up six months ago.

Chunxi watched as Songjun's petite frame vanished from view, lost in thought.

Would she, too, be called a mother?

In the afternoon, dazzling light filled the rainforest, and the air was thick with the riotous chirping of cicadas.

Chunxi lay diagonally across the bamboo bed, beneath a dark green pha khao ma (Thai sarong). Her temperature was slowly climbing, and her brain felt fuzzy. She saw her mother's despairing face, the tears in her eyes, her hysterical screams of 'My life is bitter! You don't want me or our children, why do you keep coming back?' And her father, a lazy bum who only showed up to eat and sleep at weekends. She was the eldest, so it fell upon her to fetch water, chop firewood, pick vegetables, cook meals, bathe her younger siblings, do their laundry… Busy! Always busy! Was this a family? The endless mountain of chores was the first hill she had to climb in her life. Her mother could only grumble, 'Who asked us to have such bad fate?'... Was this their fate? It couldn't be! She believed that everything would have to change, that it *could* change... Ah Xiang gave her so much strength and support... She saw a little face with soft, red cheeks, her youngest brother, eyes so bright... biting his fingers, gurgling with laughter, banishing gloom from the house... Could she once again have such an innocent face in front of her? Held in her arms, looking at him again and again... Oh, then there'd be scalding tears plopping onto his tiny forehead...

In order to avoid detection by Enemy planes, the squad dorm had green tarps spread across its roof on clear days. Trees rustled in the wind, scattering leaves onto it.

Would the seed in her stomach be cast off like those leaves?

That would be such silent anguish! A flood of familial feeling swirled in her chest, and she felt herself sink then rise to the surface, ready at any moment to be swept away or submerged!

Yet this baby would add to the unit's burdens. She'd witnessed and heard of many such situations, behaviour that breached the Organisation's discipline, opening a gap that let in so much trouble. And how would that look to the people in the farming villages?

She wanted a little Songjun of her own... But if the child were to grow up outside, its fate might be the one that befell her own mother instead! They were in southern Thailand, and the nearest town was the infamously seedy Betong. She'd heard of guerrilla brats who'd ended up in houses of ill repute, or even becoming triad gangsters...

Having a child meant eternal worry, whether or not they stayed by your side. Had Ah Xiang considered this aspect of fatherhood?

She'd agreed with Ah Xiang when he'd said, 'This is all we'll have in this life.' But what else, if not this?

Sitting up abruptly, she reached for the pitcher and guzzled down mouthfuls of cool water.

No matter what, now that they'd chosen to be part of the collective, protecting the interests of the group had to be their highest responsibility.

Most of their comrades were able to do this, and they ought to as well!

She wasn't going to debate right and wrong with Ah Xiang again. She didn't even care which of them was to blame.

Her breasts were growing sore and swollen, with a sort of bursting fullness and stabbing pain. Her nipples were hard and sensitive. For the first time she realised that the seed in her belly was clearly searching for her love and protection, and wanted her to prepare for its arrival.

In the night, she quietly massaged her chest, and found her thoughts turning to breastfeeding. Her own heart felt as unfeeling as this dark night. Didn't she deserve to be chastened for the cruelty of ending a young life?

After some hesitation, she gave in to Ah Xiang and agreed to keep the child. How many times did her thoughts waver after that? She was terror-stricken, she struggled bitterly, she shed silent tears beneath the covers at night.

… Those who chose this path ought not to have children, and shouldn't have parents either!

Now she thought how, when she first joined up, her mother must surely have wept long into the night.

> the waxing moon grows brighter night by night
> shrouded by clouds and mist, all around is foggy

Many helicopters had arrived at Jantalat Air Base. An urgent message came from the People: the Enemy's blackshirts were about to enter the hills!

HQ ordered the combat groups in the various battle zones to set out separately. The farm workers were redeployed too, and Chunxi was sent to the front lines.

She'd just recovered from her illness, the colour only now returning to her pallid face. The concerned leader asked her, 'Are you sure this is alright?'

She smiled radiantly. 'It won't be alright if I'm not there! I helped set the landmines by the crop fields, if you hadn't sent me, I'd be petitioning to go.'

Before setting out, she stopped by Ah Xiang's dorm and helped him clear out his backpack. Anything he didn't need went into a metal tub with her own nonessential items, for storage underground.

The unit might have to move camp at any moment.

Ah Xiang looked at her familiar figure, his eyes full of tenderness. Their circumstances were changing rapidly, and if they did as he wanted, the woman standing before him would have to forge through the wilderness with a big belly. It even crossed his mind that Chunxi might be this eager to set forth because of some desire for atonement. In the past, he'd have been all too willing to take her place, but now he could only be a burden to her. She even had to help him pack up his possessions. His ears burned. He felt as if a gleaming mirror were suspended high overhead, reflecting his face and showing all the grime that had accumulated on his heart.

Before leaving, Chunxi murmured, 'Don't blame me. Take care of yourself.' Her eyelids fluttered, unable to hold back the tears.

The Enemy's progress this time round was swift. In just a few days, landmines in the first battle zone began going off, followed by rounds of fire from the helicopters overhead, then the *lrrrnng lrrnng* of chainsaws cutting down entire swathes of trees, clearing space to serve as helipads from which they could evacuate injured troops.

The next day, there was an unexpected engagement at the second battle zone! News came back that there had been no casualties among the comrades, but the deafening bursts of gunfire echoed around the unit for a long time. The campsite was shielded from air surveillance, and there were strict prohibitions on noise and fire. Life was firmly on a battle footing now, and seething anxiety cast a heavy shadow over the comrades' hearts.

The cropland was between the two battle zones, a vulnerable and highly visible target. Although it was nowhere near the frontline, it could turn into a firestorm in an instant.

Ah Xiang's heart was clenched tight. Each day he studied the farm worklist, trying to gauge where things were heading.

Late one night, the unit deployed a battalion of between fifty and sixty people to slip into the crop fields where, working fast to finish before dawn, they would retrieve two thousand kilograms of cassava under cover of darkness. That would feed the unit for more than half a month.

Ding Feng returned with a package for Ah Xiang. 'From Chunxi.'

He opened it and found a handmade mooncake: cassava skin with a sweet potato filling, roasted in a pot till it turned a burnished golden brown.

It flashed across Ah Xiang's mind that the waxing moon was growing brighter night by night, and Mid-Autumn would be here in just a few days.

Another burst of gunfire at dawn! Even closer to the unit this time, coming from the direction of the crop fields. Over breakfast, the comrades debated in hushed voices, guessing the unit would soon have to move.

Ah Xiang couldn't force down any breakfast, so he went back to pack up his remaining possessions, unable to still the violent thudding of his heart.

Bnng bnng bnng—another thundering barrage of gunfire, interspersed with the occasional single shot.

The battle had waged for many hours now. The comrades' hearts were in their throats.

All was silent in the tent. Overhead, branches rustled as the wind stirred them. The sentry's footsteps were the only ones that could be heard. Everyone was still, awaiting orders.

Then the comrades saw the farming group leader sprinting back to HQ, covered in sweat, carbine swaying and still reeking faintly of gunpowder.

There were four people in the farming group, but she'd returned alone. The comrades didn't say anything, but their hearts plummeted off a cliff.

The command came—they were to go on the move right away!

A report from HQ: The crop field was under attack. Tieqiang, a male comrade, had been mowed down by the Enemy in the first burst of gunfire. The three female comrades scattered. Unable to find Chunxi and Chen Wei, a slightly older woman, the leader hurried back to make her report.

Everyone left the tent, apart from the combat group. The others went to the maildrop to wait for the two missing comrades.

The battalion needed to head southwest as quickly as possible, towards the broken road. There were quite a few old and injured comrades in the unit, and it was imperative to get them to safety before the Enemy closed in.

A little after three o'clock, the unit climbed up the watershed separating Thailand and Malaysia, the highest point in this range of hills.

The dragon ridge grew narrower the further they walked. Now and then rocks coated in jade-green lichen stretched across the path.

The mountain winds whistled, and fog wafted close to the ground.

The small pathway snaked along, obscured by staghorn ferns, wood ferns, and vines. There were no tall trees here on the dragon ridge. On either side of them, the hill fell away in a sheer drop. Past the clumps of thorny undergrowth, the ocean of tree crowns roiled endlessly into the distance.

Ah Xiang walked in front of Ding Feng. His stump had been rubbed raw by the iron leg, and was screaming with pain. Maybe the skin was broken. He walked as if his legs were different lengths.

He'd had a small bundle to begin with, but Ding Feng grabbed it from him when they got to the steep section. He even went back downhill to hack off a branch for Ah Xiang to use as a crutch.

As he walked, Ah Xiang kept an eye out, remembering the wild orchids and pitcher plant Chunxi had brought him from here. What had she said? 'You'd never have expected it, right? All the way up there on the border dragon, so hard to reach on foot—it's covered in these kinds of plants, and all sorts of flowers!'

He didn't see anything, though. Nothing at all. The border dragon was long—perhaps up ahead would be a hillside full of mountain flowers waiting for him!

They arrived at a small, flat piece of land on the hill spine. Apparently this was listed on the map as a peak. The unit took a break here.

It was not yet four o'clock, but already the setting sun looked weary and faded. The faint light seeping through the clouds was barely warm. Their faces, damp with sweat from the climb, were swiftly dried by hill breezes.

Ah Xiang gazed at the only tree on this peak: a spindly trunk about as thick as his thigh, branches reaching his shoulders. A vine he didn't know the name of had completely enveloped it and was trailing green tendrils.

He strode over and, grabbing hold of a branch, jumped to reach one of the protrusions on its trunk.

'Hey! What're you doing?' Ding Feng hurried over to stop him.

'I want to have a look from up there.'

'... Come down. I'll look for you.' Holding one hand up for shade, Ding Feng turned towards the crop field.

'No,' said Ah Xiang quietly. He hauled himself up, iron leg reaching the branches.

Ding Feng came closer. 'Be careful!' He watched as Ah Xiang parted the leaves, inching upward.

Everything was hazy. He could see nothing but fog and cloud.

The evening mist touched Ah Xiang's heart like a snatch of song: *In that faraway place is a good maiden... I'd happily be a little lamb, following by her side, I wish she would take her fine leather crop and gently whip my back.*

The next day, a commander sent Ah Xiang a dispatch:

> at dawn, Chunxi and Chen Wei broke through the cordon
> the Enemy caught them fleeing
> there was another skirmish
> Chen Wei got shot in the thigh
> Chunxi went to her rescue
> and succumbed to Enemy fire

Ah Xiang bowed his head. The nightmare had come true. He felt emptied of all strength, too weak to even speak.

The Commander put a hand on Ah Xiang's shoulder. 'Chunxi was so brave! The Enemy said to the People in the street, "If she hadn't gone back for the injured woman, we'd never have hit her." An exemplary comrade.'

> flute music swansong
> forever on this desolate hill

The haunting tones of the flute reached every corner of the campground and swirled over the treetops.

Dusk fell. Standing by the jackfruit tree, Ah Xiang played his flute, his entire self rising and falling with the music. He couldn't stop. If only he could stand here till he merged with the trunk of this great tree, remaining forever on this desolate hill.

A swansong in that faraway place.

CHERRY-RED IVORY

From a dark corner beneath the bamboo bed, Zhizai pulled out a small section of elephant tusk. Unexpectedly, along with a complicated sense of anticipation, he also felt resentment.

This wasn't how it was meant to turn out.

He shouldn't have ended up here.

★

Back in the assault force, he was naturally drawn to the border zone, to the red tent of base camp, their headquarters. He looked towards it as he did the North Star. Alas, guerrilla warfare took you where the trouble was. Soon, the wandering, hunger, and sacrifices of the assault force no longer seemed like trials, but just part of everyday life. Unless he was redeployed by the Party, nothing would have induced him to leave his comrades-in-arms.

It was during a regular drop-off, heading towards the delivery point, that he stepped on a bundle of explosives left by the Enemy. With a boom, his right foot was ripped to shreds.

Like a wounded animal, he had to be carried back to camp. In the space of a single day, he'd been completely laid to waste. How could he have imagined this would happen? Day after day, he'd forged his way through hundreds of metres of wild rainforest. And now he'd lost a foot. During the countless days he lay fighting a high fever from his injury, his mind dwelt on the burden he would now be to his comrades. This was exactly the Enemy's vicious plan, calibrating the amount of explosives to maim, not kill, so injured fighters would slow down the rest of their unit, making it easier to swoop down on them all at once! At his lowest ebb, the shadow of death seemed to enshroud him, the dark rainforest closing in on a trembling leaf on the brink of falling. At one point, he thought of ending his meagre life with a single bullet. They didn't have antibiotics, so each day he applied a poultice of boiled one-horn lilies to his leg, until the inflammation went down. The medic spent several hours a day carefully cleaning his wound, removing the decaying skin and flesh. As his condition stabilised, Zhizai's mood calmed too. Watching the new skin grow millimetre by millimetre, pink as an infant's, he felt his will to survive harden with each passing day.

Then one morning, he slipped the stump of his leg into a tube made from a sweet bamboo stem that a comrade had brought back from the distant high hills, and endured the heart-clenching pain as he put his weight onto it. With a *klik*, he took his first step. Limping slowly, he made his way around the camp, stopping to help the others as they cooked foraged vegetables and wild yams, dealt with the hunters' bounty, sawed firewood, and mended clothes. All day long, the bamboo leg chafed against the skin of his calf, turning his wound scabby and callused.

Now, he knew, he would finally be sent back to the border zone.

At the border camp, the bamboo tube was exchanged for a proper prosthetic, made by the comrades themselves. He had become, as the saying goes, 'an iron-legged general'.

Of course, there was no way he could go out on patrol. He was redeployed to the munitions workshop. In the years since then, he'd learnt a whole new set of skills: cutting off lengths of white-hot iron and beating them into tubs for food storage, quenching steel to temper it for combat knives, repurposing clear plastic tubes into bullet-holders, and of course the regular work of turning aluminium monk's alms bowls into mess tins for the comrades, as well as making scabbards, folding-bed frames, lanterns and so forth. More recently, he'd been spending entire mornings and afternoons rooted to the spot, absorbed in a particular task.

For a whole week now, he'd ignored the lunch whistle— unlike previously, when he'd clank his way up the dirt steps on his metal leg to stand in line for a portion of 'poached chicken' (actually boiled cassava) and sweet black coffee, then settle under a tree with the others to eat and chat. Now he grabbed his lunch first thing in the morning and brought it to the workshop. When he got hungry, he shovelled down a couple of mouthfuls before returning to work.

Why was this job so important? All because of something the unit's leadership said.

One day, the deputy commander came to the workshop and asked to have a look at his progress.

'What do you think?'

Deputy Commander put on a pair of gold-rimmed glasses and accepted the ivory bangle. He sat on a block of wood to examine it more closely, then closed the fingers on one hand and pulled the bangle onto his wrist. He paid attention to his health, and spent more than an hour each day practising tai chi. Even in his fifties, he was still fit as a fiddle, and could walk uphill at a steady pace without breathing hard. His sparse white hair was combed over the top of his head, and between the strands you could see his scalp, ruddy with vigour.

'Not bad!' He smiled. 'Since this is a gift, it needs to be special, something you couldn't find anywhere else. And the handiwork must be exquisite enough to compare with stuff from outside.'

Zhizai had heard that this pair of bangles was intended for a dignitary from the southern island, a gift that would open the door to negotiations.

Could that really be true?

For months now, the unit's attention had been riveted by news of peace talks. In all sorts of gatherings, big or small, discourse flowed like a river, splashing water droplets through the air, while deep beneath the surface were complicated emotions it would be difficult to put into words. He'd noticed a dozen or so comrades in the barracks unable to conceal their anxiety—there were no representatives from their country on the other side of the table.

Would they have to wait for another round of negotiations? And now he'd been dragged into the situation.

Each day, the *kik-kak* as he walked to the workshop made him think of knocking at a door.

These were Party secrets, though, and there was no way he could ask questions.

He took the bangles back from the deputy commander, and gave them a gentle wipe with a rag cut from an old pair of uniform trousers. 'I still need to polish them with toothpaste so they'll shine like the ones in jewellery shops. Only these will be more lustrous and beautifully designed!'

'Back in the day, it was his wife who made contact and arranged our meeting.' Deputy Commander gave Zhizai a meaningful look, then his gaze shifted to the wilderness outside. 'It's been thirty years. Time moves on, but emotions remain. When we send her this pair of bangles, surely she'll feel something?'

As Deputy Commander left, he patted Zhizai on the shoulder. 'Keep up the good work!'

So it was true! Even in his dreams, he'd never imagined the piece of ivory in his hands would have such significance.

He'd made all kinds of things out of ivory—a knife handle, a belt buckle, a bandoleer clip, even toothpicks—but only because he had no other materials on hand. If he'd had plastic bags, for instance, he'd much rather have melted them to make the handle. Ivory is slippery when wet, hard to keep a grip on. He swapped it for a proper handle as soon as he got back to the border zone. He kept the belt buckle, though.

It's a funny story now. Back in the assault force, their main source of meat was elephants. Nothing was wasted, from the skin to the feet to the stomach. What about the tusks? They were just a leftover part of the carcass, worth even less than the bones, which at least contained marrow and could be turned into soup. What could you do with ivory? One time, when they were cutting up deadwood to burn, they used a tusk as a wedge to split each piece before taking a saw to it. It was hard to think of other uses. As they moved on from each temporary camp, they'd dry the elephant meat and skin over a fire, and either bring it with them or bury it, leaving no traces behind. As for the tusks, they were treated like surplus firewood, abandoned with no regrets.

In their bandoleers, the commandos often stashed containers the size of their little fingers containing salt, medicated oil, Yunnan white pills, that sort of thing. No one would have ever thought of keeping elephant tusks in there.

Who had the energy to carry something so heavy, useless, and bulky?

And that's why it was so unusual that Zhizai could reach under his bamboo bed for this ten-inch section of tusk.

It wasn't originally his. After he lost his foot and had to head north over difficult terrain, his comrades had to carry his belongings, and sometimes even himself—across a river, for instance. How could he have needlessly added to their burden?

Jiefang, one of his good friends from the assault force who also happened to have been a former middle school classmate, brought this tusk back. Before heading out on another expedition, he handed it to Zhizai and said, 'Keep it under your bed, maybe you'll find a use for it! You can make something or other for me next time.'

There was no next time. Jiefang was in the advance troop of the southward expedition. He died in an attack as they were crossing Sungai Perak. He was the same age as Zhizai, not yet twenty-six.

For a long time after that, whenever Zhizai thought of Jiefang, he remembered the object under his bed.

Then came the peace talks!

A photograph to commemorate the occasion!

Exchanging letters with their families!

Carving heart-shaped ivory tablets, for the comrades to bring back home!

What an unexpected development. How to respond to this sudden turn of events?

Zhizai pulled the relic out from under his bed, unrolled the straw mat it was wrapped in, and looked closely for the first time at this ten-inch piece of tusk. He held his breath. His chest grew tight, and it was hard to get any air. He flashed back

to the morning of Jiefang's departure. The two of them had sat
on the edge of the bamboo bed. Jiefang said nothing, just ran
his fingers over Zhizai's stump, blinking, trying to comfort him
but unable to find the words.

Only when he'd cleaned the tusk did he realise with a start
how unusual it was—within the gleaming white was a blush of
cherry red, a drop of blood dispersing in water.

When Deputy Commander saw this, he ordered a pair of
bangles to be made from it.

Being flawlessly smooth and round, the tusk was ideal for
this. He calculated that by sawing it into centimetre-wide
segments with a small steel saw, he should be able to get
fourteen or fifteen bangles out of it.

That's when the trouble started. Two bangles were reserved
for the Organisation, leaving thirteen. Everyone wanted one,
whether or not they were in his squad, whether or not they
knew him well. They demanded one when he ran into them,
or even came knocking on his door to ask for one.

But he only had thirteen to give away!

Zhizai didn't want to hand this over to the leadership to sort
out, but it didn't feel right to handle the matter himself. No
matter what he decided, it would be awkward. That's the other
reason he was sequestered in the workshop, beavering away—
he was in hiding!

What a headache! How would he get out of this mess?

Sometimes he felt so stuck, he prayed Jiefang would send
him the answer in a dream. After all, he was the true owner of
the tusk!

★

When Yuanshan came calling, Zhizai had already taken off his prosthetic and was getting ready for bed.

This was getting annoying. Yuanshan had been pestering him constantly for days, and it was starting to feel as if Zhizai would *have* to give him a bangle.

The kerosene lamp flickered in the night breeze. It was very quiet except for Yuanshan's crisp *kik-kak* footsteps—he, too, was an 'iron-legged general'.

According to the other comrades, it happened a while back. Two detachments seceded from the Party and holed up in the hilltops, then sent troops into our territory. Our unit sent a patrol to investigate. Only three days into the expedition, Yuanshan stepped on a landmine left by the other side.

The comrades who witnessed this said after the thunderous explosion, Yuanshan was still standing when the smoke cleared, even though his entire left foot had been blown off below the ankle.

His prosthetic reached higher than Zhizai's because the inflammation after his injury wasn't properly treated, and he ended up with a bacterial infection that meant his leg had to be amputated below the knee. He had even more difficulty getting around than Zhizai did.

Zhizai often exchanged a few words with him, and they shared a certain amount of fellow feeling.

But that was no basis for handing over a bangle, just like that! Besides, in terms of seniority, Yuanshan certainly wouldn't be the first in line.

'Have a seat,' said Zhizai by way of greeting.

'You have to give me one of those.' Yuanshan's squad dorm was on the hillside, and he'd clearly hurried over—he was breathing hard, which made him sound curt and rather bossy.

'I only have a dozen or so—not enough for everyone.' Zhizai was getting upset with him, but managed to hold his temper. 'All the people who want one say I have to give them one—so who should I listen to? You're not the first to ask me either.'

'It's not for me…'

'I know, I know, we're all working together for the Revolution! Look at the pair of us. We've both lost a foot, and now we only have half our lives left. What's the point in fighting over a bangle?' These words had been churning repeatedly through Zhizai's mind. Many times he'd wanted to say them to the comrades badgering him, but he always swallowed them. Now they'd finally spilled from his lips; this ought to be persuasive enough.

'I… I'm going to give it to Linying's mother!'

'Linying?'

Zhizai had heard Linying and Yuanshan entered the unit at the same time, back when they were just eighteen or nineteen. A few years after that, they became husband and wife. After Yuanshan lost his foot, Linying gritted her teeth and stayed with him. They travelled together through the nadir of their lives. Soon after that, Linying was out on an expedition when a tree branch fell on her, and she was martyred at the bottom of a river gully.

'Everyone only knows that Linying and I joined up together. They have no idea…' Yuanshan turned to look at the guttering flame of the kerosene lamp. A moth hurled itself at the glass lampshade and crashed onto the bamboo table with a soft thud. 'I was the one who brought her here. She hadn't even finished school. Her ma's a widow, and Linying was her only child…'

'Oh.'

'We did it for the Revolution. Never mind losing a foot, even losing an eye or an arm would have been fine, as long as we'd stayed alive to go back... someday.' Yuanshan bowed his head. 'But some people... will never return.'

Somehow the lamp seemed to have darkened. Zhizai's vision blurred.

Yuanshan's voice faltered, and grew gradually quieter. 'I thought... I thought this bangle could be like Linying's hand, holding her ma's wrist on this last stretch of the journey. That's... that's the only thing... I can return to her...'

Suddenly, Zhizai was plunged into the dark night of the rainforest. He shut his eyes.

★

The comrades noticed Zhizai was no longer avoiding them. He still took his lunch in the workshop, but once again joined them for dinner, jovial as ever.

He proclaimed that the bangles had been equitably distributed, and not a single one was left!

Like a beam of light, Yuanshan's words had given him an idea.

He blamed himself profoundly for having forgotten Jiefang —the owner of this length of tusk! When Jiefang said 'make something or other for me', had he already had this day in mind? Zhizai and Jiefang used to be classmates, and their families were close. They joined up at the same time too. He was a month older than Jiefang, hence the names they'd come up with: Zhizai for 'determined', Jiefang for 'liberation'. Determined to achieve Liberation. But he would have to return alone! When that time came, he would visit Jiefang's parents. How would he comfort them? Which of Jiefang's possessions would he bring back as a memento? Jiefang had been their eldest son!

Then he thought of Deputy Squad Leader, a young guy from the border zone named Zhongming. Last Mid-Autumn Eve, Zhongming bought a side of pork from his village for the unit to celebrate the festival. He carried it on his back to the handover point, where he was ambushed by the Thai army's blackshirts, who left him lying dead beneath the rubber trees he'd spent his life among.

And so Zhizai decided that beginning with Linying, with Jiefang, with Zhongming, each bangle would go to a martyred comrade, as long as someone was definitely able to deliver it to their family.

He made this decision very carefully and with great trepidation.

This piece of cherry-red ivory was once a useless object, albeit dazzling in its beauty. Would it really be able to push open the heavy door leading to peace talks? Could it really stand in place of these once-living voices and smiling faces? Soothe this endless yearning, this anguish?

BURIED RATIONS

In a brand-new pullover and Bermuda shorts, packed meal in hand, Xu Kai walked down the slope, onto the stepping stones across the river, to the field by Quartermaster's hut, where quite a few people had already gathered and were eating dinner.

Everyone smiled to see him. Someone patted him on the shoulder and said, 'You're back.' The happiness in his eyes didn't need to be spoken out loud.

This warm reception reminded him how the group had stuck together no matter what. The orange-yellow sunset filling the sky wasn't just spilling onto the gently sloping banks of Three Forks River, but also illuminating every nook and cranny of his heart.

Not far away were the vast trees of the rainforest, row after row of them, a dark wall stretching endlessly into the distance. A light dusting of gold shimmered on their swaying crowns as the evening breeze ruffled the leaves, causing gentle ripples like countless tiny hands applauding, like the words surging through his mind that he wished he could pour into a listening ear.

Everyone knew Xu Kai had just come back from town after a family visit. Alongside their happiness for him, there was also a faint sense of setting down a heavy burden.

Since the Hat Yai Peace Agreement, the comrades had tried to regain contact with their families on the outside in all kinds of ways. Recently, during their first New Year since leaving the rainforest, they'd had so many visitors coming here to the village or meeting them in town. Every day, the transport team travelled over thirty kilometres of bumpy terrain on off-road motorbikes. When they got back, they'd yell out their good news before even wiping the sweat off their brows.

And yet, for a long time now, Xu Kai had been alone. He'd sent letter after letter, but heard nothing back. He eyed each visitor to the village, hoping to encounter someone even a little familiar. While his comrades were folded into the warm embrace of family, even as hot tears filled their eyes, they couldn't help being aware of Xu Kai's solitary figure slumped in a corner.

He was one of the few who hadn't yet reunited with their families. As the days went by, he grew more anxious about this, and the others worried on his behalf.

But now he was finally back after a family visit!

His former squad-mate Lim Kuan, who now had a metal right leg from the unit's workshop, strode over with a *clonk clonk clonk*, leaning slightly forward to move faster, and fell into step with him. Lim Kuan had been redeployed to carve woodcuts in the print room. He'd started gaining weight from no longer going out in the field and from the recent improvement in diet, and now had a prominent little belly that wobbled when he walked quickly. Xu Kai instinctively reached out a hand, but Lim Kuan nudged him instead with a raised shoulder. 'Hey, you're back. How come you still haven't reported to me?'

'I haven't washed the clothes you lent me. I'll return them to you when they're clean.'

'No rush. How many people were there? I heard they only arrived at the village yesterday, and now they're gone. Not even enough time to warm a seat. Where was I?' He smacked the back of his head. 'I didn't even get to see them.'

Xu Kai held up both hands. 'Exactly ten of them: my ma, auntie, cousins, some friends, and neighbours. Everyone who could be there.'

'Wow, good for you. Were there enough motorbikes to carry them all?' His beady eyes looked Xu Kai up and down. 'New clothes, I see. Did your ma bring those?'

By this time, seven or eight people had gathered around them, gawking at Xu Kai's white sweater, which had a picture of the Singapore River across the chest.

'You look different,' said one of the village council members, nodding. He held a bunch of keys in his hand and still wore his green uniform, looking at Xu Kai with some emotion, as if there might be more to his words.

'It's just the packaging that's changed,' said Xu Kai simply.

Just a few months ago, they'd still been guerrillas in grass-green, a single entity blending into the rainforest. You were issued the uniform as soon as you joined up, and the colour hadn't changed for more than ten years—for decades, in fact. Because it was compulsory, no one had ever questioned it, and everyone was used to it. Now they still wore uniform trousers as they built the village, but their top halves were a rainbow of colours. As soon as they met their families, they changed to civvies.

It was initially jarring when red, orange, yellow, and blue began showing up alongside the dark greens and mud browns.

In bright daylight, these ordinary clothes made them feel they'd lost their invisibility, which made them anxious. Some, such as this council member, continued wearing the uniform.

The Thai Army had tactfully suggested the villagers leave off their uniforms, and gave them a small clothing allowance, but…

Earlier, before Xu Kai changed into his new outfit, a strange hesitation had flashed through him—though he couldn't say if that was due to the image on the pullover, or just the fact that these were civilian clothes.

'Extra rations tonight, Xu Kai. Roast pork—come and get it!' chef Xiuhong sung out from the roof of the shed.

'It's the good stuff, go grab some!' Lim Kuan nudged him. 'Ye Rong's brother came visiting from Penang, and brought a roast pig with him. An entire pig!'

This is where the unit had settled after the peace agreement. The Party chose it for them: a level piece of land where the river forked, not far from the rainforest. Soon, this would be a place the former comrades could start their new lives—a peace village. Those waiting to return to their homelands were also staying here for the time being, a little over three hundred people.

Dinner was the rowdiest time of day.

Yet some stayed on the fringes of this bustling scene.

About seven or eight metres away, Xu Kai found a man beneath a large tree, sitting on a root that protruded a foot above the ground. His head was bent over the food he was shovelling into his mouth. From time to time, three-winged seeds like little shuttlecocks spiralled down to land on him.

He looked up, met Xu Kai's gaze, and waved his stainless-steel spoon in greeting.

Xu Kai drew closer.

'You're back.' Chen Nian raised his sunburnt face, laugh lines etched into the corners of his mouth. 'Family gone?'

Xu Kai nodded. Chen Nian was from his hometown, though they hadn't been in the same unit, and had only met in this village. He hadn't been able to get in touch with his family yet, so he and Xu Kai used to spend a lot of time together chatting. When Xu Kai finally made contact, his first thought was for Chen Nian. It had been days since they'd seen each other. Maybe he'd had good news too?

Chen Nian slowly shook his head. His eyes lingered on the image on the new pullover. He squinted, apparently mesmerised by it.

'What's that?'

'Clarke Quay by the Singapore River.'

Chen Nian straightened the fabric and leaned closer. His short, grey hair was sparse, leaving his oily scalp clearly visible. 'The hostel's gone, but the bridge is still there, and the sea is still the sea.'

'You used to live there?'

'Worked there for a while. It was called Cha Chun Tau— Lumber Jetty, back then.' He tilted his head to one side, studying the picture from another angle.

'Don't worry, I'm sure you'll find your way back. For sure!'

'What's there to worry about? It's been more than twenty years, this was bound to happen.' Chen Nian looked up. Deep lines were scored into his forehead.

'Oh, did you see tomorrow's worklist?' he said, changing the subject. 'Some of us are digging up buried rations. You should come too! How about it? You've just got back from outside, after all.'

'Of course! No problem, I'll be able to carry more than usual.' Xu Kai grinned.

'Sure.' Chen Nian smiled too. Without realising it, his eyes had drifted back to the Singapore River. Did that tiny image contain the last room he lived in before he departed, twenty-seven years ago? Could he get back the social life he'd had, and reconnect with his family? His heart swelled with anxiety and sadness he couldn't stave off.

Actually, Xu Kai had a bellyful of words he would have liked to say. Even steeped in the joy of reunion, the fears that clung to the bottom of his heart had not gone away. The question was still there. He wished he could tell Chen Nian that during this visit, he and his relatives had briefly met Secretary-General Chin Peng in Hat Yai. He'd discussed this question with Chen Nian quite a few times: Why weren't representatives from the island nation invited to the peace talks? For those from Singapore, what was the way out? Where could they call home? Would they ever be able to go back to where they came from, like the other comrades? Had they been forgotten, or did the leadership simply not want another powerful opponent complicating the situation, after the failure of the Baling Talks? And now, had they been abandoned? When they'd talked about it before, he'd said if he ever bumped into their former leader, he would ask. But at that moment, faced with the warmth of the man himself, he couldn't bring himself to. Why was that?

'Hey, Xu Kai!' Their former deputy squad leader, Liu Peng, called out. 'Turns out you buried the rations we're digging up tomorrow. We saw the map at our meeting this afternoon, and your name was on it.'

'Really?' Xu Kai's ears pricked up. 'When was that? I've taken part in so many burying expeditions.'

'When we set off from Mallow Camp—that makes it twelve years. A couple of years ago, five or six of us passed by on a patrol, and the marker was still there.' Chen Nian remained silent, and Liu Peng raised his voice. 'As long as it's still there, we'll definitely dig it up. Don't worry! You know what? Some of our comrades joined up more than ten years ago, or even twenty or thirty years, but when they come out, don't they all find their families?'

*

She was having a tough time searching for the little temple.

Back in the day, this Goddess of Mercy temple had been in Marsiling kampong. She remembered an old banyan tree by the entrance gate, shady leaves rustling and long tendrils swaying.

Now, though, she couldn't quite remember how to get there. In the last few years, she'd set foot in virtually all the temples she knew of on this small island, and even offered incense more than once at the Old Temple in Johor Bahru, at the other end of the Causeway.

She'd requested a fortune there. The temple attendant, a woman around her age, said with great certainty, 'Do not fear, he's still alive. He'll come back to you one day. These are sacred words, you have to trust them.'

Clasping her hands, she'd allowed her eyes to drift upward. The Goddess of Mercy, cross-legged on her lotus throne, looked down at humanity with her usual benevolence. Just one glance, then she shut her eyes to pray. That one look was enough to take in the purple haze that enveloped the Goddess. In the many years since, that purple glow had often drifted into her dreams.

If she hadn't believed, she wouldn't be here today.

Her oldest son had finished national service and moved out, claiming it was more convenient to be close to the factory where he was doing shift work. Then in the middle of the night, the government sent people to surround the kampong— fortunately, all they managed to seize was a stack of books and some other items. But now the boy could no longer come back every weekend like he used to, to taste his mother's sweet potato porridge. Later on, he sent someone to tell her he was hiding out on the peninsula for a while, and that was the last she'd heard for more than ten years. Then her younger son was arrested in Malaysia. The news said he was a guerrilla, and was caught with a gun on him. It didn't take them long to give him the death penalty.

She could no longer remember how she'd gotten through those days. Two tall, strapping boys, so full of life, turned to ash, to smoke, vanishing before her eyes. Every year at Tomb Sweeping, she would carefully wipe her younger son's porcelain bust with a towel, just like stroking his face, still so tender and smooth, eyes blazing with such spirit. He'd looked so like his big brother. They'd even sounded and moved similarly, not to mention the cruel way they'd abandoned their old mother. All her thoughts now rested on her older son, her only hope for what life she had left. She'd spent so many nights choking on her tears, when even hope seemed desolate as the dark, stretching endlessly and plunging into infinity.

She had meditated thousands of times on her fortune: Do not fear, he's still alive.

When the government moved them from the kampong to an HDB flat, she immediately took out a classified ad in the Malaysian Chinese papers to run for several days, notifying her son who'd vanished into thin air.

And now she actually hugged him. He was almost forty, thin with cropped hair, wrinkles starting to show. Her lucky big boy, still whole and healthy. Her tears rained heavily onto his shoulders, his chest. Back home, she gave thanks at all the temples. In the end, the divine had taken care of her, and her son had emerged from the rainforest. Now she prayed he would return safely to her side.

She placed a bunch of fresh-cut flowers in the vase on the altar. Behind the dull red curtains, incense smoke drifted languorously through the air, and many gods looked down from their high platforms. Years ago, when the kampong temples were moved, gods were gathered from all over and herded together into these shared spaces. She had no need to seek out divinity, though. As soon as she shut her eyes, there was her Goddess of Mercy, standing tall, features clear as could be.

Now she stood in silence, three incense sticks in her clasped hands. She didn't say a word, but already her tears were flowing.

For more than a week now, she'd felt as if she were moving through a dream, as if she'd woken up to find three or four thousand days had passed her by. Her son, taller than her, stood not far away. She took him by the hand, and all those missing days came rushing back. Time was no longer a gaping void. The wound could heal, and the pain would be forgotten.

She remembered the night before her son left. Durians had fallen from the tree, and she'd sent a message summoning him home. In the time it took a dog to bark twice, he hurtled down the little path. She didn't dare turn on the lights, so in the silent dark, he tasted the fresh durians then quietly departed.

A few days ago, she'd been on the back of an off-road motorbike, going along a winding mountain road to the village, the exhaust sputtering *tu tu tu*. The road twisted back and forth, a cliff on one side. She shut her eyes and listened to the whistling wind. What was brushing past her, fog or clouds or trees? If she fell, she would be smashed to pieces, yet she felt no fear. When she thought of what her son had been through, such hardship and danger, this ride was just her taking on a little of his fear and suffering.

'No matter what, when he returns, that will be a new beginning,' said the temple attendant after hearing the news, taking the fortune she'd brought back, paper yellowed after all these years, the words still clearly visible. She bent over it to chant, 'A plum branch in winter, leaves fallen and withered, but not destroyed; when the sun appears in spring, blossoms come again.

'You see? Trust in divinity and you won't go wrong. Come here.' The woman led her into a back room.

'Auntie.' Now the attendant opened a drawer and pulled out a sheet of paper. 'This man left even earlier than your child, more than twenty years ago, and there hasn't been any news.'

She took the paper, on which were a Chinese name and some numbers. She recognised the first character, Ong—her surname too. When she was just a little girl, her father had made sure that no matter what, she could read her own surname.

'Don't worry if you can't read it, just ask your daughter to send your son a telegram, asking if he knows this name. If he does, tell him to call me.

'His mother's in her eighties, you know. She came in a wheelchair asking the gods for help. And ah, this must be fate, she got exactly the same fortune as you. Number sixty-nine. Look—' The attendant traced the numbers six and nine on the back of the paper. 'Turn six around, and you get nine. It's like I said, have no fear, he's still alive, and he'll definitely turn around and come back. I told her about your son, and she begged me to get you to pass on a message.'

She held the paper tight. 'I will, of course I will.'

'The gods have eyes, and they'll protect good people,' said the attendant with great sincerity. 'Her son was involved in the unions, and fought for better conditions for the coolies. The government was going to arrest him, so he fled overnight. He hadn't been married long, and his daughter was just born— poor girl, she's never seen her father. The other day, she came pushing her grandma's wheelchair. Her name's Hongying. She's already finished university.'

The percussive *tok tok tok* of a wooden fish pierced the swirling smoke.

The attendant sighed long and deep. 'A day in the rainforest is a hundred years in the mortal world!'

★

They set out, more than sixty of them, a resplendent group!

This was a special moment. Even as civilians, they still moved in formation. They were departing the present, entering a hidden corner of history.

Monsoon season was finally over, and the tropical rainforest was at its brightest and clearest. Wild grass, undergrowth, vines, shrubs, ferns sprouting from tree branches, mushrooms among piles of dry leaves—all putting forth shoots, sprouting, extending their tendrils, propagating the species, flourishing with life and energy.

The path through the rainforest seemed exceptionally broad and sturdy. They walked along merrily, joyful voices and laughter filling the air, every step imbued with longing and affection, hearts astir with happiness that couldn't be put into words, a closeness to bygone days.

Chen Nian was exhilarated. He wasn't supposed to be in this team, and indeed didn't often get to go on expeditions, being relegated to the radio team instead. His special duties had left him cut off from the unit's external activities. No matter what, he couldn't miss the chance to go on this mission to dig up buried rations. Who knew if he'd ever get another opportunity?

He walked behind Xu Kai, who said, 'This is bizarre. Look!' He gestured at the people ahead meandering between the trees. 'Never mind that we're not in uniform, we don't even have our weapons with us. It feels odd.'

Chen Nian smiled. It was true, he'd been issued a rifle the day he enrolled, and he felt strangely dejected to be empty-handed now.

He recalled the earth-shaking explosion as they destroyed their weapons, not long ago. Such a shattering sound, as if they were blowing up his whole life.

For more than twenty years he'd been drifting, to Indonesia, Beijing, Hunan, and finally the Thai-Malaysian border. He'd willingly accepted every one of these deployments. All these sacrifices for what he believed in. If such a thing as fate existed, then his fate had always been in his own hands. Not like now, when he felt only confusion and doubt about where he'd come from and where he was going, completely powerless.

As the saying went, he'd removed his armour and returned to the land. But where was his land?

He hoped to learn more from Xu Kai about what was happening in the island nation to the south, but Xu Kai must have seen something in his sunken eyes, and instinctively changed the subject.

'You don't normally see such a large group going to fetch rations. It happened once before, during the twenty-month encirclement campaign,' said Xu Kai. 'Don't you find that strange? The Thai Army had us under siege like they agreed with Malaysia, but they also let the People bring us supplies. During that time, we transported and buried huge quantities of rations. And guess what? The stuff we're digging up today is what we buried twelve years ago!'

'So our different strategies against the Thai and Malaysian forces are paying off!' Chen Nian's smile had a simplicity that made people want to trust him.

'Apparently, in the part of the rainforest where we were active, we buried enough rations to feed the troops for more than a decade.'

'I'm really curious about how our rations can stay underground for ten or twenty years without going bad,' said Chen Nian, who had clearly been pondering this for a while. 'I'll make sure I get a good look today.'

'That's easy!' said Xu Kai, looking around as he walked on.

The team reached the top of the dragon ridge. The dry season had arrived, and the wind that rushed at them had the scent of all living things awakening. Sunlight darted around the weighty crowns of trees like little golden birds, and the chirping of cicadas filled their ears.

Xu Kai stepped out of line and pushed through the undergrowth to a tree large enough that it would take two or three people to encircle it. Its vast trunk soared heavenward, sturdy as a pillar, and its bark was covered in irregular cracks. The branches were so high up that individual leaves and twigs could not be seen, only criss-crossing lines flowing rhythmically outward and drooping back to earth.

'It's a meranti tree.' Xu Kai rapped on the trunk. Looking all around, he soon spotted an irregularly shaped object about the size of a pebble, and brought it over to Chen Nian. 'Meranti resin.' He brushed a few dried leaves off its surface. 'Break this open, mix it with used motor oil, and boil until it turns into a paste. Smear that over a beaten metal tub, then stick plastic over it to make it waterproof. A container that's treated like this will keep underground for a couple of decades without rusting, and the food in it will be preserved too.'

'That sounds simple enough.' Chen Nian eyed the lump of resin, then broke open its brittle shell with a snap, revealing its translucent filling, like amber.

'We use whatever materials we have to hand. It's easy, and it solves the problem.' Xu Kai gestured. 'Look, there are meranti trees everywhere.'

Chen Nian held on to the small chunk of resin, unwilling to throw it away. As they continued walking, he reflected that these rations could still satisfy hunger and provide nutrients after being dug up. All these years in the unit, he'd been eating buried rice mixed with cassava, which may not have been as fragrant as fresh grains, but being fluffier and softer, was more filling.

And what about people?

In secondary school, his teacher had taught him to love his country and its land, and to make sacrifices for society. That's what he'd always done. He fought against colonialism, to secure his country's independence. He unionised his workplace, so the labourers could share in the rewards. The times taught him to participate fully in life and seek progress. In the collective, he was always loyal and passionate, never once thinking about his personal interests. His fellow workers had treated him with sincerity.

He would always remember Xu Dishan's essay 'Peanuts'. At all times, in all places, he wanted to be of use to society and all people.

Yet now that colonialism had collapsed and his country was independent, he and his comrades, who'd given their blood and sweat for the anti-imperialist cause, were political exiles! Once again, history was mocking his ideals, his loyalty, and his righteousness.

On 1 February, twenty-seven years ago—he remembered it was an ordinary Friday evening—he was just about to leave the Lumber Jetty Union building to head home, when he got an urgent message telling him to flee right away.

The next day was the ninth day of the first lunar month, the Jade Emperor's birthday, a major occasion for the Hokkien community. His mother had made a lot of food and was waiting at home for him, but he couldn't delay a single minute. Turning a corner, he sprinted towards the southwestern coast, departing without having a final meal with his mother, bidding his family farewell, or hugging his daughter—who was not yet a month old. In the blink of an eye, he vanished into the vast, dark sea.

If his home was still there, he'd definitely be able to find his way back, even in the dark: past the government primary school by the side of Jurong Road, through the field in front of Hong San Temple, up the slope, take the right branch when the road forks, uphill again, then he'd hear Black Snout's familiar barking and a dark shadow charging like the wind towards him...

He'd made many inquiries since leaving the rainforest, but the road and these places were nowhere to be found on this small island of six hundred square kilometres, as if someone had rubbed Aladdin's lamp and asked the genie to remove the primary school, the temple, the street...

And his colleagues, his neighbours, his family...

A commotion from up ahead. 'They've dug up the rations!'

'They did it!' Filled with excitement, Chen Nian set aside the knots in his heart, and followed Xu Kai as they hurried over for a closer look. Would they know what these things were, freshly out of the earth? Being brought into the daylight after so many years, what world would they be confronted with?

★

Hongying pushed Grandma home in her wheelchair. The old woman drowsed, muttering in her sleep, 'Por! Hey, Por!'

She put Grandma to bed. After so many years mostly spent indoors, her complexion had grown sallow. Time left streaks of rust on her forehead, cheeks, and chin, even across her wrinkly neck.

Hongying bent to heft Grandma's lifeless legs onto the bed. Since losing sensation five years ago, her legs had now become shrivelled twigs. Yet she remembered long days of following these legs across vegetable fields, through rubber plantations, into water, over hills. All the way through her childhood, adolescence, and youth.

As far back as she could remember, it had always been Grandma holding her little hand. For a long time, she'd thought Grandma must be her mother. 'And Ba?' she used to ask. 'Where is Ba?'

Each time she asked the question, Grandma would give a different answer. She didn't understand. Grandma said Ba was still alive, but other people's bas lived with them, or at least came home during New Year and other holidays, and those families would go out to Sentosa or the zoo...

Yet her ba only existed in yellowing black-and-white photographs.

Slowly, she became aware that Grandma wasn't her mother. So where was Ma? In the same place as Ba? Grandma just shook her head and refused to answer.

When they lived in the kampong, Grandma grew vegetables, and their little wooden hut was full of dogs and cats, rabbits and chickens. She had many playmates among her neighbours, and the days passed easily. When she was in secondary school, they were moved into an HDB flat. Grandma took a job as a cleaner at the Nantah campus, and only finished work in the evening. Hongying would come home after school and sit alone, staring at the wall.

Grandma sent her to an English school. She made the most of it and got a place in a top secondary school, even winning a scholarship.

'It's safer to read ang moh books. Less to worry about,' Grandma kept saying. 'If you went to a Chinese school like your ma and ba, you'd suffer your whole life!'

Later, she learnt a few more things from a former kampong neighbour, Auntie Lim, who visited from time to time. Seeing that Hongying had grown even taller than Grandma, she said earnestly, 'You have to be good to your grandma! She's suffered a lot because of you.' Then, lowering her voice, 'After your ba left, when you were two or three, your ma wanted to marry someone else and give you another father. Your grandma said over her dead body, and insisted on keeping you with her till your ba came back. She said you're an Ong, and there's no way she'd let you take someone else's surname.'

Auntie Lim's eyes reddened. 'She's been through so much! No one knows if your ba will ever come back. Your grandma is closer to you than anyone else in the world.'

Hongying understood everything.

And now Grandma had dozed off again. Beneath her tightly closed eyes were two heavy pouches—did they contain the many tears she'd refused to shed for so long? And the deep furrows running from her pursed lips to her chin clearly indicated her resilience and determination.

Hongying took out the fortune Grandma had kept for her. She could still remember the temple attendant explaining: 'Turn six around, and you get nine. He's still alive. He'll definitely turn around and come back.'

Was that true? Call it a dream. Like Grandma, she would hold this dream close at all times.

She really had grown up. She hadn't told Grandma how much else she knew now. Reading ang moh books could be just as dangerous these days!

A couple of years ago, one of her secondary schoolmates— an English-educated older girl who was unquestionably among society's elite—had been taken from her home late one night at the same time as several other professionals—lawyers, doctors, businessmen, and professors—and held in solitary confinement until she wrote a false confession, then went on TV to apologise for what she was supposed to have done.

The whole thing left Hongying shocked and shaken. They'd only met for afternoon tea, and were trying to find a time to take part in some volunteer work overseas. Perfectly legal activities for the public good. How could someone like her friend, loved and respected by all, get written up in the papers as a member of a 'conspiracy'? And then be locked up for such a long time, without a trial?

She still couldn't believe it and found it terrifying. While following the story in the news, she'd also carried out her own research.

She looked back through her country's brief history. In the piles of old paper, she glimpsed her father, a faint shadow cast on a wooden wall by the waning sun. There were other faces she knew, the uncles and aunties who visited their kampong hut when she was little, unfamiliar but so close to her.

Grandma told her that day happened to be the Jade Emperor's birthday. 'The sun hadn't risen yet. In the dark, cold night, the dogs wouldn't stop barking. Somehow they found their way to our humble wooden hut. A dozen people surrounded the place and kicked open the front door. Your ba wasn't home. They were so angry, they knocked over all our furniture, *pring prang.*'

Hongying knew this was Operation Cold Store, a raid that had taken place across the entire island on 2 February, twenty-seven years ago. At least a hundred and ten people were held in the Internal Security Department without a trial, for so many years—more than ten, more than twenty…

Before she was even one month old.

'They woke you, and you started bawling. Maybe you knew you'd never see your ba again.'

A wound that hadn't healed yet. Blood and tears flowed for Grandma, for herself, for the father she couldn't even remember, and for her mother. Even more heart-rending, deepening the pain, were her schoolmate and friends who only wanted to give back to society, and their families, for whom this pitch-dark nightmare would continue in the garden city's bright tropical sunshine.

Her eyes fell again on her fortune, number sixty-nine. What a magical number! Could her personal circumstances, and the narrative of the nation, really turn around just like that?

★

No sooner had the team returned from digging up rations when someone shouted, 'Xu Kai! Is Xu Kai back? Telegram!'

'Here!' He let the sack of rice drop from his shoulder, and sprinted to the telegram operator.

Without asking, he knew this must be from his family. Why the rush? Another visit?

The message: 'Looking for Ong Kim Por, Singaporean. Phone number 6760XXXX.'

Chen Nian's original surname was Ong. Xu Kai's heart thumped. Turning around, he shouted, 'Chen Nian! Where is Chen Nian?'

DELICIOUS HUNGER

1.

'Do you still remember which building we lived in?' I ask.

He looks around, somewhat confused.

A vehicle rumbles past on the main road, its headlights passing across us and briefly flashing in his sunken eyes.

It rained this afternoon, and the puddles gleam faintly, dark and mysterious. The damp envelops dingy yellow streetlights, like the eyes of someone desperate for sleep, illuminating the few remaining stalls and scattered red plastic chairs, mostly empty.

A scrawny piebald brown dog limps from the shadows, head drooping as it truffles beneath the tables and chairs for something or other.

More desolate than expected. It certainly wasn't like this forty years ago!

'We lived on the third floor.' He looks at me, like opening a shutter. 'See? From our window, catty corner across the road, there was a bakery.'

I remember, of course. On Sundays, our day off, the beguiling scent of fresh-baked bread wafted over. I invariably went downstairs to join the queue, returning with a piping-hot sliced loaf that I'd devour, leaving leftovers for breakfast the next day.

This was in the mid-seventies. I'd drifted north from the foothills of Gunung Ledang, and was temporarily staying here, in a rented room in Pudu, Kuala Lumpur. It was here that I met him.

Our comrades in the Underground had arranged carpentry jobs for us both at a nearby construction site. I didn't have the skills, so I mostly helped out and carried things. After some time, the messengers connected with an armed unit, and we were brought into the hills.

At the time, there was a famous street called Wai Sek Kai in Pudu. As soon as it got dark, hawker stalls would open for business, lights blazing. For several kilometres around, you could smell the delicious aromas, hear the clamorous crowds, and feel the electric atmosphere.

'We had dinner there every evening after work.' He sips his coffee—black, just a little sugar. 'It was near impossible to find a seat. How has it changed so much?'

It really has! It was on this street that our young selves made their final memories of the outside world's delicious food.

There were far too many tempting snacks. We began on the left side of the street, working our way through the stalls, sampling all the flavours as we ate.

'Heh, you had such a big appetite back then,' I say, smiling.

Age twenty-three and twenty-four, after a full day's sweaty labour beneath the scorching sun, we were naturally ravenous by evening time. Even so, I could never stuff down nearly as much as him.

'Right? Remember how much we suka' (Malay: 'liked') 'that deep-fried pig intestine congee? How many bowls did we get through in one evening?'

'Three for me, five for you. We finished at the same time.'

'Eight empty bowls piled this high. Ha!'

He always ate a ton, and quickly too. I called him 'the python', which made him crinkle his eyes and grin, so his slightly protruding front teeth glinted in the lamplight. His laugh lines touched a faint dimple at a corner of his mouth.

'I could really go for another bowl of that congee.' Amid the wrinkles of his face, I can still make out that faint dimple.

The night before we joined up, I thought we should do something different, and tried to drag him to Kentucky Fried Chicken (which these days, seems to only be branded with its initials). He batted away my suggestion. 'That ang moh food doesn't sound tasty. It's only chicken, after all.'

I'd seen many billboard ads promising it would be 'finger-lickin' good', and insisted that we try it at least once. After we went into the rainforest, who knew when we'd ever emerge again?

'You know what happens if you eat chicken every day?' He glared at me.

I shook my head.

'You'll smell like chicken shit! Not what you expected, right?' The year before, he explained, he'd been hiding out in a chicken farm, and couldn't forget the experience of having to eat chicken every day for more than six months.

'Let me tell you something. Tan Sri Lim Geok Chan, the guy who first brought KFC to Malaysia, once got asked, "Why chicken?" And you know what he said? "Chicken is the only meat eaten by every race!" Clever, right? Isn't that the same as the United Front of the Revolution?' I felt this association would make my argument much more convincing.

'Wah! Are you saying the Revolution should be like KFC?'

In the end, we enjoyed a tasty feast. Looking at the chicken bones littering the table, I lit a cigarette and said, half-joking, 'Hey, with that appetite of yours, will you be able to cope in the rainforest? We'll have to live on wild plants and fruits, you know.'

'Look who's talking!' he said in crisp Hokkien, his mouth twitching. 'Maybe you should quit smoking? Where do you think you're going to find cigarettes in the rainforest?'

Back then, we both had this thought: We'll be waging guerrilla warfare in the hills, full of revolutionary spirit. As for what we would eat or how we would eat it, how was that even a problem?

2.

We joined up together in Perak, but before long we got separated. He stayed behind while I headed north with the trekking unit. After over a month of tramping through the hilly rainforest, we arrived at our base on the Thai-Malaysian border.

Later, I heard that the unit had needed male medics, and I was chosen because I'd studied up to Form 5. Many medical terms were in English, so I might as well put my knowledge to good use.

To start with, I found the work a little dull. I'd gone through all this effort to join an armed unit, only to end up with a syringe in my hand! Gradually, however, I came to realise that this was all in the line of work, and I ought to accept my deployment. Didn't Chairman Mao's *Three Constant Essays* include 'In Memory of Norman Bethune', the Canadian doctor who joined the Revolutionary struggle? Besides, the senior medic in the border zone had been trained in Socialist China, and then saw combat in Vietnam. Not to mention the number of lives she'd saved on the battlefield and her expertise in Western medicine, which she paired well with the traditional Chinese variety. Being able to learn from her was an eye-opening experience.

We met again more than a year later. By this point, I was a full-fledged medic. Apart from my few items of clothing, my high rucksack was crammed full of things like commonly used pills, emergency medicines, special remedies, bone-setting plasters, acupuncture needles, surgical tools, a collapsible stretcher, plus injectable supplements of Vitamin B-Complex, Vitamin B12, liver extract, calcium gluconate, and so on. One of my special duties was during handovers, when I would give fortifying shots to our comrades who'd arrived weary from fighting in harsh conditions.

I gave him a shot too, of course, even though he insisted there was no need. He'd gotten paler and much thinner since our time on the construction site. His narrow eyes blazed with spirit, and he seemed to have become both gentler and more capable since I'd last seen him.

'Are you still eating as much as before?' I asked.

He smiled and didn't answer.

The evening we made contact, there was a simple but very moving gathering. On a flat piece of land on the mountain spine, we laid a perimeter with torches made from lengths of bamboo, stuffed with meranti tree resin, which burned with a crisp *bik bik pak pak*. Dull yellow flames licked the ink-black sky, lapped at the hollowed-out yet spirited faces of the comrades. Both the trekking and guerrilla unit commanders made speeches, which heartened everyone. Near the end came the most important item: Quartermaster had allocated everyone a cup of Milo and a little cake about the size of a fist.

This was abundance indeed for our guerrilla comrades-in-arms, who subsisted on wild fruit and vegetables, and for those of us in the trekking team who'd gone hungry during months on the move.

In the midst of everyone's exuberance, naturally I went over to him. By the light of the bamboo torches, we sipped at our Milo like honeybees gathering nectar, letting it swirl around our mouths before swallowing. Next, with solemnity, we bit into our cakes.

I had no idea what this confectionary was made of: dark brown, sweet, springy yet a little chewy, deliciously scorched with a flavour that went straight to the heart.

'A few months ago, we roasted a tub of cassava flour at the Orang Asli crop field. We knew you were coming, so we saved it for today.' He took another small bite. 'I thought it would be good mixed with nangka powder' (wild jackfruit seeds, ground) 'plus some of the flour and milk powder you brought, then fried in elephant fat.'

Elephant fat! So that's what gave this its unique flavour.

'Can you believe it? In just over a year, we've already eaten five whole elephants! This elephant fat is quite something.'

Whereas here in the border zone, the most I'd gotten was elephant jerky. How must it have been, to have hunted down five elephants? I looked at him and couldn't help feeling envy.

'Well? Delicious, isn't it?'

'It's tasty,' I said sincerely, nodding.

He stuffed the final bit of cake into his mouth, then ran his tongue over his lips to pick up all the crumbs.

The hungrier we got, the more we missed all the scrumptious foods we'd enjoyed before. Crispy char siew buns from a Wai Sek Kai stall floated before our eyes. Those buns were deep-fried to the same dark golden colour as this cake we were eating now, glistening with grease, half the size of our faces. We could eat two or three in one sitting.

Recalling his appetite, I couldn't help asking—though I knew the answer—'Have you had enough?'

'Yes!' He rubbed his belly, dimpling with laughter. 'I've trained myself to have an elastic stomach—it stretches or shrinks as needed.'

We were in the same place for ten whole days. During that time, I often saw him helping out in the kitchen.

In the centre of the campsite were two cooking pots, each suspended by three wooden stakes thrust in the ground at a seventy-degree angle. Over two feet high and topped with low aluminium domes like Indian cooking pots, these bubbled away *gugg gugg* all day long.

Beneath the pots was a constant fire fed by long pieces of dry wood, all about the thickness of my calf. We never sawed these down, but stuck entire tree trunks in there. Whenever we went into the kitchen area, we had to keep stepping over these logs.

He was always sitting on the end of one of these pieces of wood, legs spread wide, bent over the wild tuber he was slicing, with more on the plastic sheet in front of him.

Sometimes I went over to help. Those foraged sweet potatoes, I knew, were all we had to eat three meals a day.

'What do you think this looks like?' He pointed at the pile of deep red root vegetables.

'Like, um, a pig's liver?'

'Correct!' He smiled. 'These are known as "stone pig livers". Have you acquired a taste for them yet?'

Actually, for several days now, my stomach had been throbbing faintly. During my morning shit, the yams I'd eaten the day before came out in a big clump, leaving me sweating with pain. I had to slowly rise to my feet before I could let out my breath.

'Well?' Without waiting for an answer, he said empathetically, 'Your tummy aches, right?'

I nodded, and he stopped what he was doing for a moment to say consolingly, 'It'll be fine. It's what we call a stomach adjustment—you're eating new foods, and still getting used to them. Stone pig livers taste bitter, so maybe that means they're a little poisonous, but they're so abundant and easy to dig up! We boil them, squeeze them dry, then boil them again. If we could add oil, salt, and sugar, they'd basically taste like mashed sweet potatoes!'

'Uh huh.' I nodded vigorously. A few days ago, I'd seen him with a large basin of soft stone pig livers, squatting by the cooking fire and taking huge bites out of them.

He used a monk's alms bowl as his mess tin, but in order to increase its capacity, he'd beaten the sides so they bulged out. He kept sticking it into the fire during this process, leaving it blackened as an arhat's belly.

'It's all the same, in the end. Get used to it, and even bitter things taste delicious,' he said.

Delicious! Before joining up, he'd chosen for himself the name Fenglei—thunder and wind—but since our reunion, I'd noticed that the comrades all called him 'Delicious', probably because that was his catchphrase. As for me, I'd chosen a name full of fighting spirit: Wuyang, raising battle. But then everyone just called me 'Little Yang'.

The time came for the trekkers to return—we'd handed off all the equipment we'd brought to our comrades in the assault force. I'd traded my newish mess tin for Delicious' arhat belly.

He also asked if he could have my National shortwave radio. 'You know how it is. Before we joined up, we'd never have dreamt of not reading the papers or listening to the news. Not having that in here—it's as painful as hunger.' He also insisted that whether or not I was part of the next delegation, I should make sure he received several batteries!

3.

More than a year later, I was back there. I hadn't forgotten the batteries, of course.

When we made contact, though, he wasn't there. I asked his comrades, and they said, 'He won't be needing those anymore.'

About half a year before this, they told me, they'd encountered the Enemy and exchanged gunfire. The medic, Sunflower, got shot in the right hand and had to drop the backpack she was carrying. When Delicious realised what had happened, he'd let go of his own bag, and with his comrades covering him, braved the Enemy's shots to retrieve their medical supplies.

'He...' My heart contracted. 'Where is he?'

'He and Shaochuan have gone out to dig up buried rations.'

Ah. A heavy weight lifted off my heart.

On this expedition, I'd been deployed to support the assault force unit, replacing Sunflower as their medic, so she could accompany the trekkers back to the border zone for more training. When I arrived, I found out she also needed treatment for her injury.

Even after her recovery, she was left permanently unable to bend her elbow, and life was difficult for her. There were rumours of a Comrade Li Liang in our border zone who was a genius at herbal remedies. Perhaps he could help? When she spotted me, Sunflower asked about him.

'It's true,' I said with certainty. I'd studied herbal medicine with Li Liang, and had witnessed him healing a similar arm injury.

I have a clear impression of how these remedies were made: every batch of medicinal herbs was wrapped around a newly hatched chick, which was said to enhance their efficacy, the whole bundle heated and applied to the wound.

'He'll have to break the bone again, though.'

'I'm not scared. As long as he can cure me.' Sunflower's face was resolute.

'What's Shaochuan doing here?' I asked. Half a year ago, I'd attended his assault force unit when his malaria flared up. I recalled his pallid face, his purplish, trembling lips.

'We're always heading to Dyan River to search for food. That's their territory, and how could we get through without a Landmine Lord to tell us where the mines are? So the leadership sent him over.'

Delicious and Shanchuan returned, bearing not buried rations but two bags bulging with wild rambutans.

'Goddammit, a black bear dug up our stores again,' Shaochuan raged to the gathered comrades, breathing hard and not bothering to wipe the sweat off his forehead. 'Two fourteen-gantang tubs, completely gone! We walked thirty or forty metres before we found the containers dumped on the hillside.'

'They were chewed to pieces,' Delicious went on. 'We tried to see if we could salvage any rice or salt, but there was nothing—not one grain!'

Everyone's face sank, and we sighed deeply. I'd heard of such things happening, but this was my first time witnessing it. Black bears made a lot of mischief—Enemy Number Two.

So now there was a waist-high heap of rambutans in the kitchen area, bright red and bristling with hair, bringing some joy at the successful link-up. Everyone knew where there were rambutans, there would be other wild fruit.

After I'd gotten my share of rambutans from Quartermaster, I went straight off to find Delicious. As he and Shaochuan were both single, they'd set up their hammocks side by side.

Although it wasn't quite accurate to say Shaochuan was single; he was already married with children while underground. Back then, he'd worked as a contractor at the construction site, which gave him the opportunity to hide and resettle other underground comrades when need be. Then a senior officer was arrested and gave up Shaochuan's name. Now that his cover was blown, he had no option but to enter the rainforest. I asked how his wife and children felt about him joining up? He tilted his head to one side and narrowed his eyes as he drew vigorously on his cigarette, then he held up his wrist to show off his Titoni watch. 'See? She got me this before I came inside.'

They were in the middle of lunch: wild yams. The mess tin that Delicious had swapped his old one for was now also a blackened arhat belly.

'Oh right, I brought your batteries—though apparently you've lost my radio.'

Shaochuan, a talkative man, butted in. 'Right? Good thing we had Delicious here—we'd have been in bad shape if we'd lost our medic supplies. No antibiotics, nothing to treat gunshot wounds. Speaking of which, how is Sunflower's injury?'

'Shame about the radio. I hadn't even had it for six months.' Regret showed on his face.

'Losing your own backpack is no big deal—the main thing is you saved communal property. Anyway, the Organisation should compensate you.' Shaochuan always spoke his mind. 'There are three things we can't do without in the unit: a radio, medical supplies, and a big pot for communal meals. You only know how serious it is when you lose one of these.'

'I heard you're not going back with the trekkers?' Delicious asked me.

'Yes, Sunflower will be laid up for a while, I'll be here for a year or so.'

'Ha! That's what I heard first thing this morning. Guess what I brought you?' Shaochuan bent down and began rooting through his possessions.

'You need this, or you'll be in trouble.' He held up a bundle of shrivelled leaves and waggled them at me. 'Know what these are? Wild grape leaves. Chop these up and roast them—and you can smoke them like tobacco. You quit after crossing the border dragon, didn't you?'

Shaochuan was smiling so hard, his eyes were pressed into slits. From between his teeth came the reek of tobacco, something I hadn't encountered for a while.

He and I were among the small number of comrades in the unit who indulged. As a medic who smoked, I felt a certain amount of pressure. Still, I was certain this despised habit wasn't affecting my duties in any way. Now here was someone showing a little understanding. I felt a flicker of warmth.

Tobacco made from wild grape leaves. I wanted to give these a go.

'Call that a present? Rambutans look nicer, and they're better for you too.' Delicious grabbed a handful of the crimson fruit and thrust them at me. 'Have more. I ate my fill while I was up the tree.'

'Sure, they look pretty, and they taste pleasantly sharp.' Shaochuan swallowed. 'But the flesh doesn't come off easily, and it's a shame to spit them out.'

'I just gulp them down, seed and all.' Delicious laughed, revealing the small gap between his front teeth. 'Otherwise all you get is a mouthful of juice. How many would you have to eat to get full that way?'

'Ha! Who asked you to gorge yourself like that?'

I'd only just settled in, and even before I had the chance to examine a single comrade or give anyone an injection, an unexpected medical issue cropped up!

This was on my third day. Shaochuan came up to me at dawn and said, 'Delicious has a problem. He can't shit.'

'Wah! What's going on?'

'Ever since we came back that day, he hasn't been able to. His stomach is hard as rock, and his face is turning green. I tried to get him to see you, but he says he's fine. You should go to him.'

Delicious was curled up in his hammock. I touched his forehead—it was scalding. He was clutching his belly, and sweat glistened on his forehead and nose. The pulsing of his purplish veins was clearly visible through his skin.

I held his icy hand. 'Stomachache?'

He nodded.

'It must be the rambutans! Over the last few days, he's gobbled dozens, maybe a hundred,' Shaochuan said.

'You mean the rambutan seeds?' I asked.

'What else could it be?' Shaochuan gestured with finality. 'I kept warning him, but he said he'd be fine as long as he drank plenty of water. "Rambutan seeds aren't poisonous," he said, and "they tasted better than yet more yams." Now what?'

I scratched my head. I'd never heard of anything like this! During my years in the border zone accompanying the battalion's mhor (Thai: 'doctor') and learning from them, I'd encountered my fair share of strange ailments, but never a blockage caused by wild fruit. My first thought was that I'd left a small packet of milk powder with Quartermaster for safekeeping. Maybe that might have an effect?

Another day passed, but we were no closer to a remedy. Sunflower suggested feeding him raw oil to induce diarrhoea, and everyone helpfully offered their stores of elephant grease. Yet still Delicious squatted beneath a tree, holding his belly, face contorted in agony. No movement.

My diagnosis was a pile-up of rambutan seeds must be blocking his bumhole. So I tried sticking slivers of soap in there to smooth the way. Delicious tried loosening things with his finger. Still no shit, but now he was bleeding from back there.

This dragged on for several more days. Delicious was on the brink of collapse. He didn't even have the strength to squat any longer. All day long he lay in his hammock, tossing and turning, moaning… At times, he looked as though he was about to lose consciousness.

One morning, I noticed Sunflower pulling a burning coal from the fire with bamboo pincers, so she could sterilise a syringe. With a jolt of inspiration, I quickly asked Command for permission to carry out a special operation: pulling seeds from his bum with forceps.

I asked Shaochuan to be my assistant. After setting up a makeshift operating theatre with tarps, we set to it with our sterilised tools, grabbing and plucking, pushing and tugging. In the end, we finally managed to pull those rambutan seeds one by one from Delicious' bum.

Standing to one side, Shaochuan counted: seventy-eight seeds, seventy-nine seeds, eighty...

Then, with a flourish, he presented the 'good news': 'They're all out! Eighty-three of them.'

I wiped the sweat dripping down Delicious' face, then hurried to get him on a drip.

He regained consciousness, but his body remained weak and he was unsteady on his feet.

Commander handed me his little packet of oatmeal—he'd been issued one by the Organisation—and told me to use it to nourish Delicious. I cooked the oatmeal in his arhat belly mess tin and Delicious ate it in small mouthfuls, not speaking.

I thought back to the Thai-Malaysian border, where we were able to plant crops in our own patch of rainforest, as well as scavenging for cassava and fruits nearby. Sighing, I said, 'Is there really nothing else the assault force can do, other than ask the rainforest for wild yams and vegetables?'

'If you want cassava, ask the Orang Asli; if you want staples like rice or oil, salt or sugar, ask the Underground.' Shaochuan was squatting against a tree, puffing away at a cigarette rolled from wild grape leaves. He looked up at me, squinting. 'Both are risky, though.'

'...'

'If we hadn't been buying and delivering rations for the assault force, the Underground ring I was in wouldn't have been smashed. I had to escape in the middle of the night and come here! Oh, I was going to ask you—' Getting worked up, Shaochuan stubbed out his cigarette against a root. 'When our leader comrades sent you to lectures, did anyone speak about how the Underground struggle in the cities needed to be "invisible and ingenious, lying in wait for a long time, gathering strength"?'

'Yes, they did!' I answered smoothly, though my brain had turned into mush. Could he be right? When I was underground, I'd transported rations for the assault force too!

How could we not? The rainforest, even in the villages, didn't produce grains! It's not like you could eat rubber seeds.

'I think—it's not that Chairman Mao was wrong when he said, "We will encircle the cities from the countryside, and seize power through armed violence." But our villages don't produce the food we need, and we don't have a separatist regime, so what else can we do?'

What indeed.

Delicious finished the oatmeal, spoon clunking against the mess tin.

'This is the only way.' Shaochuan grinned mischievously at Delicious. 'Ask the rainforest for food. And make sure not to swallow any more rambutan seeds.'

The trekkers returned to the border zone, and after clearing away all traces of the encampment, we departed too.

HQ held a meeting with all the comrades. The unit was going to move into a large crop field by the Northwest River, which we'd heard had once been a Malay kampong that the British Army forcibly relocated during the early days of the anti-colonial struggle. The trees they'd left behind were in the midst of bearing fruit.

Commander took off his army cap and said, 'The leadership agrees that, if conditions permit, blast fishing can take place to make salt fish and fish jerky. Or hunt down a couple of elephants and dry their meat.' Although his words were reserved, a smile beamed from his face.

Shaochuan had already been to the location, and couldn't stop chattering about it after the meeting, full of beans.

'I bet you haven't tasted durian since you joined up? That place is a durian orchard. There'll be so many fruits on the ground, more than you can count. Eat as much as you like, we'll never run out. We can make pickled durian, or have it with mixed grains, first class!

'The hillside is covered in duku and langsat! You can make a meal of bananas, or toast them dry. When you've eaten the jackfruit flesh, the seeds can be powdered and used as flour—they're even more fragrant than the ones from wild nangka.

'Have you ever seen fish holding a conference? Look in the pond and you'll see big and small schools of them, layer after layer. Toss in an explosive, and boom! Even if you had four hands you wouldn't be able to scoop up a catch like that.

'Dried fish, sardines, saltfish—which do you like best? To tell you the truth, the tastiest treat is fish salted inside a bamboo stem, after a week or so. Believe it or not, I prefer it to fresh fish.'

As Shaochuan spoke, he actually started drooling, and had to wipe his mouth with the back of his hand. 'Don't laugh! You'll be like the mouse who fell into the vat of rice. Delicious, this is your time to shine—you'll be crying out *delicious, delicious* all day long. Ha! No fear you'll be eating rambutan seeds now.'

Everyone burst into laughter as Delicious blushed.

'You know who first brought me there? One of the Orang Asli! Right at the start, I asked him how far we'd have to walk.'

This was the key question. Everyone pricked up their ears.

'He said oh that's easy, just count three jackfruit trees and you'll be there. Sounds close, doesn't it?' He paused a moment, then slapped his thigh hard. 'Goddamit, I walked and walked until the sky was almost dark—and that's when I finally reached that third jackfruit tree he was talking about! Heh.'

Shaochuan's eyes sparkled as he talked, and through them we could see this mythical land of plenty appearing in the midst of the rainforest, like something from a legend.

Everyone's heart stirred, and we felt vigour in our legs. Hill after hill, river after river, we would move full speed ahead.

4.

And now we could hear the mighty river, rumbling like thunder.

We saw trees in full blossom, great swathes of roiling foliage like a vast green ocean.

Beneath the suddenly clear sky, all around us coconut trees stretched above the groves like flagpoles.

The bright equatorial sun was back, pouring scalding light down onto our heads and backs.

This scene felt both familiar and strange. Compared to the dark, soaring rainforest we were used to, these shrubs seemed low and shrunken as toys left behind by some child. They shimmered a little in the rising heat, scarcely seeming real.

I stared blankly. Delicious turned and met my eyes. We both seemed momentarily lost. Was he, like me, recollecting the construction site, and those other days in the outside world?

We were both silent. He was holding a folded pha khao ma, fanning himself with it. As for me, I undid another shirt button.

Sweat ran down the inside of my uniform like wriggling caterpillars, humid and irritating, just like my feelings.

We began moving faster. With Shaochuan as our advance scout, we covered each stretch of road in just half an hour, and no one complained.

When we stopped for a break, he doubled back to us, carrying something in both hands, which he held out to Commander. 'Look!'

Seven or eight mangosteens, each a little larger than a ping pong ball, off-white and topped with squarish green stems like children wearing adults' hats, eye-catching purple-red sepals underneath.

'A shame they're not ripe,' I thought. We had a mangosteen tree back home. Frowning, I said, 'You can't eat those—they'll be astringent, and if you get any of the yellow juice on your clothes, it'll never wash out.'

'They're edible. Sweet and fresh, absolutely delicious.' Shaochuan automatically looked at Delicious as he said the word. 'Leader knows about this, right?'

Sure enough, the next time we went to the unit, we made camp by a brook where five or six mangosteen trees grew. We plucked the rice-white fruit and held them in the water as we sliced off their peel, swirling them around till the river had sluiced away the sap, leaving translucent lobes of glistening flesh.

Shaochuan had been right.

Even as he stuffed his mouth, he found the time to crow, 'An old comrade taught me this! How could I be wrong?'

It had taken us a while to find a campsite.

We needed somewhere close to water, but not at a swamp, where the landscape would be disadvantageous to us. We ended up at a three-pronged fork in the river, fifteen minutes' walk from the crop field, on a not-particularly-wide hill ridge.

Commander made a few rounds of the perimeter, then gathered everyone to remind us that military alertness had to be our first priority. He made sure our sentries were in place front and back, then sent Shaochuan and Delicious out to patrol the hillside.

The twelve of us were split into three groups: fishing, gathering, battle readiness.

I was in the latter, so I stayed back at the campsite and helped deal with each day's spoils.

After just a couple of days, our tiny campground was piled high with all manner of fruits.

The scent of durian hung heavy in the air, and the appetite it induced in us got us all worked up, whether we wanted to be or not.

We really did eat fruit for every meal. Then, still chatting about food, we'd slice up more fruit to be dried for rations. Unless they were on sentry duty, our comrades' hands barely stopped moving.

Down one side of the dragon spine, we set up a wooden rack on which we could grill fish for jerky, dry banana chips or jackfruit seeds, or roast elephant meat. Next to it stood a pile of firewood, sawed into four-foot lengths.

Tropical fruits tend to be heaty, so I asked Delicious to keep an eye out while on patrol. If he saw any elephant's foot, ganda rusa or wild banana vines, he should bring them back so I could stew them and give the cooling brew to the comrades.

This was the most well-fed I'd been since joining up, including my time in the border zone. The mouse who fell into the rice vat, as Shaochuan would say.

Colour came back to the comrades' faces, and our conversations grew lively and laughter-filled.

What a mystical thing civilisation is. Foods that our ancestors carefully selected from the natural world, after some alteration, were perfectly suited to our digestive tracts, and their nutrients were immediately turned into energy. As for everything else, you could force it down, but it would only make you ill. Nothing compared to a mess tin full of stone pig guts and a durian segment!

This abandoned kampong could be called a ruined civilisation. After a few days, we seemed to have returned to regular life.

The weather was scorching, this close to the rainforest. No sooner had we got back from bathing in the gully, than we'd be covered with sweat again. Even so, the heat was like that perspiration, a joyous drenching.

The first time he checked the snares, Delicious returned with a large deer on his back. He'd only set this one the day before! With that exclamation, he hurried off to make his report to HQ.

It turned out they'd bumped into some Orang Aslis out gathering fruits—he thought they were from the minority Jahai tribe. They spotted our patrol first, and immediately vanished without a trace.

'I followed their footprints for a stretch—there were maybe four or five of them. The path was blocked by shrubs and vines. They were able to go straight through, but we couldn't. We didn't even see them getting away.'

Commander—he was quite dark-skinned, and it was rumoured that he was part-Thai—frowned even harder at this news and stroked his stubbly chin without saying a word.

After talking it over, HQ decided not to decamp for now; we would go on high alert to keep our location from being revealed, and set a cordon of landmines in the dip between two peaks on the dragon ridge. Blast fishing and hunting would be put on hold—we would survive on snares and foraging for the time being.

Even without fishing or hunting, we brought in a good amount of food each day over the next couple of weeks: a twelve-gantang aluminium tub of pickled durian, two bamboo baskets of roasted jackfruit seeds, wild boar jerky—we'd caught three of them in a single day—and a few dozen pounds of dried fish.

All the comrades were quietly calculating how much they would each have to carry on the return journey.

Delicious said HQ was sending him across the river to find a suitable spot to bury some of these rations. If all went well, and we spent the rest of our time here hunting and gathering, our food supply for the next year might be sorted!

This thought filled the comrades with spirit; their hands now had endless energy.

Near the end of a day, Delicious and Shaochuan sat by a tree cleaning their rifles, shirtless because of the oppressive heat. Shaochuan stood and rubbed his gently protruding belly. 'Aiyoh! If this keeps growing, soon I won't be able to walk.' He mopped his damp forehead. 'I'm even sweating grease!'

I tapped him on the shoulder. 'Hey, watch out! Don't forget: Military alertness above all. You'll be in trouble if we hear gunshots, and you can't find a uniform that fits you.'

Shaochuan burst into laughter. 'Out here in the belly of the rainforest, the Enemy will have to attack by air. When we hear the helicopters going *pah pah pah*, we'll have plenty of time to pack our things and get away.'

5.

The landmine went off as I was drying the last batch of laundry just before dawn.

As the faintest glimmers of light came into the sky, the ground shook and a boom hit our eardrums, jolting the whole camp awake as if from a nightmare.

Out of nowhere, Commander was standing behind me shouting, 'Grab the clothes! Grab the clothes!' Then he was sprinting like the wind with the battle group behind him, heading for the sentry post, calling behind him, 'Pack up the cooking pots and waterskins.'

Shaochuan and Delicious, whose hammocks were closest to the kitchen area, leapt to the ground and headed for the firepit.

Png png—png! The sentry's gunshots were met with a whole barrage from the hillside. The Enemy was coming at us from both sides!

The campsite was still hidden in the gloom, apart from the flames from the kitchen area—which is where all the Enemy gunfire was aiming.

Shaochuan tipped a waterskin over the firepit—

Pahh chhh—a plume of bluish smoke rose into the air.

Delicious pulled the huge cooking pot off its stand, turned it over, and dragged it aside.

Meanwhile, our comrades were returning fire.

I stuffed the clothes I'd managed to retrieve into a rucksack, and quickly took my position behind a tree.

The Enemy's explosive shells landed *pik pik pok pok* on the soil and shrubs all around.

Mortars came down in all directions, and dawn arrived to the sound of explosions, descending through the gun smoke.

This was my first time in the line of fire, and my heart felt as if it might leap from my chest. I pressed myself against the tree, M16 on my shoulder, and surveyed the hillside as light filtered through the trees. The *ziuw ziuw* of bullets whizzed past me, but which direction were they aiming?

'Get a good look. Push them!' Shaochuan's voice came from behind me. Out of the corner of my eye, I saw him and Delicious shoving waterskins and other kitchen equipment into the biggest cooking pot.

Pnng! I pulled my trigger, and the bang steadied my tremulous heart.

In the distance I could hear the *hrrnng hrrnng* of a helicopter, getting louder as it approached!

Up ahead, the combat team covered each other as Commander directed the rest of the comrades to pack up their things, preparing to descend the other side of the ridge.

With an enormous boom, a shell exploded very close by. More passed overhead, rustling through the branches.

'Hit the ground!' yelled Shaochuan, a moment before a mortar landed in the centre of our campsite. *Huwwnngg!*

My calf felt numb for a second, then a stabbing pain sliced through it. I looked down and saw a deep gash from a piece of shrapnel.

I glanced back at Delicious. He was holding up Shaochuan, who was slumped on the ground with a hand pressed to his bleeding forehead, bright red gushing over his face.

Hunched over and gripping Shaochuan by the armpits, Delicious effortfully dragged him towards a nearby tree.

Limping, I went over to help.

'Goddammit,' said Shaochuan, smiling grimly. 'I got hit in the head—so how come I can't move my legs?'

Another shell landed behind me.

The Enemy's gunfire was coming thicker and faster. All around us, bushes were quivering as bullets struck them.

Our entrenched comrades fiercely returned fire. In the midst of his exertions, Delicious let out a low grunt of pain, cutting through the chaos of gunshots. His legs collapsed beneath him, and his right hand fell to his side. 'I've been hit!'

Blood spattered onto my face and my mind went blank. I didn't know which of them I should grab hold of.

'I can still walk,' said Delicious. 'Help him.'

The helicopter was right overhead now, its *pak pak pak* filling the sky.

Only now did Shaochuan notice my injured leg. Shoving me aside with his blood-smeared hand, he said, 'I'm not leaving. Keep Delicious safe and carry the cooking pot. Quick, move!'

As the chopper swept the treetops, they rained leaves down on us.

'Give me your hand grenade!' Shaochuan screamed over the huge waves of sound and air swirling around us, so insistent I couldn't have refused.

I did as he asked. He took off his watch and stuffed it into my shirt pocket.

It was full daylight now. There was movement in the shrubs around us. The Enemy was surrounding us.

I regained my position against the tree and began firing. Meanwhile, Delicious was creeping close to the ground, cooking pot on his back, down the far hillside.

Dimly, I heard the call to retreat and regroup.

When I passed by Shaochuan again, he'd managed to drag himself over to a sapling, and bright blood stained his whole body. He sat with his legs together, two hand grenades resting between them.

I paused for a second, thinking I should say something, but he waved me on. 'Go! Quickly, move!'

Only ten of us made it out, three injured. The cut on my thigh wasn't deep, and I was easily able to stop the bleeding by winding a puttee around it. Delicious had been hit in the right wrist, and a white fragment of shattered bone stuck through the profusely bleeding wound. He dropped the cooking pot and fell to the ground, face pale as paper and eyes rolling back, looking like he might faint at any moment. I hurried over to clean and disinfect his wound, bandage it and give him an injection to stop the bleeding.

Huaizhen, a petite woman from Guangxi, was the most badly hurt: a bullet had gone into her belly, and one side of her trousers was stiff with blood and bodily fluids. Another comrade was carrying her piggyback, and her head lolled against his shoulder as she blearily cried out, 'Water! Water!'

But we couldn't give her a drink—we needed to continue our retreat. From past experience, comrades suffering blood loss would grow extremely thirsty, but as soon as they'd had some water, they'd lose the remnants of their strength, and would have to be carried on a stretcher rather than piggyback. This took far more energy, bashing through the rainforest.

I did everything I could: gave her shots for the pain and for the bleeding; then to stop her from fainting, I put a small segment of Korean ginseng in her mouth and told her to chew it slowly, so the juice would trickle down her throat.

Ah Zhi hadn't made it out—as he plunged into battle, he'd been shot in the head and martyred on the spot.

Shaochuan held the rear for us. As we descended the far side of the dragon ridge, we heard the Enemy screaming in shock, then two grenades exploding in quick succession.

All the rations we'd so carefully prepared had been abandoned with the campsite.

Not far away, we could hear mortars and machine guns, and shells whistled over our heads. Painfully, we forged our way through the rainforest.

The treetops were like thick clouds, shielding us. Dappled shadows fell over us; we couldn't have pushed them away even if we'd wanted to.

6.

We all thought the same way back then: when we go into the rainforest and become guerrillas, we'll be fuelled by revolutionary fervour. Who cares what we'll eat or how we'll get food? How is that even a problem?

Truly.

Looking back now, I realise how many questions actually revolved around eating.

I look at Delicious, bent over his barely sweetened coffee (I still like calling him Delicious). For some reason, this sight reminds me of the nonsense impromptu rhyme we came up with.

This was back in the assault force. I'd finished treating a patient, and headed for the kitchen area, where—wah! Such an alluring aroma. I took a deep breath, and exclaimed,   'Tasty!'

Squatting nearby, chopping wild yams, he immediately retorted,   'Tasty

   Tortoise guts fried with ginger, with snake belly.'

Shaochuan chimed in,   'Don't be hasty—'

                         'It's better than royal jelly!'

Delicious grinned, revealing the gap in his gleaming front teeth. That's the image now fixed in my mind.

Beneath his wrinkles and liver spots, I can still make out the same features.

'I still remember that cake.' Without realising it, my thoughts have begun to wander. 'The first time we met in the assault force, at the welcome party, we all got pieces of cassava cake fried in elephant fat. To this day, I haven't tasted anything better.'

The hand holding the coffee cup stops moving, and he is silent for a while. 'Maybe so. I can't think of anything more delicious either.'

'Without hunger, nothing tastes as good,' I mutter.

'Remember the wristwatch?' Delicious abruptly says. 'The Titoni watch that Shaochuan gave you?'

Yes, after we left the rainforest, because Delicious lived close to Shaochuan's hometown, he was dispatched to return the watch to the family.

Delicious sighs. His voice grows heavy as he says:

'I met Shaochuan's wife and son. Their son's at Universiti Tunku Abdul Rahman…

'His wife said:

"I gave my husband that watch because I wanted him to be steadfast. I wanted him to make it through. How could I take it back now?"'

GLOSSARY

1. SNARE

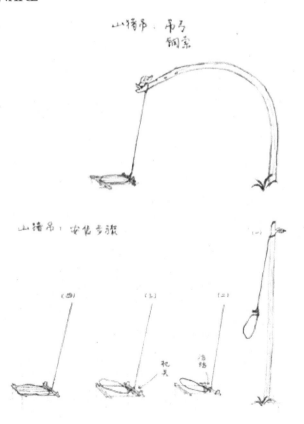

Wire snares were the main source of the unit's meat. As long as you had the apparatus with you (a metal noose and trigger mechanism), you'd be able to set a snare anywhere in the rainforest. All you needed was a length of tree branch about the thickness of your wrist and three metres long. You'd find an area where wild animals were active and dig a little trough, thrust one end of branch deep into the ground and fix the snare to the other, pulling it back into the depression so the branch bends into an arc, its tip attached to the trigger mechanism. As soon as an animal stepped in the depression, the branch would spring back, tightening the noose around one of the creature's limbs, preventing it from escaping. (As seen in 'Spell', 'Prey', 'Wild Mangoes', and 'Delicious Hunger'.)

2. METAL LEG

From the mid-seventies onwards, more comrades began having their feet or lower legs shattered by landmines. When this happened, they had to walk with the aid of crutches. Some in the assault forces made artificial limbs out of bamboo stems. Then Comrade Aiwu lost a leg to a mine and was redeployed to the munitions workroom. He and the comrades there all agreed that they should study the materials available to them and work out a way to make a prosthetic limb, which they called a 'metal leg'. This invention would make the daily lives of their comrades with missing limbs much more convenient. After countless rounds of adjustments, they managed to produce a lightweight alloy, which they turned into a leg with a wooden sole attached, and soft rubber at the other end to cushion the stump and reduce friction. (As seen in 'Buried Rations', 'In the Line of Work', and 'Cherry-Red Ivory'.)

3. TRESTLE STOVE, COOKING BASIN

火炉撤
煲锋

The so-called trestle stove consisted of three pieces of wood, each about the thickness of an arm and sharpened at one end so they could be thrust into the ground at a seventy-degree angle in a triangular shape, on whatever piece of flat land had been designated the campground kitchen. These served as stands for cooking basins, which came in a set of three (collectively known as 'Indian pots' and stored by stacking them into each other). Each had a lip around the edge between one and two inches wide, exactly the right size to balance atop the sticks. After making sure the supports were in the right position, we'd level off their tops with a saw, then place the basin atop them right over the fire. (As seen in 'Delicious Hunger', 'Wild Mangoes', and 'Mysterious Night'.)

4. ROAD-SWEEPING STICK

扫路棍

In the rainforest, trees grow particularly tall and slender, in order to reach as much sunlight as possible. Find a suitable young tree trunk, cut a length about the height of a person, shave off the extra branches, leaving only a couple cut down to three inches and forming a V-shape. With these, you'd be able to brush away any footprints left behind, fluff up leaf piles that had been trodden flat, and otherwise destroy all kinds of tracks. The person wielding this implement was called the 'road-sweeping general' and always went last in the detachment. Yellow bush and ebony tree wood were the most suitable for this, both being sturdy yet flexible. (As seen in 'Wild Mangoes', 'Magic Ears', and 'Mysterious Night'.)

5. HAMMOCK

A thick, strong piece of twill fabric, six feet long and two feet wide. Dyed green for camouflage. At either end, the cloth was connected to seven nylon strings, each comprising two braided strands, fanning out from a metal hook that, in turn, was connected to a rope or chain wrapped around a tree trunk. At either end, short wooden bars kept the hammock spread open; these split in two for easy storage.

There were three components to each hammock: the fabric, the rope, and the wooden bars. Some comrades also had an additional thin cloth layer underneath, to keep ants away and hold in the heat. Each comrade was assigned a hammock, and we had to bring it with us on every expedition. These hammocks lasted a lifetime. (As seen in 'Delicious Hunger', 'Wild Mangoes', 'Magic Ears', and 'Mysterious Night'.)

6. BAMBOO BASKET

In addition to rucksacks and metal tubs, the unit often also used bamboo baskets to transport items. These came in a variety of shapes, and could be woven tightly or loosely, to transport cassava, canned food, other fruit and vegetables, chickens and so on—all of which would be carried on our backs. These baskets were made of nothing but bamboo. We'd slice bamboo stems into inch-wide strips, scrape away the insides to leave the hardy outer skin, and weave those into baskets roughly a foot and a half wide, a foot long, and three feet tall. Within a week, the bamboo would have dried out and turned brown, at which point the basket would be ready for use. If we were in a hurry, though, we pressed them into service right away. (As seen in 'Wild Mangoes'.)

7. WATERSKIN

行军水袋：背水袋
储水袋

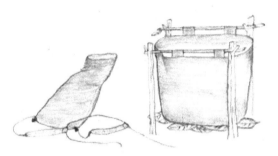

We wouldn't have been able to cook in the wild without a supply of water, but it would have been strategically unwise to set up camp by a lake or river. Instead, we made use of waterskins, large ones for storage as well as smaller, more portable ones. These were made from thick, hardy tarpaulin, coated with green paint on both sides for another layer of watertightness. In the outside world, similar fabric is used to make lorry covers. We constructed these with great care, ensuring they wouldn't leak a single drop of water. These were basically the water tanks that sustained our troops, and no camp kitchen could do without them. (As seen in 'Wild Mangoes' and 'Delicious Hunger'.)

8. MESS TIN, WATER BOTTLE

飯盒

水壺

Our word for 'mess tin' was 'fankok', from the Hakka dialect that many older comrades spoke. Each of these was large enough to contain a meal for one. To start with, we bought and repurposed the aluminium containers used by monks as begging bowls. Later, we learnt that aluminium was bad for the health, and switched to stainless steel. Both were flexible metals we could beat into whatever shape we needed, making covers and handles. As for our water bottles, we bought those from the outside world. (As seen in 'Delicious Hunger', 'Wild Mangoes', and 'Hillside Rain'.)

9. RUCKSACK

We made these out of used fertiliser bags we found discarded outside rubber plantations, resewing the sack material into backpacks. Each comrade got two of these, one for personal items, one to carry rations when they needed to be transported. Around the middle was a band attached to which were two shoulder straps, also made of sack material, a little over an inch wide and two feet long, fixed at the other end to the bottom corners of the rucksack. The top was cinched with a piece of string that could then be tied to the centre band. (As seen in 'Wild Mangoes', 'Delicious Hunger', and 'In the Line of Work'.)

10. GUN RACK

挂挖枪

We'd choose a sapling of about human height and remove most of its branches, leaving only three or four at different heights and pointing in different directions. These we'd whittle down to two or three inches, turning them into pegs on which we could conveniently hang our rifles, small bags, caps, and so on. (As seen in 'Swansong in that Faraway Place'.)

11. IVORY ORNAMENTS

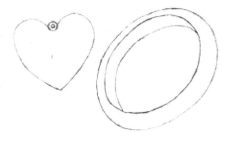

During our days in the guerrilla unit, ivory had no value to us, though we sometimes carved it into belt buckles. On the eve of the Hat Yai peace agreement signing, some units took the elephant tusks they'd been holding onto and carved them into heart-shaped pendants, which they polished to a shine and presented to the comrades to bring home as mementos. Others carved ivory into bracelets, for use as gifts. (As seen in 'Cherry-Red Ivory'.)

12. GUERRILLA LIGHT

These were usually made from stainless steel welded into an oval or rectangular container, about three or four inches high, small enough to be held in one hand. The hollow in the centre would be filled with kerosene. The top narrowed to an opening less than an inch wide, to which a neck with screw treads was welded, with a spring to which the lamp wick was attached. When shut, the wick would be safely tucked inside, and the lid would prevent the kerosene from leaking. Unscrew the lid and the wick would pop out to be lit. These lamps were used after dark when carrying out medical treatment, rifle cleaning, general tidying, or other tasks. Some also had a retractable lampshade to shield the flame from wind. Because these were indispensable items in guerrilla life, we called them 'guerrilla lights'. (As seen in 'Swansong in that Faraway Place' and 'Wild Mangoes'.)

13. TRICK LURE

马骝钓

Take a small piece of red plastic and heat it over the fire till it gets soft, thread it onto a fishhook and knead it into a ball that will bob up and down in the water. Tie the hook to your fishing line. When you reach the river, break off a length of young bamboo to use as a rod, and tie the line to it. Toss the line into rapidly flowing water and swish it back and forth. Drawn by what they think is a freshly fallen berry, the fish will rush over to eat it, allowing your hook to pierce their mouths. This was a trick we played on the fish, so we called this a 'trick lure'. We generally managed to catch a dozen or more fish in a couple of hours, each six or seven inches long. (As seen in 'Wild Mangoes'.)

14. COMBAT KNIFE

腰刀

We couldn't do without our combat knives—we needed them for most of our daily chores, and they were effectively the 'second firearm' of rainforest life. Each blade was about ten inches long, made by a munitions specialist heating steel plates in a furnace until molten, then tempering and forging them into shape. The handle was either made from ordinary plastic bags, melted down and pressed layer by layer into a mould, or else carved from wood. A sheath would then be made from meranti wood, fitted to the dimensions of the blade. In the decades since the peace agreement, when the comrades have had occasion to use these knives, the blades have proven to be just as sharp as ever, and their sheaths remain uncracked. (As seen in 'Magic Ears', 'Spell', and 'Mysterious Night'.)

15. METAL TUB

藏粮桶: 14平方桶（装米56公斤）
40开斜桶（装米160公斤）

These food containers came in a variety of sizes and were
made of galvanised iron (for storing rice, sugar, etc.) or
stainless steel (for oil or medicine). We had them in eighty-,
forty-, fourteen- and ten-gantang versions (a 'gantang' is
about 2.7 kilograms). After each tub was constructed, it
would be coated in a mixture of kerosene and meranti tree
resin, which when heated formed a substance similar to
asphalt. We would apply this over the surface of the tub
while still warm, then paste a pre-cut plastic sheet over that,
making sure to get rid of any air pockets. This ensured the
tubs would be completely waterproof. Despite the humidity
of the rainforest, tubs treated in this way could keep buried
rations safe for over a decade with no problem. (As seen in
'Buried Rations' and 'Delicious Hunger'.)

AUTHOR'S NOTE

AN ENCOUNTER WITH MYSELF
by Hai Fan

I have no idea whether, by publishing this book, I'm doing the right thing at the right time.

After my return to Singapore, friends would come by to visit, and they often suggested that I write down my experiences. I always responded with a smile and nothing else. I truly didn't have the inclination, nor the energy.

At the time, the most important thing for me was settling down. I had neither a secure place to call home, nor a steady job, nor any money (I only had two hundred Singapore dollars to my name when I came back)—and I still had to face an ongoing court case! How could I have dared to even think of sitting idly at a desk with a pen in my hand?

Ten years passed in a blink, then twenty. In 2014 I put together some of my writing from my time in the rainforest in the previous century, and added to it a diary of my first days in the peace village. Together, these made up *What the Rainforest Told You*, 'a little book that is hard to classify' (in the words of the historian and writer Phoon Yuen Ming), because 'it begins with six short stories, but the final sixty pages are journalistic essays titled *As If the Rainforest Knew*' (Li Zi Shu).

This was a gesture of farewell. I only brought out this book to commemorate my time in the rainforest, to present stirring sounds and images from back then in tales like those in *1001 Nights*, so people could hear the voice of someone who'd lived through this period of history and was closer to the truth. I'm very grateful to Mr Chong Ton Sin of Gerakbudaya for being willing to publish this little book.

I'm even more thankful to Li Zi Shu. As she recalls, 'After reading *What the Rainforest Told You*, I got all worked up and sent Hai Fan an email asking him to please definitely continue writing!' She meant what she'd said, and took the initiative to recommend two stories from the book to the literature section of *Sin Chew Daily*.

Dong Qin, Phoon Yuen Ming, Tuo Ling, and Li Guoliang all wrote reviews of the book; Dr Wong Lih Lih interviewed me and included this material in her essay 'A Hidden Pearl: The "Undercurrent Literature" of Communists Writing in Malaysian Chinese Literature'.

I'm touched by them, and deeply moved.

By that point, I could be said to have spent some time on the path of literature, and I had the desire to keep expressing my thoughts and feelings through words, as well as the raw ability to do so. My return to a normal person's life had now lasted a quarter of a century, many more years than I'd spent in the rainforest. There was distance between me and the past. I was no longer the way I was when I first returned, full of conflicting emotions that tangled around me, with no hope of resolution.

With kind, warm-hearted encouragement, would I be able to awaken these events that had lain dormant for so long, beneath layers of time and memory?

And so, I reordered my life and began spending my free time quieting my heart and looking back, thinking deeply, sweeping clean the small roads that lay buried beneath fallen leaves. I prepared to step into the rainforest again.

I wrote from the middle of last year to this April or May, and produced seven short stories. After showing these drafts to good friends, I received their encouragement and valuable feedback. Later, these pieces were published in the literary supplements of *Sin Chew Daily*, *Nanyang Siang Pau*, and *Hong Kong Aesthetics*. Enthusiastic friends scanned and shared them as PDFs with their acquaintances, posted them online, and so on. The responses left me even more heartened, and that's when I began thinking about publishing a short story collection about the Malayan Communist Party.

Once again, it was Li Zi Shu who made an introduction, this time to Got One Publisher, who agreed to take it on.

I asked Zi Shu if she would write an afterword contextualising the book, and she replied, 'I feel like I would be the obvious candidate for the job.'

I'm sure there are other people I'm forgetting to thank, which happens when you publish a book.

Life is a single-lane road, and each of us walks through different landscapes. Even if you're travelling alone, you'll have different identities on different stretches of this road. Could there be a magical pathway that would allow us to meet with our past selves? To pick up these memories and rip them to shreds, mix them together, sculpt them again... Could this not be a process of getting to know ourselves?

And so I am publishing this book at this time, not just to obey the urgings of my heart but also to hear the responses from readers and the life around me. The stories beyond the stories.

—Hai Fan
15 November 2016

DEAD PIGS, BURIED RATIONS, YESTERDAY'S PEOPLE
by Li Zi Shu

He was exactly as I'd imagined him.

In 2012 I met Hai Fan for the first time, though he was using a different pen name back then. He was the moderator of a literature panel I was on in Singapore. I'd taken part in countless events of this nature, and right away I found this person a little unusual—his voice was resonant and he uttered each word with great force, very unlike the gentle cadences I was used to from soft-spoken literary folk. He was also extremely slim with a ramrod-straight back, and his skin was so leathery he must have spent countless months and years out in the elements. Behind thick glasses, his eyes were blazing. My intuition told me he didn't fit in this setting, nor in the Singapore I knew.

In 2012 Singapore, Hai Fan's appearance felt too unostentatious, his words too sincere, his enunciation too clear. His eyes hid nothing, and the flames of idealism flickered within them. I couldn't work out how old he was, but he must have been at least middle-aged—so why still so naive?

Later, I went to see a Singaporean scholar friend at his office, and his assistant (a former MCP guerrilla) pulled a slim volume from the shelf and pressed it into my hands: *What the Rainforest Told You.* 'These stories are very well-written—the author must surely have been a guerrilla himself, but I don't know who he is.'

I glanced at the name on the cover: Hai Fan.

My friend could be said to be an expert in the Malayan Communist Party (MCP or Magong)—he'd spent many years archiving historical materials related to this movement and knew a few of the key players, including the now-deceased Secretary-General Chin Peng, whom he was friendly with. And yet he had no idea that there was a writer within the MCP ranks named Hai Fan.

A couple of days later, I found myself at the home of the man who'd moderated the panel, and he gave me a book of his, modestly claiming it was a 'clumsy piece of work'. Sure enough, it was the same book I'd seen in my friend's office, *What the Rainforest Told You*. A little awkwardly, Hai Fan asked if I could let him know what I thought, while entreating me to please keep his secret and not to reveal his true identity. I solemnly promised, and felt smug as I accepted the book, as if I'd intercepted a crucial intelligence report.

Compared to the MCP members I'd previously met, the man before me came the closest to my mental archetype of a Malayan Communist. He'd spent the best and most precious years of his life in the rainforest, where time moved slowly and it could be difficult to tell the present from the past. Now his rifle had been destroyed and he'd had to set down his rucksack full of ideals, emerging into the outside world to find it so greatly altered that he could no longer recognise this mortal realm. He'd only ever been an ordinary soldier, and he departed empty handed, learning all over again how to make his way in a completely unfamiliar society, working hard to become a 'contemporary person'.

For someone who'd walked long distances across the hills carrying fifty or sixty kilograms of rations on his back, the broad, flat city roads proved much more of a challenge, and even the faintest shadows beneath his feet felt too burdensome.

One of the stories in this collection, 'Spell', deals with burdens: specifically, a wild boar weighing over a hundred kilograms. In order to preserve the creature's warm blood to turn into pig blood soup later, three comrades take turns carrying it, stumbling along with great difficulty, until the whole thing goes arse over tip, leaving them battered and bleeding, and breaking someone's glasses. When the dust settles, the wild boar is dead. Just like that, their vision of an invigorating cauldron of pig blood soup evaporates into nothing.

These stories are about a war that got absorbed into its era, and the torment of a struggle with no future. After so many years of service and sacrifice, the lives of the comrades become as weighty and burdensome as that dead boar, its blood already cooling. In 'Spell', the three comrades have no choice but to hack the boar's carcass into portions so they can carry it, but decades of struggle are a different beast, one that cannot be butchered, one whose burden can neither be shared nor set down. Hai Fan walked out of the rainforest with this weight on his back, and still seemed to be carrying it as he staggered around this towering, spotless, obsessive-compulsive, haughty island-state.

I read *What the Rainforest Told You* in a single night, and the next day I emailed Hai Fan to tell him how delighted and excited I was by it. Next, I wrote a recommendation and sent it to the literary section of *Sin Chew Daily*, along with a couple of the short stories from the book. To be frank, although I'd written about the MCP in my own fiction, I'd never previously enjoyed any of the writing I'd read by MCP members, the true 'Magong literature'. As I wrote in my essay 'A Neglected Talent in the Rainforest':

> Whether we're reading Jin Zhimang's *Hunger* or He Jin's *The Mighty Wave*, we understand that these tomes are of more historical than literary value. [...] Due to the urgency with which these works serve ideological needs, they have the strong reek of propaganda about them, and the writing is often somewhat unsophisticated, full of hackneyed cliches, lacking in aesthetic sensibility, and would surely be judged to have fallen far short of the exacting standards of literature.

I was excited to learn that the field of Magong literature was not as arid as I'd feared; in this man was the potential for a gushing geyser. *What the Rainforest Told You* might only contain six short stories, but each is better than the last, crafted with just as much artistry as other contemporary Malaysian fiction, and in addition, they are a form of 'outsider writing' containing the breath of the forest and hills, plain but never dull, with a kind of wild beauty. Even though their subject is the figures of the unit (whom one might, looking at them through today's eyes, regard as a little archetypical), their emotions are sincere, their simple words are stirring, and they have a grandeur to them. Over thirty years ago, while he was still in the rainforest, Hai Fan wrote stories like these—but not many, and with few opportunities for publication. He then stopped writing for many years, and so didn't earn the literary recognition that Jin Zhimang and He Jin did, which allowed them to be seen as representatives of Magong writing. In my eyes, Hai Fan is the equivalent of the rations put in storage by the guerrillas, buried underground for a decade or two without going bad, and as in the story 'Buried Rations', his writing 'may not have been as fragrant as fresh grains, but being fluffier and softer, was more filling'.

After *What the Rainforest Told You* was published, with the assistance of the *Sin Chew Daily* recommendation, it received a fair amount of attention (especially in old leftist and former MCP circles), encouraging Hai Fan to continue writing and to push open the door to his memories, doubling back along the road of time and walking slowly through past events he'd never spoken of or perhaps wanted to forget, like the characters in 'Buried Rations' who 'were departing the present, entering a hidden corner of history'. This part of history had been deliberately left blank, but after the signing of the peace agreement, the seal of many years was broken, and all kinds of people were able to step forward with vivid recollections, gradually bringing it into focus. For the literature of Singapore and Malaysia, this previously forbidden corner turned out to be rich with buried rations, but only the people who'd actually taken part in the burying, the 'people of yesterday', knew where to dig them up.

Hai Fan was one of these yesterday's people, and not only does he know where these treasures are buried, but we must acknowledge with some sadness that it's highly probable he's one of the few remaining people who possesses the tools and abilities to dig them up!

The eleven stories in this collection describe the lives of guerrillas in the rainforest, including quite a few notable individuals: a closemouthed man with magical hearing abilities, an Orang Asli trapper whose reverence for the rainforest allows him to commune with nature, a superb fisherman who needs no rod or bait, a physically small comrade able to carry sixty-kilogram loads over mountain roads, a woman who can easily identify all kinds of fruit trees amid the profusion of jungle flora, an incredibly brave fighter able to withstand anything 'in the line of work'. While doing battle, survival took precedence over all else, and writing stories seemed completely useless. After setting aside their battle gear and leaving empty-handed, though, this rainforest stoicism was no longer needed, and the comrades found that they lacked a scribe who could record their history and bring memory to life. The emergence of Hai Fan broke this long-standing drought, and we finally had a worthy successor to Jin Zhimang and He Jin.

After *What the Rainforest Told You*, Hai Fan continued writing stories of MCP life, which were published in Malaysia, Hong Kong, and elsewhere. Seven of the stories from this collection were written between 2015 and 2016, and their originality is testament to Hai Fan's aspiration. Having resumed his writing practice after many years, he looked back unflinchingly at the past, and after publication, faced the scrutiny of his old comrades. Compared to his earlier works, these new pieces are more considered and wide-ranging, with a broadening of subject matter. Although written with great care, they are perhaps also more mannered, with the author's fingerprints more visible. Among these stories, 'Swansong in that Faraway Place', one of the longest, tells the lyrical story of a battlefield romance, delving into both the characters' inner psychologies and outer circumstances, not to mention a tender description of sex, although its meticulousness ends up feeling overly deliberate. The love story in 'Wild Mangoes' is more moving—it might be simpler, its characters and story more contained, and yet every detail gleams, giving it greater literary power.

Setting aside affairs of the heart, Hai Fan also writes about hardscrabble existence in the rainforest, much of which has to do with searching for food. 'Delicious Hunger' revolves around eating, the deer and bear in 'Prey' end up in the comrades' bellies, the three men in 'Spell' refuse to waste so much as a drop of pig's blood, and even 'Wild Mangoes' has food as its inciting incident. Then we get to 'Buried Rations', in which the peace treaty has just been signed, and the comrades in the peace village leave off their uniforms one by one—trading them for civilian clothing brought by their families—and more than sixty of them set off in high spirits to dig up the food they buried twelve years ago. The gravity with which food is treated in these stories goes to show how arduous the guerrillas' lives were as they waged lone battle in the rainforest.

Hai Fan lived such a life for more than ten years. I believe he saw and heard, experienced and thought far more in those years than is contained in these eleven short stories. We will have to wait for him to gather more material, and to share it with us in an even more mature voice. In addition to awaiting his retrieval of more deeply buried rations, I also hope he will bring his focus closer to our moment, and write about what happened after leaving the rainforest, when he and his comrades returned to the homes and societies they'd left behind. As Hai Fan's friend, I long for the day when this former MCP member labouring under the weight of a pig carcass will finally be able to encounter himself within his own words, and have the courage to be reconciled with this other self.

—Li Zi Shu

Li Zi Shu is a Malaysian Chinese author. Her books include the novels This Timeworn Land *and* The Age of Goodbyes *(both translated into English by YZ Chin) as well as short story collections, flash fiction collections, and essay collections.*

ISBN (paperback): 9781917126021

ISBN (ebook): 9781911284994

A catalogue record for this book is available from the British Library.

Cover Art: Sim Chi Yin

Cover Design: Amandine Forest

Art Direction: Kristen Vida Alfaro

Typesetting and E-book production: Abbas Jaffary

Line Editor: Tice Cin

Copy Editor: Alyea Canada

Proofreader: Alice Frecknall

Acquiring Editor: Kristen Vida Alfaro

Publishing Assistant: Nguyễn Đỗ Phương Anh

Publicist: Trà My Hickin

Marketing Manager: Trà My Hickin

Managing Editor: Mayada Ibrahim

Rights Director: Julia Sanches

Publisher: Kristen Vida Alfaro

Made with Hederis

Printed and bound by Clays Ltd, Elcograf S.p.A.

This book has been selected to receive financial assistance from English PEN's PEN Translates programme, supported by Arts Council England. English PEN exists to promote literature and our understanding of it, to uphold writers' freedoms around the world, to campaign against the persecution and imprisonment of writers for stating their views, and to promote the friendly co-operation of writers and the free exchange of ideas. www.englishpen.org

ABOUT TILTED AXIS PRESS

Tilted Axis Press is an independent publisher of contemporary literature by the Global Majority, translated into or written in a variety of Englishes.

Founded in 2015, our practice is an ongoing exploration into alternatives to the hierarchisation of certain languages and forms of translation, and the monoculture of globalisation.

We focus on contemporary translated fiction and also publish poetry and non-fiction. Our editorial vision, *Translating Waters*, is shaped by the complex movement of language, stories, and imaginations. Often fugitive and always trailblazing, our authors and translators challenge how we read, what we think, and how we view the world.

Building and nourishing community is part of our publishing practice. Inspired by the Afro-Asia Writers' Association, literary collectives, and grassroots organisations, we seek collaborative and interdisciplinary projects that expand what constitutes the literary and build on existing solidarities across the globe.

tiltedaxispress.com
@TiltedAxisPress